SHARON A. MITCHELL
INSTINCT

VINCI
BOOKS

By Sharon A. Mitchell

When Bad Things Happen

GONE

TRUST

SELFISH

INSTINCT

REASONS WHY

MINE

SANCTUM

Vinci Books

vinci-books.com

Published by Vinci Books Ltd in 2025

1

The publisher and the author have made every effort to obtain permissions for any third party material used in this book and to comply with copyright law. Any queries in this respect should be brought to the attention of the publisher and any omissions will be corrected in future editions.

A CIP catalogue record for this book is available from the British Library.
Paperback ISBN: 9781036707538

The EU GPSR authorised representative is Logos Europe, 9 rue Nicolas Poussion, 17000 La Rochelle, France
contact@logoseurope.eu

Chapter One

Fifteen years ago, in Mexico

"I'm sorry, but I just can't do it." The nanny stood in the doorway with her suitcase at her feet. "I still think there's something wrong with that baby."

"The adoptive agency gave her a clean bill of health."

"I'm used to infants, but there's something different about this one. She screams and does not take comfort from being held. Yet, she eats okay." She picked up her suitcase and headed for the door. "She's been fed, changed, and is in her crib. I'll send for the rest of my things." The door closed behind her, only to open a moment later. "My boss says they won't send anyone else here. You'll need to try a new agency if you want another nanny." Then she was gone.

"How can a creature that small make such a racket?" Anita held her head in her hands and raised tearful eyes to her husband. "Looks like it's just us, alone with the baby tonight." Her shoulders drooped. She'd

1

never felt so helpless; it was time to face facts. "We made a mistake, didn't we? A big mistake."

Roman ran his hands through his hair, leaving it in spikes, despite the pomade. "It looks like it. This was not what we expected. She's already driven away three nannies in as many months. We didn't think we'd have to be hands on with the baby, at least at this stage of her life. Later on, yeah, and we can afford to hire help. But no one wants to stay with this child."

"What are we going to do? This is not the life we imagined."

He hated seeing the despair in his wife's eyes. Their idyll of being parents was not working, despite the money they'd paid out. The sum had been enormous, but if it gave them their dream of a little girl, so be it. This child was not what they had had in mind.

Roman strode to his desk and picked up his phone. Scrolling through the contacts, he selected the number he wanted. Putting the phone to his ear, he waited until the cultured voice of the receptionist picked up. "This is Roman Baltez. Put me through to Alejandro." The look of gratitude on his wife's face told Roman that he was doing the right thing. They'd tried, but parenting was not for them. Or at least parenting this little girl. She could go back.

As he hung up the phone he muttered, "God help the next people who take in this child."

Present Day, California

Running her fingers through her hair, Cynthia stared at the computer screen. Surely, she read the numbers wrong. A simple spreadsheet, a straightforward budget. How hard was that to decipher?

Opening another screen, she tapped in the credentials

to her online bank account. Carefully, she compared all the deposits for the past month. No, she hadn't missed any. She pulled up the statement for the previous month and the one before that. The same. The exact same deposits happened each month. Of course, they did; she knew that, but hoped for some pleasant surprises.

She needed to get a handle on their expenses. Even if math was not her strong suit, she knew that spending more than they brought in would not work for long.

Cynthia unclenched her jaw. Grinding down her teeth would only create another bill. Maybe if she could just have enough concentrated time to figure this out, she could come up with a solution. She sighed. Shouldering this on her own felt like wading through setting concrete. A mess.

Enough. She needed to think about something else. She'd go exercise in the basement; that would clear her head.

"Mommy!"

Good grief. She'd only been working out down here for fifteen minutes. She blew the hair out of her eyes.

"Mom! Come see."

Sigh. She knew Amy would not give up. Slowly she lowered her legs, while gripping the pole firmly. She practiced one of her landings, pleased with how smoothly it was coming. She shut off the music and headed upstairs. Despite money or not, despite needing exercise to manage anxiety, her daughter needed attention.

"Mommy, that truck is huge!" Then Amy looked at her mom and laughed. "Have you been hanging upside down again? Your hair's all over the place."

Cynthia joined her daughter, both kneeling on the

couch, arms resting on its back, looking out the window at the truck angled so its open back door pointed at them. "It's a moving van. Guess that house sold and we're getting new neighbors."

A sedan and an SUV drove up, parking along the curb. A teenaged girl and woman got out of the sedan, and a man from the SUV joined them. The three stared at the house; the young girl looked bored; the man proud. The woman wore weariness on her shoulders. Reaching into the back seat of the car, she lifted out an infant car seat.

Cynthia sympathized. Moving was a pain, even if someone else carried your stuff into the house for you. It'd be even harder with a baby.

The family disappeared inside their new home. Movers carried what looked like pieces of a bed frame into the front door. Soon the teen left the house and climbed the ramp into the back of the moving van. Cynthia watched as the girl first checked the house, then searched for a box, seeming to check the labels. She found the one she wanted near the door of the van. Pulling something from her pocket, she crouched and worked at the bottom of the box. Hearing footsteps, she rose and casually placed something in her back pocket, pulling her shirt over it, one tail not quite covering the object. To Cynthia, it looked like the handles of a pair of scissors.

Next, the movers brought a couch and rocking chair into the house. The third mover, a slight young fellow, began shifting the smaller boxes. Picking up one carton, the one that had interested the girl, he took two steps toward the ramp when the cardboard bottom gave way, spilling its contents, shattering them as they fell. There was nothing but the sound of smashing china, then one heartfelt profanity.

4

The man and woman rushed out the door, the woman giving a moan at the carnage. Their daughter stood to the side with a smirk.

Six hours later, Cynthia and Amy rang the doorbell at their new neighbors' house. It took a while for the door to open, even though she could hear voices and footsteps.

Maybe this wasn't such a good idea after all. They could always chuck the pizza in the trash can if they didn't want it. Finally, the door opened, and a girl gave Cynthia a bored stare.

"Yeah?" the girl asked.

"Hi. I'm Cynthia Blythe and this is my daughter, Amy. We're your neighbors." She indicated the direction of her house by pointing her chin. "I see that you're just moving in and thought how tiring that is. Since you might not know what's available in the neighborhood, I ordered a pizza for you." She held up the boxes. "They're the best around. I didn't know what kind you'd like, so I got their selection assortment. It gives slices of six different types."

Amy held up a smaller box. "And these are their cinnamon sticks. They're the best, although you have to eat your pizza before you get to try one. That's what mom always said, although I don't think it's fair."

The door opened wider, and a woman stood behind the girl. "That's so sweet of you. We haven't had time to even think about food."

"What's that delicious smell? I'm starving." A deeper voice approached from the hallway.

The woman turned to him. "Looks like we have a welcome surprise from a new neighbor." She turned back to

Cynthia and held out her hand. "Hi. I'm Barbara McDaw. This is my husband, Howard, and our daughter, Natalie." The adults shook hands. Natalie looked like this was all beneath her, and her viridescent green eyes looked right through Cynthia.

"Nat, will you take these into the kitchen, please, and try to find some plates?" To Cynthia, she said, "Will you and your daughter join us?"

"Oh, definitely not. You don't need company right now. I just thought I'd welcome you to the neighborhood and bring you a snack." She took Amy's hand and turned to go. "Oh, there's a takeout menu stapled to the pizza box. They have a twenty-five percent off coupon for first-time orders."

"Thanks so much. We really appreciate this. I feel like I've been around the bend and up a pole."

"A pole?" asked Amy. "Do you have a pole, too? My mom has one, and she hangs upside down on it when she dances."

Cynthia died a little inside. There was no stopping Amy, short of slapping a hand across the child's mouth.

"A pole? Dancing?" Howard smirked.

Barbara elbowed her husband in the stomach.

There was nothing for it but to explain and try to salvage the situation. "It was a joke, at least at first. My husband bought me pole dancing lessons for Christmas. He bet me I wouldn't go. So, I did. And it wasn't bad. There's an amiable group of women there and we had fun. So, I kept going. Then for my birthday, Hugh installed a pole in our basement."

"I bet that was more for your husband's benefit than yours." This earned Howard another elbow jab from Barbara. Undeterred, looking over Cynthia's shoulder, he asked, "Where is he?"

6

"I'm a widow." Cynthia had found that there was no easy way to say this.

"Ouch. Sorry. I really put my foot in it that time. My apologies," said Howard.

"That's fine. You had no way of knowing." She put her hand on Amy's shoulder to steer her away from the door. "Well, welcome to the neighborhood and enjoy the pizza."

As they walked back home, Amy asked, "Do you think that girl is like Bonnie and doesn't talk? That would mean I have four friends who don't speak - Bonnie, Timothy, Daniel, and now Natalie. Do you think she'll be my friend?"

"She looks quite a bit older than you, so I'm not sure if you'll be friends in the same way that you are with Timothy and Daniel. And your other friends do talk, just not very much."

"How come?"

"Lots of different reasons. Talking is easy for you, some-times way too easy it seems." She smiled at her daughter. "But it's not easy for some kids to say what they're thinking. They communicate in other ways. They are all speaking more and more, though."

"I guess." She skipped, holding her mother's hand. "Doesn't matter. We get along fine, and I can talk for all of us."

Several days later, Cynthia sighed as they drove up their street. It had been a long day so far. Life was harder when you had to do all the errands and manage on your own, on top of being both mother and father to Amy. It had not been her plan to be a widow before her thirtieth birthday.

She glanced in the rear-view mirror at her daughter.

Sure, Amy was drowsy and quiet now, but she'd rouse as soon as the car stopped, raring to get going again. If only there was someone to spell her off sometimes. If only she could have some time to herself.

Whine, whine, she thought. Suck it up, buttercup.

Up ahead were people on the sidewalk. Oh, no. It was her new neighbors, and it looked like they'd pass by just about the time Cynthia's car would pull to a stop. Drats. She was tired, and in a mood to feel sorry for herself. Making nice with people she didn't know was not part of the plan.

Of its own accord, her foot eased from the pedal. As if those few seconds would make any difference. She flexed her hands on the steering wheel and straightened her spine. Barbara seemed a nice enough woman. She had just moved in and knew no one. Cynthia knew what loneliness felt like; she should make the effort to be friendly. She forced her lips into a smile.

Pulling into their driveway and stopping, Cynthia popped the latch on the trunk as Amy hopped out of the car.

Barbara and Natalie, walking along the sidewalk, approached their property. Barbara indicated the stroller Natalie pushed. "This is sometimes the only way we can get him to take a nap."

Natalie moved the stroller with a jerky back-and-forth motion. Her mom stilled her hand, saying, "Easy, or he'll wake up again. We don't want *that*."

Natalie abandoned her little brother, crouching down in front of Amy. "Hey! Remember me? I'm Natalie."

Cynthia thought this a vastly different Natalie than the sullen teen she'd met when the family first moved in.

Teenagers. She hoped it would be a long time before she went through that stage with Amy.

Taking Amy's hand, Natalie stood. "Mrs. Blythe, would you like help with your groceries? Amy and I can bring them in while you and mom visit."

"That would be lovely, thank you." She fished her keys from her pocket, handing them to Amy. "You remember how to open the lock?"

Natalie intercepted the keys. "That's all right. I'll open the door for her." She reached into the trunk for two bags. "Come on, Amy, take a few of the light ones."

Turning to Barbara, Cynthia said, "What a lovely daughter you have."

A corner of Barbara's mouth lifted. "She has her moments."

As soon as Natalie unlocked the door, a small, furry creature charged out to greet his people. "Blitz!" Amy yelled at her dog.

"He's supposed to wait to be invited out," Cynthia explained. "It's a work in progress, especially if we have left him inside alone for a while." She grabbed his collar as the little dog stretched his front paws on the stroller, trying to peer inside.

Natalie slung her arm across Amy's shoulders as they returned for their second load of groceries.

"Ow!" Amy pulled sharply away from Natalie, rubbing her scalp. "That hurt! Why'd you do that?"

"I'm so sorry." Natalie smoothed her palms down both sides of Amy's head. "Your hair got caught in my watch strap. I'll have to be more careful."

"No, it didn't. You pulled my hair!"

"Amy!" Cynthia was mortified. "It was an accident, could happen to anyone. I've snagged my own hair on bracelets before." Turning to Natalie, "I'm sorry she reacted like that. Looks like your brother's not the only one who could use a nap."

"Mo-omm," protested Amy. "She did so do it on purpose."

"Hush. Just get those groceries in, please." Embarrassed, she apologized to Barbara. "Amy's usually easy to get along with, but it's been a long day of errands and I guess she's cranky. I hope Natalie won't take offense."

"No worries. They might be our kids, but that doesn't mean we have total control over them. Natalie has her irritable moments, too. Actually, more than just moments, some days. Don't ever try bringing a new baby into the life of a fifteen-year-old, then moving her to a new location."

"Was it hard for her to leave her friends?"

"She didn't really have friends."

Natalie looked out Cynthia's kitchen window. Yes, her mother and Cynthia were still in the same spot, talking about old lady things, she supposed. She watched Amy emptying bags and placing the groceries on the kitchen table and counters. The items to go into the fridge were on the right side of the table. Natalie began unpacking things as well. To Amy, she asked, "Why'd you do that?"

"Do what?"

"Try to get me in trouble."

"You pulled my hair!"

"Now, Amy." Natalie stroked the child's head. "Does that even make sense? Why would I do something like that?"

Amy pursed her lips, her eyes narrowing.

They heard the voices of their mothers getting closer,

the front door opening, the gentle bumps as they got the stroller through the door, then footsteps in the short hallway leading to the kitchen.

"Amy," Natalie warned loudly. "Be careful with those eggs."

There was a splat, then silence. Clear, viscous fluid oozed out of the upside-down egg carton, followed by blobs and streams of orangey yellow, like a sunset over an ocean.

"Oh, Amy." Cynthia watched the goop spread across her clean floor.

"What? I didn't do anything." Amy pointed at Natalie. "She did it."

Across the room, Natalie raised her hands, palms extended outward. She backed up even farther from the mess until her back hit the stove. "I'm way over here. I wasn't near them. I told you to keep things back from the edge of the table."

"You didn't…"

"That's okay, girls," Cynthia interrupted her daughter. "Accidents happen. I'll get this cleaned up." Turning to Barbara, she said, "Around four or so, Elizabeth, our neighbor, is coming over for coffee. Why don't you join us? We'll be on the patio out back."

Rustling and sounds of irritation came from the depths of the stroller. Barbara used the entrance to the kitchen to turn the contraption around. "Sounds nice. Maybe I can get this little guy down for a decent sleep by then."

As Natalie brushed by Amy, she gave the girl a pat on the head, a big grin, and a wink, then held the door open for her mother. "Bye, Mrs. Blythe." She smiled to herself. Her job here was done.

Cynthia stooped to drag the garbage can and cleaner supplies from beneath the sink. Straightening, she glanced out the window. Was that the same car she'd noticed before? Why was it driving so slowly down their street? Squinting her eyes, she tried to see the driver. Too far away. Maybe a dark-haired man, but the sun glinted off his windscreen, making it hard to tell. It was a quiet street, with not a lot of non-local traffic. Strangers stood out. This car didn't, though - just a nondescript, white SUV. She'd ask Elizabeth if she'd noticed the car.

Chapter Two

Barbara arrived at Cynthia's alone, opening the side gate to join Cynthia on the patio. "Liam's down for the count, finally. I love my son, but never more than when he's sleeping."

Cynthia laughed and raised her glass of iced tea. "I get that. Amy looks like an angel when she's asleep." She gestured to the insulated pitcher on the round glass table. "Want some?"

As they settled in, Cynthia said, "It must be nice to have an older sister like Natalie to help with the baby."

Barbara hesitated. "Yes. Mostly, or at least sometimes. It's been a hard adjustment for her, going from being an only child to sharing our attention with a demanding newborn."

"How old is she?"

"Fifteen."

"That's a long time to be the only child."

"She, ah, hasn't been with us quite that long. She was almost three when we adopted her."

"Lucky girl."

"Yes, I think she was. Before coming to us, she'd been in a number of homes and things didn't go well for her."

"Oh? How so?"

"It sounds like she was a difficult baby." Barbara sipped her drink. "This is good - not too sweet." She surveyed Cynthia's child-friendly yard. "She was certainly a difficult toddler when she came to us. But we were committed. If we took a child into our home, she was ours."

"Looks like things worked out for you."

The silence dragged. "Sometimes I think yes, sometimes no. It's been tough on her and on us." Unsure whether to say more, Barbara hesitated. After all, she hardly knew her new neighbor, and this was rather like airing their dirty laundry. Still, she needed a friend; Natalie needed a friend. "Natalie's different."

Cynthia smiled. "Aren't we all?"

"No. I mean yes, but not in the way that Natalie's different. Some things are harder for her."

"I have two friends whose children are autistic. The way those kids experience life isn't easy for them, or their parents."

"I bet." She thought about that. "Autism. I never thought of that word in relation to Natalie." She shook her head. "No, I'm not sure it fits, but then I don't know that much about autism. Still, there's something about Natalie."

"Have you taken her for counseling?"

"Been there, done that, got the t-shirt. We've tried many times over the years, with different therapists. At first it was for us, helping us find ways to parent this child who always seemed so unhappy."

"You must have done a good job because I've seen her smile often in the short time I've known her."

"Yes, well, that might mean something, and it might not."

Cynthia tilted her head to the side and lowered her eyebrows. "What do you mean?"

"Oh, nothing. I'm maudlin today - comes from lack of sleep."

"Hey," a voice called from the side of the house. "You out here, Cyn?"

"Yeah, we're out back. Come have a seat."

A slight form rushed past his mother. His head swiveled, looking for Amy.

"She's in the house, Timothy. Go find her, then I have a snack ready for the two of you."

Elizabeth approached the two women. She stopped in front of Barbara. "Hi, I'm Elizabeth Whitmore. That whirlwind who flashed by is my son, Timothy."

"Barbara McDaw. My husband, Howard, and I moved in with our son and daughter last week. We're two doors down that way."

"Good. More kids for Timothy and Amy to play with."

"Not sure how well that will work. Natalie's fifteen and Liam is only four months. Might be awhile before he can compete in their games."

"The time goes fast." The screen door slammed shut. "Sort of like with those two." Amy and Timothy raced across the lawn to the swing set, hopped on and pumped their legs.

"Oh, to have that energy." The women conversed about everything and nothing, watching the kids play.

"Maybe I'm lazy or getting old," said Elizabeth, "but

I'm pleased to sit here and watch them play, rather than playing with them."

The other two agreed. "Sitting here with adult company is nice, too."

"If you ever want a break, I bet Natalie would be willing to babysit," offered Barbara. "She doesn't know anyone here yet, so has plenty of time."

"Yay! A babysitter right close by. That's great to know. It's nice to go out for an adult meal with Brendan, without Timothy occasionally."

"Brendan?" asked Barbara.

Cynthia stilled and tilted her head toward the back door. "Did you hear something?"

The other two listened. "Not really," said Elizabeth.

"I'll just go check inside. I need to bring out the kids' snacks now, anyway. Anyone care for wine instead of more iced tea?"

Carrying the tray with their empty glasses into the kitchen, she stopped short when she saw Natalie doing something at her kitchen counter. Cynthia glanced at her front door, positive that she'd locked it. Ever since her friends' troubles of the past year or so, she'd been vigilant about that.

"Hi!" Natalie seemed pleased with herself. "I noticed you were getting something ready for the kids and thought I'd help."

"Ah, thanks, but you didn't need to do that." Thinking over what Barbara had said and not said, she blurted, "How did you get in here?"

"That's why I came over." From the back pocket of her

jeans, she produced a set of keys. "You gave me these this afternoon when I helped Amy bring in the groceries. I forgot to give them back to you." She regarded the key ring. "Looks like your car key is on here, so you'd have missed it soon enough."

Holding out her hand for the keys, Cynthia relaxed. That made sense. After Amy dropped the eggs, most other thoughts had fled their minds. "Thanks." Cynthia deposited the keys in a dish by the kitchen door.

She loaded one tray with a bottle of pinot grigio and three wine glasses and another with salami, cheese, and crackers, plus juice for the kids. "Would you like some?" she asked Natalie.

Natalie eyed the wine tray. "Sure, thanks."

Cynthia smiled. "I meant the juice and crackers."

"Oh, yeah." Her eyes twinkled. "Can't blame a girl for trying."

They left the kitchen together, heading for the back door, each carrying a tray. "Just a minute," said Cynthia, putting down her tray. "I better make sure that the front door is locked."

Natalie smirked, continuing to the back door, the cheese tray in her hands.

Using her elbow to disengage the back door latch, Natalie backed out of the door, steadying the tray carefully.

"Natalie! What are you doing here?" Alarm filled Barbara's eyes. "Where's Liam? You're supposed to be watching him."

"Relax, mommy dearest." She patted her left hip. "I checked on him right before I left. He's dead to the world. And I brought the baby monitor with me."

"You what! *I* have the monitoring unit right here." She pulled it from her pocket. "Let me see what you have."

Natalie held out the rectangular unit.

"Nat! That's the base unit that stays in his room so we can hear if he awakens. Geez, girl. You know that."

Natalie took a half-step backward, shoulders hunching.

"Give me that," her mother ordered. By this time, Cynthia had joined them. "Sorry, but I need to go check on Liam. Natalie left him alone. Thanks for the refreshments, Cynthia, and nice to meet you, Elizabeth."

When she left, Natalie placed the tray gingerly on the table. "Guess I blew that."

Cynthia felt for the dejected girl. Putting her arm across Natalie's shoulders, she gave a little squeeze. "I'm sure there's no harm done. He was only alone for a few moments. Your mom's just worried."

"Yeah. She worries a lot. Sometimes, when I try to help, it doesn't work out." She studied the patio tile at her feet. "Sometimes it feels like I can't do anything right."

"Well, you can help right now," Cynthia said. "Would you mind going to tell the kids that their snacks are ready?"

Brightening, Natalie straightened and headed for the children on the swings.

"That was awkward," said Elizabeth.

"Barbara said that the transition from being an only child to having a baby in the house has been rough on Natalie."

"I think at her age, I would have loved having a little brother or sister around."

"Maybe. Barbara implied things haven't been easy for Natalie."

"Then she fits right in here." Elizabeth's droll tone went with her eye-rolling.

It didn't take long for Amy and Timothy to deplete the plate of crackers and cheese and to down their drinks.

"May we be excused?" Amy was on her best behavior. She knew that if her mom and Timothy's remained occupied, she and Timothy could keep playing longer.

Cynthia nodded.

"Aren't you the polite little girl," Natalie beamed at the child.

Amy looked uncertain, but her brow cleared as Timothy tugged on her hand and they returned to the swing set.

"Maybe I'll go push the kids on the swings for a few minutes," volunteered Natalie. "Give my mom a chance to cool off." She pressed her lips together and followed the children.

First, she approached Timothy, wrapping her hands around his where they grasped the chains of the swing, looming over him.

Timothy squirmed violently, twisting back and forth with a loud, "NOOOO!"

Instantly Elizabeth was out of her seat and across the grass. "Timothy," she admonished. "A simple 'no' would have sufficed. No need to yell."

She pulled Natalie aside. "I apologize for my son. He didn't mean anything personal by that. It's just that he does not like to be touched, especially by people he doesn't know well and when he's not expecting it."

"Really?" Natalie raised her eyebrows. "I thought little kids were cuddly."

"Not all kids."

"Sorry. I didn't mean to make him uncomfortable." She toed the grass. "It's not my day. I'm messing up all over."

Elizabeth squeezed her arm. "Not your fault; you couldn't know." She nodded at the swing set. "But I bet

Amy would appreciate a push." She left the kids to it and headed for the patio.

Brightening, Natalie smiled. "Do you want a push from the front or the back?" she asked Amy.

"The back."

"All right, then." Natalie positioned herself directly in front of Amy. She put her hands on the child's waist and gave a gentle push backward.

After studying Natalie, a moment, Amy wiggled her legs as her swing arced backward. "Higher," she instructed.

With the older girl planted directed in front of her, Amy spread her legs wide as she came close. Her legs safely passed on either side of Natalie, doing no damage.

"Clever girl," smiled Natalie. The gleam in her eye was difficult to decipher for the eight-year-old.

Placing her hands on either side of Amy's ribcage, Natalie squeezed as she pushed.

"Ow!" Amy yelled.

"Amy, play nice," came from her mother.

"She hurt me!"

"Amy," came her mother's warning tone. "Be kind to our guest."

Chapter Three

In Mexico

It wasn't working. Nothing worked. The kid had two modes - hollering or tantruming. Three modes, really, and the third was slightly preferable. The silent mode. Who knew that a four-year-old could give you the silent treatment? But to Germaine, it felt good when Jordy employed it.

The playroom was the stuff of kids' Christmas lists, with every toy advertised for preschoolers. They'd spent a fortune on the outdoor play area, a child's paradise. But not for this boy. When they'd ask him what he wanted, he'd say, "Bonnie."

Who the hell was Bonnie? When they questioned if she was Mommy, he'd wail and yell for Bonnie. Sometimes he'd ask for Benjie, but mostly just Bonnie.

The kid was morose. He'd pick up a toy that was adored by most children. Germaine and Emma, so excited to be adopting this little boy, spent hours setting up a marble run toy, supposedly the envy of the sandbox set (or rather, they'd had staff set it up, but still…). The battery-operated ride-in truck should have been a hit. How many four-

year-olds had their own powered vehicle to drive around the expansive grounds of an estate? The truck got a glimmer of attention, but nothing sustained, nothing like the excitement they'd expected. Instead, the kid chose to sit in the sandbox, sifting grains through his fingers.

Germaine would do anything for his wife, including opening his home to a stranger's child. Married for almost twenty years, they'd never been blessed with a baby. While Germaine could live with this, Emma couldn't. Germaine hoped that as they grew older, the urge to have a family would lessen. It hadn't. If anything, his wife's obsession grew.

When they'd explored every fertility specialist that money could buy and still no pregnancy, they discussed adoption.

They led a good life and had the money to indulge their desires. But now that they were in their forties, the demands of a newborn might be too much, even with hired help. They liked their sleep. So, they'd settled on adopting an older toddler, a child who slept through the night, one who was out of that messy diaper stage, one who talked and could entertain himself for periods of time.

The private adoption agency kept them appraised on new children coming into their care, but none seemed right until Jordy. He'd been raised with his birth mother who, because of circumstances, was willing to give him up so that he could have a better life than that which she could offer. Now that took love.

There had been little time - less than two days' notice that they could have Jordy, the child of their dreams. But with a staff like theirs, getting ready to accept a boy into their home was not a problem.

The problem was now that he was here.

They'd expected there to be an adjustment period; of course there would be. But kids were adaptable, and what child would not want to be in this house?

It was almost like Jordy was depressed. What could a kid who had only been on this earth less than five years have to be depressed about?

The bakery was local, convenient, always fresh, and delicious. Best of all, it was kid friendly.

Elizabeth and Timothy arrived early and chose a table for six. Being in kindergarten, Timothy was only in school for half-days. Cynthia would join them soon after she picked up her daughter, Amy, from school. Bonnie would be with them; she spent her days at Cynthia's, being tutored on an independent study program from school.

From behind the counter, Ellie, the owner, waved at Elizabeth. She raised a finger, signaling that she'd be there in a minute to take her order. Ellie poked her head into the kitchen. "Jeff, your buddy, Timothy's here."

Shortly, a young man in a chef's hat and apron appeared at Elizabeth's table. "Hey, little man." He squatted beside Timothy's chair. "Ready to go choose your treat?"

Without speaking, Timothy put down his iPad, took Jeff's hand, and went to inspect the glass-fronted display case. Ellie's policy was that a child received a free goodie each time they visited.

Jeff waited patiently as the boy carefully considered each offering, both palms flat on the glass. Despite the array of treats, Jeff knew which one Timothy would pick - the same one he devoured last time, and the time before that.

On their first visit, his mother had encouraged her son to try a chocolate eclair. Timothy enjoyed the first bite, the rich pastry, and the smooth chocolate topping, but when the Chantilly cream oozed out onto his hand, that was a different story. Jeff got some textures were just icky, no matter how they looked or tasted. Seeing Timothy's panic at the white, sticky goo on his palm, Jeff arrived with a damp cloth to wipe it off, and the offering of a gingerbread man instead.

Timothy reminded Jeff of his nephew, Kyle, who had been choosing nothing but gingerbread men as his treat for almost six years now. Yep, Jeff was right. After all those minutes of deciding, Timothy chose one of the gingerbread men with plain white icing. Ellie had a plate with a paper doily and napkin ready. As Timothy raised his eyes to Ellie, then returned them to the cookie he wanted, Ellie picked it up with tongs, deposited that cookie on the plate, and passed it over the counter to Jeff. With a flourish, Jeff presented it to Timothy. The child's grin rewarded them both.

Taking careful steps, Timothy held the plate in both hands and made it safely to the table he shared with his mom. As he set it down, Ellie called to him.

"Timothy, your hot chocolate's ready."

At first Elizabeth had been uncomfortable with the child handling their drinks. What if he spilled it and made a mess on the floor?

Jeff had pointed to the mop and pail in the corner. "That's what that's for," he explained.

The hot chocolate made it to the table, with only a slight amount slopping down the side of the cup.

While Jeff chatted with Timothy about his iPad game, Ellie used the spray bottle she kept under the counter to wipe the handprints off the display case. She firmly believed that this was the most pristine piece of glass in the city, since she polished it so often.

The bell over the door dinged as Amy, Bonnie, and Cynthia entered. While the latter two approached at a sedate pace, Amy barreled over to Elizabeth and Timothy, the way she did everything. Giving Elizabeth a quick hug, she gushed over Timothy's gingerbread man, even though it was now missing one leg.

"Ready?" Jeff asked her.

That was all the invitation Amy required. She'd been here once before. She raced to the counter, stopping herself with both hands spread against the display case glass.

Ellie smiled at her. That's what spray cleaners were for.

Squatting down, Amy began her inspection with the bottom row of goodies, slowly straightening to see what each shelf offered, her flattened palms rising each time, too. Unlike Timothy, her tastes varied depending on, well, who knew with Amy? Today it was a Boston cream donut.

Ellie served it on a glass plate with a paper doily but added two napkins; this could be a messy treat. The donut made it safely to the table.

Bonnie sat, hands carefully cradling her drink, periodically glancing over her shoulder toward the display case. The sign said free treats for kids twelve and under. Bonnie was in her thirteenth year, sort of borderline in her mind. She dared not presume.

Ellie noticed Bonnie's reticence and motioned her over. First looking to Cynthia for permission, Bonnie slowly rose and approached the counter. These were situations she hated. Her mother would tell her that if she didn't speak, she could not eat. Restaurants were the worst when they'd try to make her talk to strangers. Bonnie couldn't, she just couldn't. What if she said the wrong thing? What if she stuttered? Once, when she had given her order, her mother said how selfish she was, ordering something so expensive that the others now couldn't get what they wanted. Another time her mother told her she'd get fat and waddle everywhere if she ate that.

There were so many choices on display, all looking

good. But they didn't have price tags. How would she know which was all right for her to have?

Ellie watched the girl's indecision. This seemed more than just deciding between which treat looked most appealing. "Anything," she explained. "You can choose from any of these." Watching carefully, she thought that the child's eyes lingered on the cinnamon rolls. "I'll tell you which is my favorite. These right here." She used her tongs to point out the gooey cinnamon rolls. "Want one?"

Bonnie's head nodded even before the girl seemed to realize that she'd indicated a choice. Her startled eyes rose to Ellie's. Was she in trouble?

"Excellent choice. Just give me a few seconds to warm it up in the microwave. I like the way the butter melts on it when it's hot." The child still looked uncomfortable. Maybe she needed to feel useful. "It looks like Elizabeth's coffee cup is empty. Would you mind taking this carafe to her, please?" Bonnie's half-smile told Ellie she was on the right track. "But come right back for your cinnamon bun."

Amy and Timothy squirmed in their seats. Treats devoured, they were ready for action. Sitting sedately was not cutting it.

As soon as she finished serving her customer, Ellie came over. "There's a play area in the back corner. The kids are welcome to use it."

"Oh, no, thank you," Elizabeth immediately responded. "I'd rather keep them here with us."

Amy was already out of her chair and headed for the area Ellie had pointed out. It took Timothy only seconds to follow.

Ellie scooped up Elizabeth's and Cynthia's cups and said, "Come with me. Bonnie, can you carry your own, please?" She set the cups down on a small, two-seater table, just a few feet away from the two-foot wall surrounding three sides of the play area. "Now you can watch the kids." She pulled over a third chair for Bonnie, telling her, "There. You have a choice of sitting with the ladies, or closer to the kids."

After looking to Cynthia for permission, Bonnie perched on the padded ledge bordering the play area.

"Either we're not that interesting, or she's had enough of me," remarked Cynthia. Bonnie spent weekdays at Cynthia's house, being homeschooled. Bonnie's previous school attendance was spotty; Cynthia, a teacher, was plugging those gaps and getting the girl ready to re-enter the school system next fall.

Timothy and Amy made good use of the toys on the shelves for a while. Although they usually played well together, being in a confined area only lasted so long, and they grew irritated with one another. Before Elizabeth or Cynthia intervened, Bonnie took a jigsaw puzzle from a shelf, spread the pieces on the rug, and began putting it together. Soon she had a little body on either side of her, helping. Bonnie grinned over at the two moms.

Elizabeth mouthed, "Thank you!"

Cynthia said, "That child is amazing. She intuitively reads situations and knows how to respond. Many kids her age are only concerned about themselves, but that's not Bonnie."

"Murph and Anna lucked out when they decided to foster her."

Bonnie's smile widened as she looked over the puzzle

pieces. There had been little praise in her life, and she was still not sure how to receive compliments. Still, it was nice to receive approval rather than complaints.

Chapter Four

In Mexico

"Germaine, do something," insisted Emma. *The nanny resigned and no amount of pay inducement convinced her to stay.*

As Germaine kept saying, this was not working. Nothing worked since this child came into their lives.

Germaine was a problem-solver. That's how he excelled in his business. He was a take-charge guy but didn't want to be hands on with this little boy. Neither did Emma. That's why they had staff.

He picked up the phone. "Give me Alejandro Ramon."

"Sally, change of plan. I've got a job for you to do."

Sally peered at Alejandro from under her lashes. She was painting her toenails and didn't like her concentration interrupted. "A job? I thought I was your partner."

"Partner? What gave you that idea?"

"That was the plan when I came down here with you. I was to help manage the operation."

"There is no operation now, thanks to your daughter."

"And your ex-wife, Anna."

"It's gone now. That stable is history, and we need to lie low with the others. That's why we have to look after the adoption side. Can't have unhappy clients telling their friends not to use us." He stood up and took a step towards the door. "It's simple economics, babe."

"What's that got to do with me?" Sally inspected her delicately manicured nails. "I need to make an appointment." She pointed to her left ring finger. "The flower on this one's off center."

"It's your son," Alejandro said. "The older brat. He's giving his new parents a hard time and their second nanny walked out on them. They need a new one by tomorrow."

Sally crossed her legs, allowing her skirt to ride up. She dangled her mule from the toes of the foot with the dried nails. Good. She'd diverted his attention.

"Get dressed," Alejandro ordered as he stood up, adjusting the pleat in his pants. "We'll drive there now, get a hotel for the night, then show up at their place first thing in the morning."

"We? Why me? Can't you go by yourself?"

"Hardly. I'm not nanny material."

Sally stared at him.

"But you, my dear, you are." Alejandro took satisfaction at the look of dismay on Sally's face. "You are your son's new nanny."

"No! I'm not good with kids. That's why I gave them up." An awful thought struck her. "Are both boys there?" One child was terrible enough, but two toddlers? She shuddered.

"No, Mommy Dearest. Your younger son is doing just fine in his new home. Your older brat is not, and I can't afford to have dissatisfied customers."

"What's wrong with him? He wasn't that bad of a kid."

"He's messed up, they say. He yells and tantrums and won't interact with them. Nothing they've tried to bribe him with works. When he's not raising holy hell, he's demanding Bonnie."

"Then get Bonnie here."

Alejandro just looked at her. He shook his head. "Yeah, right. How do you propose we do that? She's surrounded by watchdogs now, and the cops are all over this." He warmed to the topic, his ire rising. "You said you could control her. You said she was under your thumb. Yet when Anna showed up, that kid abandoned you to run with Anna." He laughed, the cruel sort that showed no humor. "What does that say about your mothering?"

"Bonnie's a fickle child. Or that Anna chick brainwashed her."

Alejandro tilted his head and regarded Sally through narrowed eyes. "Whatever. We're leaving in fifteen minutes. Pack if you want, or not." He looked at his watch. "In exactly eleven hours from now, you'll be a nanny." His eyes became intense. "And you'll do a good job of it."

Amy was at school. Bonnie worked away at the dining room table. Supervising Bonnie's independent school program was a godsend. It brought Cynthia some much-needed cash, and she liked to think that she was preparing Bonnie for her return to school next fall.

Cynthia was grateful that Bonnie was an independent sort of kid. Once she understood a lesson, she worked diligently on her own. That left Cynthia a few minutes to herself. On the computer monitor in front of her, she studied the resume she developed. Pitiful, she thought. It wasn't bad on the education side and the initial years of her teaching. But once she became pregnant with Amy, her work history stopped. Sighing, she shut the window. Staring at it wouldn't make it look any better.

Checking that Bonnie was doing all right, she opened the back door and went onto the patio. Earlier that morning she'd cut the lawn using her rotary mower. She loved the whirring sounds that came from it, instead of the noise an electric or gas motor would have made. If she didn't let the grass get too long, it was easy to push the mower through the greenery. She filled her lungs with the clean spring air. The scent of freshly mown grass clippings lingered. In the lilac bushes near the back fence a robin sang to his hoped-for mate.

A mate. She'd believed that she'd mated for life when she married Hugh. She thought they'd grow old together, watch Amy grow up together.

The sound of wailing broke her reverie. She realized the crying had been going on for some time, but the volume now ramped up. Ah, how she remembered those times when baby Amy had done that, and how thankful she'd been that there were two of them to cope on those occasions.

The screaming came from the McDaw's house. How loud must it be in their home if she could hear it this loud from two doors away? Poor Liam. Poor Barbara. At least she wasn't alone.

Oh, but she'd seen Natalie walk off down the street a while ago. And Howard worked away part of each week. Maybe Barbara was alone.

Not her problem, Cynthia thought. Going back inside, she poured herself a glass of iced tea and offered one to Bonnie. Sipping, she realized she could hear the baby crying, even though she was now indoors.

She debated, casting her eyes to the ceiling. She really, really didn't feel like it, but she knew what it was like to be alone.

Putting her glass in the refrigerator, she told Bonnie she'd be back in a minute. Maybe Barbara was fine; if so, she really would be back momentarily.

The front door wasn't latched. Not good. She'd have to tell Barbara about the trouble her friends had experienced, and the need for vigilance. There was no answer to her knock. She rang the bell again. Opening the door, she poked her head in, calling, "Knock, knock." Nothing. "Barbara?" She could hear Liam shrieking from upstairs.

Shutting the door behind her and pressing in the lock button, she advanced, calling out to Barbara. "Barbara? It's me, Cynthia. The door was open. I knocked, then let myself in."

From the top of the stairs Barbara appeared, a screaming baby in her arms. Cynthia didn't know which of their faces were wetter with tears. Grabbing the banister, she took the steps two at a time. Reaching the landing, she reached for the baby. "Here, let me take him for a minute. You look like you need a break."

For a second, Barbara grasped Liam more tightly to her chest, then closed her eyes and held out her arms. She surrendered. "Thank you."

Swaying with the unhappy infant in her arms, Cynthia tried a smile. She hoped that her body language conveyed more than her words. It was hard to be heard above the lung power this kid possessed. "Mothering's great, but we could all use a rest from it sometimes."

"No kidding." Barbara scrubbed her cheeks with her palms. "Sorry. I'm a mess. Usually I'm better at this, but I can't get him to stop crying. It's been going on and on."

Peering at the child's red face, Cynthia asked, "Do you think he's sick?"

"No, at least I don't think so. He was fine earlier today. I left to get some groceries, and Natalie stayed with him. When I came home, he was like this. Natalie said she had no idea what started it."

"Is this strange for him?"

"Very. He has his moments, but usually he's a pretty typical baby."

Just then, a strange noise emanated from the child. Then vomit erupted from his mouth, spewing over Cynthia's shoulder, splatting on the wall behind her.

Then silence. Either the event shocked Liam silent, or getting rid of his stomach's contents stopped his distress.

Turning, Cynthia and Barbara surveyed the coagulating mass trickling down the wall, oozing into the carpet.

No stranger to infants' projectile vomit, both women ogled the mess.

"What did he eat?" It looked like nothing Cynthia recalled from Amy's babyhood.

"Natalie said she gave him applesauce because he seemed hungry."

This didn't resemble any applesauce either of them had seen before. Passing the now quiet baby to Barbara, Cynthia stepped closer, crouching down to inspect the ooze. "Yeah, I see how it could have been applesauce not too long ago, but what is this darker stuff? It looks gritty." If she didn't know better, she'd say it was coffee grounds. No way could that be right. "I wonder if he got into something?"

It was almost like Barbara's eyes shuttered. Her body language spoke wariness. "He's crawling now, so yeah, he could have gotten into something. Natalie might not always be as attentive as she should when she's watching him." Just then, the baby's stomach spewed again. This time he shrieked along with it, gurgling, then choking.

"I think we should take him to emergency. This doesn't look right."

Eyes wide with fear, Barbara nodded.

"I'll run home and tell Bonnie where I'm going, then meet you at your car."

Grabbing her cell phone and purse, Cynthia explained to Bonnie, giving her the option of coming with them or waiting here for Anna to pick her up. Bonnie preferred to stay. Dialing Anna's number, Cynthia explained what was going on. Anna would take Amy home with them. Carefully locking the door behind her, Cynthia ran to Barbara's car and got in the driver's seat.

At the hospital's emergency department, the once again screaming baby, plus the sample of the emesis they'd carefully scraped from the wall, ensured that they received prompt attention.

Hours later, Liam slept peacefully in a tiny crib while his mom stood guard. The doctor had just delivered the news. The medical team pumped Liam's stomach to rid it of any remainders of the meal he'd ingested. The lab analyzed the contents they'd brought in, plus supplemented it with other offerings Liam expelled. Yes, he'd ingested applesauce. But he'd consumed a sizeable amount of coffee grounds along with his meal. While Liam currently had a sinus tachycardia of 140-160, this was decreasing. The prognosis was that he'd be fine. No more coffee for him, though. The physician's final advice was to keep the child away from the garbage can where they threw their coffee grounds. Or maybe compost them.

Barbara was quiet on the way home. Cynthia assumed her neighbor relished the quiet now that her son was feeling better.

Staring straight ahead, Barbara's voice was low. "We throw our coffee grounds in the garbage. I keep the garbage can under the kitchen sink. The cupboard door has a child lock on it. We know Liam is too young to open the cupboard doors, but we thought we'd install the child locks now, so that we'd get used to them."

"Maybe you forgot today."

Barbara shook her head. "I remember doing it. I thought at the time that the garbage can was almost full and that once Liam went down for his nap, I'd take it out and put in a fresh bag."

"Maybe he got into something while you were grocery shopping."

Now Barbara turned to look at Cynthia. "Our coffee machine grinds our beans fresh every morning. I keep the beans in the cupboard above the coffeepot. There is no way Liam could have gotten up there."

They drove in silence for a few minutes.

Barbara added, "Just like there's no way he could have gotten into the coffee grounds in the garbage can."

Chapter Five

Cynthia pulled up the program on her computer. She was still feeling her way through this, but felt the Know Your Money app might help.

This was new to her. Her husband had handled their finances since their marriage almost ten years ago. Their salaries went into a joint account, but since he made more money than Cynthia, she was content to have him balance their budget. He steadily added to their savings account, although this slowed down when Cynthia stopped working when she became pregnant with Amy.

Then Hugh became ill. Most of their bills were on an automatic payment system. Rather than a major life insurance policy, he had mortgage insurance. Upon his death, their house was paid off, thankfully. His job benefits provided a small life insurance policy that had kept Cynthia and Amy afloat up till now.

Biting her lip, Cynthia studied her computer monitor. She pushed her hair behind her ears. As she bent over her keyboard, those pesky locks fell forward again. She hated her hair at this length. It was too short to stick up in a bun or ponytail, yet long enough to brush annoyingly at the back of her neck. Just one more thing she was waiting in limbo for.

After carefully inputting the funds in their savings account and faithfully recording what they spent each month, she now had a handle on their money situation. Although they lived modestly, Cynthia knew things could not go on as they were past this coming year.

Once over the shock of losing her husband, she was grateful that he'd had the forethought to ensure that their home would be paid off upon his death. That seemed a major burden taken care of. She believed they needed little to live on. But bills continued to come in. There was the car payment that would last for two more years. That same car had needed new tires, which ate into her savings. After the problems her neighbor, Elizabeth, and their friends had with possible child kidnapping, Cynthia had to have a security system installed in her house before she felt safe. Another expense - a big one initially, then there was the monthly fee.

Never extravagant, Cynthia used to give groceries little thought, buying what she felt they needed and what took her fancy. Now, she saved those cash register receipts, carefully inputting each and every one into the Know Your Money program. Every time she filled up with gas or got an oil change, she recorded it. For the past two months, she had even recorded the little things, like coffee and donuts at the bakery.

The news was not good. She doubted that knowledge was power. Now that she knew exactly how much money they spent in a month, she tried to economize, but it didn't make a big difference. It cost her and Amy far more to live than the interest on their savings generated. Each month, they dipped heavily into the principal, which whittled down alarmingly fast.

By Christmas, there would be nothing left. Nothing at all.

Cynthia mused about the vagaries of communication. While speaking was difficult for Bonnie, the girl successfully communicated her thoughts and needs. Sometimes it took some guessing, but Bonnie was patient with her.

Right now, they were working on a lesson about written expression. While communicating orally was tough for this student, she excelled at writing. It was almost like the act of writing freed her to express her thoughts.

Cynthia pondered the idea of introducing Bonnie to voice dictation. She wondered if dictating in private, into a microphone, and seeing her words appear on the computer screen would be a helpful bridge to becoming more comfortable speaking. The next time Murph picked Bonnie up, Cynthia would ask his thoughts on this. Since he was a psychiatrist as well as Bonnie's foster father, they'd follow his advice.

The ringing of the front doorbell interrupted her thoughts. Checking through the peephole, Cynthia saw Barbara. Glancing at Bonnie, the girl gave her a thumbs up, then returned to her writing. Unlocking the door, Cynthia greeted Barbara.

"Hi," said Barbara. "I wanted to thank you for what you did yesterday. I was so frazzled from all his screaming that my brain didn't even reason that he needed medical attention. I really appreciate what you did, and all of your help."

"You're welcome. How is he today?"

"Back to normal. He slept little last night." She rolled her eyes. "Would you believe I didn't either?" She pulled back the blanket in the stroller. "See? He's fine now, if more tired than usual. That's okay though; we can all use the rest."

"Care to come in for a coffee?"

Busy positioning the stroller along the side of the entrance hall, Barbara didn't see Bonnie until she walked by the kitchen doorway. "Sorry," she apologized to Cynthia. "I didn't mean to interrupt."

"It's fine." Steering Barbara into the dining room, she introduced them. "This is Bonnie Ramirez. She's the daughter of some friends. Bonnie's on independent study from school this year. I'm a teacher, so we're working together. She's a brilliant student."

Bonnie smiled shyly, then returned to her writing.

After pouring the coffee into mugs, Cynthia and Barbara settled in the living room.

"So, you're a teacher?" Barbara asked.

Cynthia nodded. "But I haven't taught for a few years, since before Amy was born. I'm thinking of getting back into the career though now that Amy's in school full-time. When Bonnie came to live with my friends, they wanted to homeschool her but weren't sure how to do it. She's a good kid. I've taught young teens before, so I offered. Besides, it's a way of getting my feet wet again."

Cynthia could see the wheels churning in Barbara's brain. "Do you like it?" her neighbor asked.

"Yes," Cynthia replied. "I enjoy it almost as much as when I had a classroom."

"Is it full time, like school days? Do you get paid by the hour?" Barbara jerked backwards. "I'm sorry. I didn't mean to be so personal."

Cynthia answered more slowly. "Yes, we mostly keep school hours, but it varies somewhat, depending on our schedules. And yes, we have an hourly agreement." She didn't say what she was thinking - why are you asking?

"Forgive me if I'm too forward. Any advice you give would be great. Natalie is not in school now. At her last school, she had a rough time. There were bullies, and she was ostracized and targeted." She stared into the soft beige liquid in her mug. "Mean girls and all that. It got so bad that it wasn't just at school anymore but spilled into the neighborhood as well." She looked up at Cynthia. "That's the main reason we moved - to get her out of that environment and give her a fresh start."

"That's tough. Bullies can make life miserable for some kids. If it's not noticed and stopped right away, it can be difficult for educators to tackle."

"Yeah, well, tackling is not something they did. In fact, some of the teachers seemed to side more with the bullies than with the victim. They accused Natalie of things and sometimes punished when she says it wasn't her fault at all."

Cynthia made the appropriate noises. What could she say?

"Understandably, Natalie is reluctant to enter a school again," Barbara continued. "She says it will be even worse if she's the new kid, entering in the middle of the school year."

"Yes, that can be tough. If you met with the teachers ahead of time and explained things, they might work out a plan with you."

Barbara shook her head. "I'd be willing to try that, but

Natalie isn't. You don't know Natalie. Once her mind if made up, there's no shifting her. Howard says we should just make her, but I don't know. These past few years have been so hard on her."

"These early teen years are rough on many kids."

"If only that was it. Natalie's whole life has been tough. She spent her first few years bouncing from home to home, with no one to call her family, before she came to us. Because of her background, she didn't settle in easily and we all had a few rough years. Lots of screaming and tantrums, not quite the parenting vision we dreamed of. But we were determined to see it through. After all, we'd made a commitment to this child. It wasn't *her* fault all the things they had put her through. Then things smoothed out, but got rougher again when adolescence hit."

"I'm sorry you've struggled." Cynthia thought of her worst days with Amy, and they paled compared to anything Barbara and her daughter had been through.

"We've talked about homeschooling. I know it's not a permanent solution, and she needs to be with other kids, but just for this year. It would give her a break from school and time to adjust to this neighborhood, maybe make some friends before returning to school in the fall."

"Sounds like a plan."

"Except, I can't see how we'd do it." She nodded in the stroller's direction. "Liam, even though he's generally a wonderful baby, takes up a lot of time. I'm not sure how I'd direct Natalie in her studies. I'm not a teacher and I have no idea how to follow a curriculum or get her through her work."

Ah, thought Cynthia. I see where this is going.

"I know it's a lot to ask." Barbara took a deep breath. "Is there any chance that you'd consider teaching Natalie?"

She turned her head toward the dining room. "I realize that would mean dividing your time between the two girls. Even if you could only help Natalie part time." Her eyes pleaded with Cynthia. "Would you consider it? We'll pay you whatever you think is reasonable."

Chapter Six

Peace reigned in the bakery. With few other customers at this time of day, it was quiet, just what Cynthia and Elizabeth sought.

"I was chatting with Barbara the other day," said Cynthia. "She says that Natalie had a rough time at her last school. Lots of bullying. They moved here to give her a fresh start but aren't sure if they'll put her in school now or wait until fall. Barbara says that the poor kid was traumatized." She paused while Ellie refilled her coffee cup.

Elizabeth could see the teacher in Cynthia reaching out. "Poor kid. Did you offer to homeschool her as well?"

"The idea crossed my mind, and Barbara asked, but I thought I'd talk to Anna and Murph first. Plus, I want to get to know Natalie to see if she'd be a good fit with Bonnie. She's my priority."

"How's the teaching part coming? You were worried since you've been out of the profession for years."

"Bonnie's a dream to teach. She's sharp. This was a good way for me to ease back into being an educator."

"Can you see yourself back working in a school?"

"I'd better. Doubt that I'll have a choice."

Elizabeth tilted her head at her friend. "Why do you say that?"

Cynthia sighed. Her situation was so different from Elizabeth's. "Money," she confessed. "I have to support us."

Elizabeth colored. "You haven't had a job since I've known you. I just thought that when Hugh died, his money, or insurance, or whatever, meant that you didn't have to work." Elizabeth had inherited enough that she and Timothy were comfortable.

"Yeah, well, that was the case for a while. Hugh set things up so that we'd be okay for a couple of years. Until I got my feet under me, he said." She grimaced. "It's taken me longer than he expected for me to find my feet. This past year, we've been burning through the principal. We have less than a year's worth of savings left, if we keep spending at the rate we're going now."

Talk of money made Elizabeth uncomfortable. It fell under the category of personal things one kept to oneself. Finances were not something she'd had to worry about, ever. But she could see that her friend needed to talk. Swallowing her discomfort, Elizabeth tried. "What will you do?"

"I thought about selling the house. I even talked to a real estate agent. She thought that I could get a decent price for the place. I've been punching that number into a bunch of online calculators to see how much I could take out a month without touching the principal. Even if I invested what I got for the house, I'd still have rent to pay or mortgage payments on another place we'd get. I don't want Amy to have to change schools, so I'd want to remain in this area and places aren't cheap. I'd only be a couple of hundred dollars ahead."

"What else can you do?"

"Going back to teaching makes the most sense. It's not a great paying profession, but I'd make more than I would waiting tables or clerking in a store."

Elizabeth nodded.

"Besides, it's the only thing I'm trained for."

"Did you enjoy teaching?"

Cynthia's warm smile lit her face. "Yeah, I did. And I was good at it." She colored. "It felt like I was, anyway. The kids seemed to respond to me."

"Sounds like you have a plan, then."

"Not really. It's not that simple. Just because *I* want a teaching job does not mean that there's one available for me, or that they want me." Her brow furrowed. "I've not been in a classroom in over eight years. A lot changes in that amount of time. And even if I got an interview, what do I say when they ask what I've been doing for the past eight years?"

"You've been raising a child. You looked after a sick husband. You did important things."

"Thanks. It felt so at the time. Now, I'm not so sure."

Ellie came by to warm up their coffee. In the play area, Bonnie bent over the puzzle on the floor, Amy and Timothy working on either side of her.

Cynthia nodded at Bonnie. "She may be just what I needed to get back into teaching. Because of Bonnie, I've had to dive back into the curriculums. When I apply for a job, I can say that I spent the past year teaching, even if it was just homeschooling."

"And if you take on Natalie, too?"

"I used to teach middle years. If I taught both Bonnie and Natalie, I'd cover the full gamut of the middle years curriculum."

"Aren't middle years young teenagers?"

"Yes."

"And you actually *liked* that?"

The twinkle in Cynthia's eyes said that she did. "I loved that age group. They're such fun. One minute they're coming across all grown up, then in a flash they act like little kids. It's like they're trying on all sorts of personas, and none of them quite fit. It's fun to help them explore different things, and to maybe have a hand in shaping the adult they'll become."

"Sounds like you're the ideal person for the job then."

"Now if only you were on the hiring committee..." She twisted a napkin in her fingers. "There's another thing. If I tutored Natalie as well as Bonnie, I'd not only be gaining experience, and padding my resume, but I'd be bringing in a bit of money as well. Money we can use."

"Maybe you'd be doing Natalie and her parents a real favor as well. Sounds like they might need you."

"Maybe." She hesitated.

"What's stopping you?"

"I need to talk to Anna and Murph about it first, but I don't think they'd object. Still, there's something about Natalie. I don't know, but something's different."

"What? Are you saying that you might have a friend whose kid is different?" Elizabeth's tone dripped sarcasm.

Cynthia laughed. Elizabeth's son was autistic, as was their friend Keira's little boy. Anna and Murph's foster daughter Bonnie had a diagnosis of selective mutism. Kids who were outside the norm were nothing new to them. "Maybe it's because Natalie is in her mid-teens, and I've forgotten what kids that age are like. Or maybe it's because she's been through so much bullying." She shrugged off her misgivings.

"What's your instinct tell you?"

"It says that I could use the money, and the experience, and that kids are kids."

"Then trust your instinct."

———————

What's wrong with me, Cynthia wondered. I used to handle rooms of twenty-five grade seven students with no problem. Well, she smiled. With not too many problems. The problems, the interactions, were what made the job so interesting.

So why was she fussing about the thought of teaching both Bonnie and Natalie at the same time? That was just *two* kids, and Bonnie was a teacher's dream. They already had their routines figured out and worked well together. How hard could it be to bring one more kid into the mix?

If she took this one, it would be a commitment. She realized how lucky she'd been. For the last eight years, she had the luxury of overseeing her own time while managing a household. What was she? Spoiled? Selfish? Lazy? Why was it so hard to commit to teaching two students, five days a week? If she was lucky enough to get a teaching job in a school, she'd have to be away for those hours and more, anyway. Most women these days worked out of the home and still looked after their homes and families. Was she getting soft that she was reluctant to step up like most people did?

Suck it up, Cynthia, she told herself. You have no choice but to get a job. They needed the money. Tutoring was a way to ease into the workforce. At least she'd still be at home, and it was only two students, not two dozen. They weren't babies; the girls would work on their lessons, giving

Cynthia time to do some things. Like develop her resume. Running a small home study program would look good on that resume. Well, not good, exactly, but better than the blank space that filled up the last eight years of her job history.

Cynthia tried to cling to the memories of being in a classroom. I was good, she reminded herself. The kids liked me and responded well. My colleagues respected me. It was nice talking to adults during the day. When she was in the classroom, she'd not doubted that she could handle the job - that never entered her head. So why did she wonder if she had what it takes to teach two young teens?

Maybe it was because these weren't just any students. They were both wounded from circumstances life had thrown their way. Her mother deserted Bonnie. Then they snatched her little brothers from her life, their whereabouts unknown. She was in a good place now, living with Anna and Murph, but the first twelve years of her life had been rough.

It sounded like Natalie had equally troubled early years, before coming to Barbara's home, then experienced devastating bullying. Did Cynthia have what it took to work with these troubled kids?

Anna and Murph seemed to think so, or at least they trusted her with Bonnie. And, as a social worker and a psychiatrist, they should know.

What was the alternative for Natalie? Barbara doubted they could convince Natalie to return to school this year. Fair enough, the kid had been through a lot. It took a highly motivated student to teach herself at home; how many fifteen-year-olds were like that? Barbara and Howard didn't seem to think they could teach their daughter. If Cynthia didn't, who would? Her efforts couldn't be worse than nothing, could they?

Money. How Cynthia hated dwelling on that topic. In an ideal world, she'd volunteer to teach both Bonnie and Natalie, helping out friends because she could. But she needed to make money. Anna and Murph didn't seem to have a problem with paying her; in fact, they refused to agree to Bonnie coming if they didn't pay Cynthia the going rate. It seemed crass to accept money from friends.

Anna solved that. Rather than hand over a check monthly, she arranged automatic deposits that arrived in Cynthia's bank account on the first of every month, just like a regular paycheck would.

Could Cynthia look Barbara in the eye and quote her the hourly rate that Murph and Anna paid? Cynthia had been at a loss as to how much to charge, so Murph researched the going rate for qualified tutors. At the time, it seemed way too much to Cynthia. After all, she was doing something she loved for a child she was fond of. The money helped, though. And if she took on Natalie, her income would double.

Bonnie was a vulnerable child. She was only now finding her way, starting to sometimes speak around those with whom she was most comfortable. How would throwing a new girl into the mix affect her? Murph and Anna needed time to think about this; Cynthia's commitment was to Bonnie first. If the child's foster parents thought it would harm her, then Cynthia would tell Barbara no.

And what about Bonnie? She flourished under the undivided attention she received at home from Anna and Murph and when she was with Cynthia. Too often in Bonnie's young life she had been pushed aside, rather than the center of someone's attention.

Would she feel that way now if they added another student to their daily routine? Just when the child's confidence was growing, Cynthia would hate to do anything to undermine that. But Bonnie was a kind child; look how she interacted with the younger children of their friends, and how she'd been with her little brothers.

While Bonnie's well-being was most important to Anna and Murph, Amy was central to Cynthia's world. How would Amy feel about two girls being in her home each day while she was away at school? Used to being the center of her mom's world, would she be jealous?

Geez. So much waffling. When did I become such a ditherer? I'm just chicken, Cynthia told herself. I hate to move out of my rut. But things have to change in my life if I'm to support our daughter. Hugh would expect it of me.

Enough. She was disgusting even herself with the doubts volleying in her head. She pulled out her phone. "Anna? Hi, it's Cynthia. I wanted to run something by you."

Not ten minutes later, her phone rang.

"Hey, Cynthia," Murph said. "Anna told me about your idea. I agree with her and think it would be great for Bonnie to have another student there with her. It'll be a gradual introduction to when she returns to school next fall. She needs to start rubbing shoulders with other kids and just one is a great way to begin, especially when it's under your supervision."

There. One argument out of the way. If Anna and Murph didn't object to her taking on a second student, what was stopping her?

Unbidden, another avenue opened in Cynthia's thoughts. What if there was more to Natalie than was obvious, and she'd not been so much a victim? What if there was some basis to all those rumors Barbara hinted at?

Cynthia chided herself. Of course, there was basis. Maybe Natalie had worn the wrong-colored socks or shirt. Those kinds of things could make her a target among adolescents. Even so, there was something about Natalie...

Cynthia grimaced. What was the matter with her? She *liked* kids.

How could she allow herself to have nasty thoughts about a fifteen-year-old? Don't blame the victim - she's a young girl and deserves a chance. Of course, something would seem off with the kid; she was in defensive mode after all she'd been through. What kid wouldn't be bitter after being picked on? She just needed people on her side.

Right?

Chapter Seven

Curled up on her sofa, Elizabeth watched Brendan play on the floor with Timothy. The two of them took their Lego world-building seriously, one with his tongue peeping between his lips, the other with a furrowed brow. For a man who spent nine hours that day on police work, he certainly had time and energy for this little boy. She contrasted that to Jackson, Timothy's father. She had to stretch her mind to think of a time when Jackson had played on the floor with Timothy, or played with him, period.

She glanced at the clock on the mantel - definitely past Timothy's bedtime. "Sorry to break this up, guys, but it's bath time."

"Ahhh," the wail was about to begin.

"You heard your mom, chap. We'll finish this next time. Let me move it onto the coffee table so it's safe."

Timothy wasn't giving up that easily. He had one bargaining chip to prolong the evening. "Story?"

Brendan ruffled his hair. "Sure, kid. As long as your mom says it's all right, I'll read you a story."

"Head to the bathtub, and I'll be with you in a minute."

Timothy obeyed his mother.

Brendan grimaced as his eyes met Elizabeth's. "Guess I should have checked with you about the story before I said yes. Sorry."

Uncurling herself from the sofa cushions, Elizabeth gave him a hug. "Of course, it's all right. Anytime. He loves it when you read to him."

As she left the room, Brendan followed. If only, he thought.

"B, B," a little voice hollered from upstairs. "B, come."

Taking the steps two at a time, Brendan tapped on the bathroom door.

Elizabeth opened it. "I don't know how you're going to get out of this. He loves the baking soda submarine you brought him and wants to show you how it works."

As Brendan rolled up his sleeves and kneeled beside the tub, Elizabeth warned, "You might get wet."

Hard to tell which of them had more fun, but finally Elizabeth called a halt to their play. "Time, guys. It really is way past lights out time."

Brendan lifted the slippery child out of the tub, into the towel his mom had ready. The kid might only be five, but he weighed more than you'd think, especially when wet. He wondered how a woman as slight as Elizabeth managed this every night.

He waited in the hallway while Elizabeth dried and dressed the boy in fresh pajamas.

The bathroom door opened, warm steam following

Timothy out. Immediately, Timothy grabbed for Brendan's hand, pulling him into the bedroom. "Sit," the child instructed, pushing Brendan onto the side of the bed.

Crouching in front of his bookcase, Timothy carefully selected, then rejected three books before pulling out the one his hand had originally touched. Clutching the book with one hand, he scrambled over top of Brendan on the bed, tucking his legs under the covers and pushing the pillows up against the headboard. He patted a pillow, looking expectantly at Brendan.

Settling himself back against the pillow, Brendan took the offered book, Where the Wild Things Are, by Maurice Sendak. A well-thumbed fave, from the look of it. As he turned to the first page, there was a tug on his left arm. Timothy raised Brendan's arm high, tucked himself into the man's side, then lowered the arm around his shoulders. He snuggled the child into him as he began reading.

After tidying up the bathroom, Elizabeth returned to her son's bedroom. Leaning against the doorframe, she watched the two males who were most important to her. Again, her thoughts went to Jackson. Had he ever read to Timothy? She thought not. Yet, in the less than two years Brendan had known them, he had read to the child countless times.

They looked good together, she thought. After all they'd been through, Timothy, like her, did not give his trust easily, but with this man, he was fully at ease and wanted - no, demanded - his attention. A change in cadence and tone interrupted her reverie.

Brendan's voice grew quieter, and his reading slowed down as well. His voice almost at a whisper, he glanced at the sleeping child, placing a kiss on the top of his head. Carefully, he lowered Timothy's head to the pillow, eased himself off the bed, and drew the covers over the little boy's shoulders. Noticing Elizabeth watching, he said, "I guess I bored him to sleep. We didn't even finish the story."

"Next time," she said. "I'm sure he'll hold you to it."

"Yeah, next time." Reluctantly, Brendan returned the book to the shelf, smoothed the covers one last time, and headed to the hall. Turning, he gave a last look at the slumbering boy before pulling the door almost closed. The carpeted stairs hushed his footsteps.

In the living room, Elizabeth held out a bottle of beer toward him. "Want one?"

"I want… something." Wiping his hand down his face, he paced the room. "Look, I'm not very good company right now. Maybe I'd better go."

Stricken, Elizabeth immediately went into contrite mode. "I'm sorry. I know he can be a bit much. You spent all that time playing with him when you've had a long day at work. Just because he asks something, you don't have to do it. He loves you, but he has to learn that he cannot command your attention whenever he wants."

Brendan stopped mid-stride and looked at her incredulously.

She hurried on. "I'll get a better handle on it, I promise. We'll set boundaries. He shouldn't act like he owns you, that he has rights to your time. That's my fault for letting this get out of hand. I'm sorry." She held up the beer as a peace offering.

Now Brendan scrubbed his face as he paced. "You don't get it, do you?" He stopped with his arms widespread and faced her. "You really don't get it."

Elizabeth had never heard that tone of voice from him, at least not directed at her.

"The fact is, I love that kid. I cherish every minute that I get to play with him. I'd read to him every night for the rest of his life if he'd let me. If you'd let me."

Elizabeth started to speak, but he held up his hand.

"Let me finish," he told her. "I need to get this off my chest." He paused a minute, calming himself, collecting his thoughts, and resumed pacing. "All my life, I've been a determined kind of guy. I figure out what I want and go after it." He gave a quick glance Elizabeth's way. "I know you've been through a lot, both you and Timothy. Life's sucked for you in lots of ways, but you've come back strong. I admire that. I also know how important it is to you to stand on your own feet."

Again Elizabeth opened her mouth, and he silenced her.

"Sorry, but I need to get through this," he apologized. "I respect the life that you've built for you and your son. I don't want to interfere with that." He took a big breath and let his shoulders sag. "I just want to be a part of it."

He couldn't look at her now. "I'm not annoyed at playing with Timothy, bathing him, reading him a story, or tucking him into bed. What bugs me is not having the right to do that, the right to be a part of his life."

He stopped in front of her. "I want more. In fact, I want it all. I hate, absolutely hate having to walk away each night."

Elizabeth tensed.

"I get it, or at least I used to. I understood when you didn't want Timothy to see me here in the morning and I could only stay over if he was away on a sleep-over. But I don't want to sneak around. I don't want to have to hide from Timothy the fact that his mom and I are a couple. Or at least, I hope we are."

Elizabeth nodded; her throat too full for words to squeeze by.

He was a freight train that could not be stopped. "I hate feeling that I don't really belong, that I don't have the right to be part of your lives." The expression in his eyes changed as he used his thumb to wipe away the tear winding its way down her cheek. "Don't cry. Please. I'm not trying to make you feel bad; I just need you to know where I'm coming from."

Elizabeth dug her fingernails into her palms, anything to keep the threatening tears at bay. This man wasn't just mad at her, he was hurting. It was her fault, and she hadn't even realized it.

He continued. "You need time - I get it. We're not exactly moving at the same pace here, but I can wait. It's not that long ago that you were married, that you had a different life. Me, when I figure out what I want, I go after it. It's killing me to hold back, to take it slow, hoping that you'll come around to my way of thinking one day."

She reached out a hand to him.

He stepped away. "You know where I'm going with this. You know what I want. I'm all in. If you don't feel the same way, or think that's the direction you're heading, then tell me. Tell me before it'll wrench my heart out to have to walk away from you and that kid."

Tears cascaded down Elizabeth's cheeks.

He couldn't stop now that he'd come this far. "I understand your need for independence; I admire it. I'm not trying to take over, or control you. I just want in, to be a part of this new life you're building. I'm not asking for a commitment today or even soon; I'm not that much of an idiot. I know that I'm way ahead of you, but if you can't see us together one day, and I mean fully together, then tell me soon so that I can back away with some shred of pride." He strode to the door and was gone.

Seconds later, his voice came through the door. "Lock up."

After she clicked the two deadbolts and set the alarm, his footsteps sounded on the porch, then the walkway. Seconds later, his car started up and pulled away.

Chapter Eight

Cynthia hated herself for waffling. It seemed that since Hugh died, all she'd done was hesitate. No, that wasn't quite true; she'd been a dithering mess since they received the diagnosis that Hugh had cancer, terminal cancer.

He'd been strong for her while he could, then she'd needed to be strong for Amy. At four, Amy had had a hard time accepting that Daddy couldn't play with her the way he used to, then the fact that he was gone, and never coming back.

At first, Cynthia justified her choices, saying she needed time to grieve and get used to her new life without her husband. Who could argue with that? But after several years, she could no longer drift.

Squaring her shoulders, she left her house and pressed the bell beside Barbara's front door.

"Hi," she said when Natalie opened the door. "Is your mom home?"

"Yeah." Leaving the door open, Natalie walked away. From the back of the house, she yelled, "Mom!"

Uncertain, Cynthia stood in the doorway.

A minute later, Barbara stood at the top of the stairs, startled to see Cynthia there. "Sorry, I didn't know you were here. Is that why Natalie yelled for me?"

"I suspect so. She didn't say."

"Well, she's in a mood today. Teenagers."

Great, thought Cynthia. What was she letting herself in for? Best get on with it, but maybe with one slight change.

"I've been thinking about what you asked, about Natalie joining Bonnie and me for homeschooling."

Barbara looked like the weight of the world lifted from her shoulders. "You'll do it, then?"

Cynthia nodded, but with some caveats. "First, I'd like some information about Natalie's past schooling. Do you have any reports from her last teachers?"

"Do I ever, although I'm not sure how relevant they are."

Frowning, Cynthia found that odd. "It will help to know how she was doing in her subjects."

"We have her report cards, of course, but we talked to the school more about behavioral issues than academics." Worried that she'd said too much, Barbara explained. "The behaviors had to do with the bullying and harassment that Nat suffered. Sometimes she fought back." She glanced away, then back. "Will that change your mind about teaching her?"

Cynthia shook her head. "If what she did was a reaction to being bullied, that shouldn't be applicable when there are just two students together, and Bonnie is a sweetheart." More firmly, she said, "There will be no bullying in my house."

Barbara closed her eyes momentarily and let the breath she hadn't realized she'd been holding. "Thanks, that's good to hear. Our daughter's been through so much. Making a friend, one who is kind, will mean a lot to Natalie."

"The girls might be friends, even if Natalie doesn't join us for homeschooling. Bonnie's a lovely girl, who has not always had it easy, either. The two might get along well."

From upstairs came the sound of an infant's cry. "Natalie," Barbara called. "Can you see to your brother, please?"

No response.

Louder, "Natalie."

They could hear the teen's sigh all the way down the hall. "Why do *I* have to? He's *your* kid."

Barbara's eye couldn't meet Cynthia's. "I'm sorry," she mouthed. "This has been a hard change for all of us. Excuse me a minute." Barbara walked to the back of the house and disappeared through a doorway. Her low voice spoke.

"*Fine*. All right, I'll get the kid, but next time it's your turn." Without glancing at Cynthia, Natalie trudged up the stairs to where the baby's cries grew stronger.

Barbara returned. "Sorry you had to hear that. Ever since the bullying got bad, Natalie's been moody. We moved to get away from all that, but now that we're here, she's probably home too much with just us. Young people need to be with others their age."

"Some kids struggle when they're out of a routine as well. Even some students who don't enjoy school, do better with the structure it imposes on their days. Too much spare time can grow old." That reminded her of what else she wanted to talk about. "Natalie and I don't really know each other, or how well we'll work together. There are four months left in the school year. Why don't we take this a month at a time and see how things go? At the end of the month, either of us can call a halt to our arrangement. Sound alright?"

Barbara was ready to agree to just about anything. Even though admitting it made her feel like she'd once again lost her shot at Mother-of-the-Year Award, having Natalie out of the house for a good chunk of the day would be a blessing. The hourly rate Cynthia charged was so definitely worth it, for many reasons.

"Would you have a minute to step over to my place and look at some of the ideas I have on where I'll start with Natalie?"

Relieved to have a commitment from Cynthia, Barbara would agree to anything. Putting her hand on the banister and one foot on the stairs, Barbara called up to Natalie. "I'm going to Cynthia's for a few minutes. I'll be right back. Thanks for keeping an eye on Liam for me."

"Whatever," was the response that drifted down to them.

Glancing at her watch, Cynthia said, "We have just a bit of time before Amy gets home from school. My friend, Keira, is bringing her. She, Elizabeth and I take turns picking up the kids from school." They spent the next while looking over the curriculum for Natalie's grade. "We'll start here and see how comfortable she is with the concepts. If there are any holes, we can backtrack and get her caught up."

It was Blitz who alerted them to the fact that they would soon no longer be alone. "Brace yourself," Cynthia warned Barbara. "Amy's here."

Balancing on his hind legs, Blitz's front paws windmilled at the front door. Unlocking it just as the doorbell sounded,

Cynthia caught her daughter as Amy barreled through the door. Sparing her mom only the briefest of hugs, she was on the floor, rolling around with her little dog.

Standing on the porch was Keira. "Guess I don't need to tell you that Amy's home."

Amy held Blitz away from her face long enough to ask, "Can Daniel come in and play? Maybe we can go get Timothy, too." In kindergarten, Timothy was not in school full days the way Daniel and Amy were.

"Sure, why not? That is, if it's okay with his mom." She raised her eyes to Keira's.

"For just a bit," said Keira. "I need to get home to finish some work, but we can stay for a half hour."

"If you've got stuff you need to do, why don't you leave Daniel here with us for a few hours?"

"Really?" asked Keira. "That would be a lifesaver." She returned to the car and escorted her son, Daniel, into the house. Keira worked from home on freelance software engineering contracts.

Bonnie had already packed up her work and left the dining room. Once Amy arrived home, the school day was over for Bonnie as well. Now she entered the role she most enjoyed - entertaining the younger children.

"Bonnie," yelled Amy, launching herself into the older girl's arms. Over Amy's head, Bonnie and Daniel shared a smile. Neither were as demonstrative as Amy, but they appreciated each other's company.

Yanking Bonnie and Daniel each by a hand, Amy led them into the living room. "What shall we do first?" she mused. Since neither of the other two spoke much, Amy kept up a monologue of their options, settling on a set of jigsaw puzzles. All three plopped onto the floor near the toy box and bookshelves.

Barbara took a seat at the opposite end of the living room while Cynthia prepared coffee for them. Watching the three little heads working together so intently, she hoped that one day her own children would find such camaraderie. So far, that pleasure had not been part of Natalie's life.

Barbara tensed as a sound she recognized got closer. Cynthia's doorbell pealed, but Liam's screeching would have announced his presence, anyway.

As the women hurried to open the door, Natalie's frustrated tone greeted them. "Will you stop, already? Can't you do anything but scream?" She ceased jiggling the stroller as her mom reached into it to pick up the crying baby. "He won't stop crying!"

Cynthia could feel the problem through the blankets. "He's soaked. Didn't you think to change him?"

"That's gross. If the kid pisses himself, that's not *my* problem."

"Natalie!"

"Well, it isn't." She'd started to leave, but heard to excited little voices as Amy, Daniel, and Bonnie came to the door to see what was going on.

Instantly, Natalie spun back, her face relaxing into a beaming smile. Bending her knees to be more on the children's height, she asked, "Who do we have here?"

Amy didn't return the brilliant smile.

Opening the door wider, Cynthia invited Natalie in.

Dropping to one knee, Natalie patted the top of Amy's head. "Hello, little one. Are you being careful with eggs these days?"

Amy jerked away. "I'm not little and I didn't drop those eggs."

"Amy," Cynthia chided her daughter. "Be polite to our guests."

Amy looked away.

"Natalie, this young man is Daniel, a friend of Amy's. His mom is a friend of mine."

Natalie held out her hand to Daniel. He shrank back.

"He's shy with people he doesn't know," explained Cynthia. "He's a great kid. He's here often, so you'll get to know each other."

From behind the younger boy and girl, Bonnie hung back.

Cynthia motioned to her. "I'm glad you're here, Natalie. I'd like you to meet Bonnie. Bonnie's here during the school week, working on an independent study program with me. When you join us next week, you'll be working together."

Natalie's smile dissolved. "Next week?" She turned to her mom, scowling. "What's this about?"

Barbara dreaded an explosion; things could go either way with Natalie. "I haven't had a chance to tell you yet. You know how your dad and I've been discussing home-schooling? We were hesitant since neither of us is qualified."

"No kidding," muttered Natalie.

Ignoring that, Barbara continued. "So, we approached Cynthia to see if she'd be willing to take you on, along with Bonnie. Cynthia's a teacher and has taught your grade before."

Natalie tilted her head to the right, surveying Cynthia, then Bonnie. As if deciding, her smile returned. "Thank you so much," she said to Cynthia. "I've been worried about missing months of school. I appreciate this."

Cynthia smiled warmly. "We'll have a good time together, the three of us." She put one arm around Bonnie.

Natalie regarded Cynthia's arm and speculated on the

closeness of those two. Putting on a concerned expression, she asked, "Are you sure I won't be intruding?"

"Not at all," Cynthia assured her. "Bonnie must get sick of just my company during the day. Someone closer to her age will be welcome. Isn't that right?" She directed that last question to Bonnie.

Dutifully, Bonnie nodded, pressed against Cynthia's side, her gaze not leaving Natalie's. The two girls took each other's measure. Bonnie's eyes remained steady, her mouth in a straight line.

Game on, thought Natalie.

"She must really be ill," said Anna next Saturday evening. She poured cups of tea for herself and Murph and set them on their oak slab kitchen table.

"Yeah. This is the first time she's turned down the opportunity to spend time with Amy, Timothy, and Daniel. She's like a mother hen with those three."

"I thought she seemed quiet all week. Something's off. I've asked if something's wrong, but she freezes, and I don't want to push. Maybe she's been incubating a bug." They shared a smile. Bonnie had a diagnosis of selective mutism. Oral communication for her was a source of acute anxiety. "But it was only when she heard that she'd share babysitting duties with Natalie that she admitted to feeling sick."

"Do you think she hid that from us when she thought it was her responsibility to look after the kids?" While Murph could intuitively decipher some of Bonnie's possible motivations, it was hard to always need to guess.

"Wouldn't surprise me. That's something Bonnie would do."

"We've tried to get her out of that parentified role, but they have ingrained it in her all her young life." Murph spoke from his background as a psychiatrist.

"Or, I wonder if she felt usurped because Natalie would be there as well?" The social worker in Anna looked at the social dynamics of situations. "It would be so much easier if she would talk to us more."

"Easier on her, as well."

Chapter Nine

"Not going."

Elizabeth looked at her son. While Timothy's speech was coming, he more often relied on nonverbal methods to get his message across. The fact that he spoke those words meant it was something important to him.

Elizabeth stood by their front door with her purse looped over her shoulder. She, Cynthia, Anna, Keira, and Barbara were going out for dinner, just the five of them. No partners, no kids. They had planned this for weeks. She tried reasoning with Timothy. "You knew about this. You can't stay home alone. Mommy's going out with her friends. You'll stay at Amy's and play with her, and Daniel while we're gone. Natalie will babysit you."

Timothy shook his head.

Losing her cool would not work, but they were going to be late. Thank God her friends would understand, but still…

Remembering her strategies, Elizabeth pulled out the social story she'd created days ago. Through pictures and words, the story described the kids playing at Amy's house while the women had an evening out. Setting the story in front of her son, Elizabeth began reading, then realized her mistake.

The story had Bonnie watching the kids. But Bonnie wasn't feeling well. Rather than cancel their outing, Barbara had suggested Natalie as a babysitter. Since Natalie already knew the kids and lived just two doors down, it was the perfect solution. Luckily, Natalie agreed.

Timothy shook his head again. He pointed at one picture in the social story. "Bonnie."

"I know Bonnie was supposed to stay with you, but she can't. She's sick." Why hadn't she remembered to change the social story, rather than throwing this surprise at Timothy? He never reacted well to unexpected changes.

"Want Bonnie."

Hastily, Elizabeth scrolled through photos on her phone, searching for one that had Natalie in it. Surely there was one here from when the kids played in the backyard. There. Yes. Natalie was pushing Amy on the swing, with Timothy beside them. She showed the picture to her son.

Timothy's eyes narrowed and his little chin thrust out. "No! Don't like her."

Swallowing her sigh of exasperation, Elizabeth clutched her last thread of patience. "Timothy, you hardly know her. Of course, you like her - we all do."

"Hurt Amy."

"No, Amy's not hurt. It's Bonnie who doesn't feel well." Glancing at her watch, Elizabeth saw there was little time left. She hated being late. Her mother taught her that was the height of rudeness.

"Look, Timothy, we're going. You're staying at Amy's house, and I'll be back in a few hours." Taking his hand, she shut and locked the door behind them and marched next door to Cynthia's house. She hated dumping a disgruntled kid on Natalie, but Timothy would come around. He loved playing with his two best friends, Amy and Daniel.

Apparently, Timothy was not the only disgruntled child. A glance at Amy's tear-streaked face told her all was not well in this household, either.

"What have we here? Looks like another grumpy-pants." Natalie grinned at the parents. "Don't worry. They'll snap out of it, and all will go according to plan." Her plan.

Elizabeth raised her eyebrows to Cynthia, asking, "Her, too?"

Timothy glared at Natalie, ignoring the adults. He took Amy's hand and led her to where Daniel sat on the floor, absorbed in his pile of Legos. Over his shoulder, he shot a look at the mother, then at Natalie, before turning his back on them and hunkering down with his friends. The three little heads formed a clique, barring any other members.

Natalie put her hands on the backs of Cynthia and Elizabeth. "Shoo. It's fine. We'll get along great. You get on your way, and we'll see you in a few hours."

Barbara said, "You're sure you're all right with this?"

"Positive. I've got your cell number and Cynthia's. I'll call if there's anything I can't handle. And Dad's just two doors down if I need help."

Keira didn't see the problem. "Let's get this party on the road. Anna will already be there waiting for us. The kids will amuse themselves."

That's right, they'd better, thought Natalie. She had plans. Using an incognito browser, she planned to spend the next few hours surfing the web on Cynthia's computer. Plus, you never knew what juicy tidbits you'd find rummaging around on someone's laptop. She'd learned stuff about her dad that way, stuff that might come in handy one day.

———————————

Several days later, Natalie and Barbara waited until Cynthia answered the door. Brushing past her mother and baby brother, Natalie entered Cynthia's house. Reaching for Amy's hand, she ignored the little girl's efforts to pull back. Spying Daniel hanging back in the hallway, Natalie put her other arm around his shoulders, propelling the kids to where she saw puzzle pieces spread out on the floor. Chatting cheeringly to the two children, she shot a look at Bonnie, who trailed behind them.

Bonnie perched on the edge of the love seat, near the action but not taking part. On the floor between the two younger children, Natalie guided them with the puzzle so encouragingly, so animatedly, that Amy forgot her pique and returned to her usual cheerful self.

Watching them, Barbara's heart melted. This was Natalie at her best. "She loves kids," she explained to Cynthia. Nodding at her now-slumbering son, happy with a dry diaper, "… just not ones this young. Once he's moving around and able to play, she'll be a great big sister."

"She certainly is attentive to the kids." That reminded Cynthia of something else. "Have you seen a white SUV parked along the street? It looks like there's a man behind the steering wheel, but he just sits there. I've noticed him a few times."

Barbara shook her head. "Sorry." She nodded at the baby cradled in her arms. "This guy keeps most of my focus directed his way. I hardly ever glance out the window."

A scratching at the patio door told Cynthia that Blitz

was ready to come back inside after doing his business in the backyard. She rose to let him in. The little dog raced into the room, eager to be with the kids. He ran straight for Amy, his favorite person in the universe. His trajectory took him right over top of the puzzle they were patiently constructing. It was tricky to get the pieces to remain connected against the plushness of the carpet. Natalie was busy trying to keep the bits connected as the children attempted to fit the pieces.

"Why you little…" began Natalie as puzzle bits disconnected and scattered. Then she tempered her tone. "Ah, you didn't know what you were doing, did you?" She attempted to rebuild one corner of the puzzle. That accomplished, she reached over to pet the dog, pulling him off Amy's lap and onto her own. Blitz struggled to get away, but Natalie's firm hand kept him in place. He yelped from the pressure. "You have to be careful," Natalie gently explained to him. "You don't want to ruin our puzzle, do you?"

Blitz whined deep in his throat and squirmed.

"He likes me best," said Amy. "He wants to come to me."

"He's getting used to me," said Natalie. She kept one hand on his back and another on his left paw.

Daniel backed away, sensing something.

"No, he isn't," insisted Amy. "Let me have him."

The dog's whine turned into a yelp, then a bark, and his struggles to evade Natalie's hold intensified.

"What's the matter with him?" Cynthia stood and approached. "He never makes noises like that."

As Natalie released her grip, Blitz scooted away, yelping with each step. He hobbled on three feet over to Cynthia, collapsing onto his haunches.

Picking up the tiny dog, Cynthia cradled him to her

chest. "He's acting like he's hurt. I wonder if he got into something in the backyard." Carefully, she inspected him.

It was Amy who noticed his foot. The outside toe on his front left paw stuck out at an odd angle. "Mommy! Look at his toe. It doesn't look right."

Hoisting Liam over her shoulder, Barbara came closer to look. "That claw looks broken. I didn't notice when he came in. He seemed to run okay then." Liam started fussing.

Natalie came over, concern all over her face. She reached out to gently stroke the top of Blitz's head. "Ah, poor little guy." The dog squirmed in Cynthia's arms, trying to avoid Natalie's touch. "I wonder if he caught a nail in a carpet loop and twisted it."

"I need to get him to the vet's office."

"Sure, you go," said Natalie. "I'll look after the kids." She smiled at Bonnie. "Won't we, Bonnie?" She turned to her mother. "You'd better take that baby home. We've got this here."

"Thanks so much, Natalie. That's sweet of you."

"Mom, I'm going with you. I don't want to stay with *her*, and Blitz needs me."

Ignoring her daughter's rudeness to deal with another time, Cynthia agreed. "Yes, you can help me with Blitz, Amy. Go get his carrier, please."

Placing Liam in his stroller, Barbara reminded Natalie to call if she needed her.

Natalie put her arm around Bonnie, snuggling the younger girl into her side. "Bonnie and me, we're a team."

With a sideways jerk, Bonnie pulled out of her embrace.

Lying in bed in the early hours of the morning after Brendan so abruptly left her house that evening, Elizabeth's gaze followed the shifting shadows on her ceiling. She barely registered the gusting winds outside, blowing the branches, casting ever-changing patterns of light coming in through the partially opened curtains.

She never forgot to shut her drapes at night. Ever. Well, at least not since their ordeals. Before that, worry about their physical safety had not occupied such a large part of her mind.

Tears flooded her eyes, soaking her pillowcase. She didn't notice or bother trying to wipe them away.

Brendan. She'd hurt that man. She had no idea their situation bothered him.

She was content with how things were, happy even. After her ex-husband Jackson's betrayal, she had not believed she'd ever trust another man, let alone let one in. But she did, and she had. Her hands fisted the bedsheets. Jackson - the man who had vowed to love and honor her, had tried to have her killed. He'd been willing to leave their son motherless, in order to get his hands on her money. If she'd known he wanted more access to her funds, all he'd needed to do was say so. The money meant little to her, but obviously it meant a lot to him. Everything.

But he was gone, locked up, and could hurt them no more. Daddy had tied up her finances so that she was protected, and she and Timothy were comfortable. Although he'd pretended to be civil, Daddy had never warmed to Jackson, even years after their marriage.

Brendan was nothing like Jackson; she felt that to the very marrow of her bones. She unclenched her hands.

But then, she'd put her faith in Jackson, too, hadn't she?

Surely, this time was different; this man was different in every way that mattered.

Her teeth clamped together in frustration. What was wrong with how things were? She and Brendan enjoyed each other's company. They spent many evenings and most of his days off work together. She thought they had fun, had a good thing going. All of them. He was so good with Timothy, and the kid loved him.

At first, Elizabeth had tried to keep Timothy and Brendan apart. Men had threatened and harmed Timothy, and she couldn't risk letting him get hurt again. But slowly, almost without her knowing it, Brendan had gotten under their skin, gently, seamlessly becoming an expected part of their lives.

She'd thought they were fine. Why couldn't this be enough?

But for Brendan, it was not. Obviously. Happy in her own bubble, she'd had no idea how he felt. For someone who prided herself on being aware of others' feelings, she'd really missed the boat this time.

She cared about Brendan, she truly did. He was a great guy, and her life and Timothy's were better with him in it. Because *she* was happy, and Timothy was happy, she'd assumed that everyone in their little triad felt the same.

Not so, as she'd learned tonight. Her complacency hurt Brendan.

Elizabeth had spent much of her life pleasing others. After her brother's death, she followed the lead of her parents, shutting down her feelings of loss.

She tried to be the perfect child, pleasing Daddy whenever possible. She followed his suggestions, only deviating twice that she could recall. Once was in choosing her college major. The second was when she became engaged to Jackson, resisting Daddy's probing into whether she knew the man well enough. Sigh. Daddy had been right.

Then, with Jackson, she tried to keep her man happy, as cliched as that sounded. He was the one away working much of the week, so she made his time at home as relaxing and stress-free as possible.

It wasn't enough.

Then there was Timothy. His few short years of life had been tough on him and on her. Not so much on Jackson, in retrospect. He didn't join them at medical appointments, monitor the child's meds, or tend him through the seizures.

Her tears slowed as resentment and anger took their place.

She was fine with appeasing Timothy when he was ill, and all children required care and attention. But she was done appeasing men. What good had it done for her? She'd let Daddy manage her life and yes, even after she and Jackson married, Daddy had still arranged much of their lives, at least financially. Relying on men had not done Elizabeth any favors, not prepared her for managing on her own.

But she was strong, or at least had become strong. During their kidnapping, she'd done what she had to do to keep herself and her son alive.

After learning the extent of Jackson's betrayal, she did what she needed to protect herself and Timothy. Never again would she be under a man's thumb. She could stand on her own.

But Brendan. Her shoulders slumped. He wasn't like

Jackson, and he wasn't like her father. He didn't expect her to do things for him; in fact, more often *he* did things for her.

Never had he tried to take choices out of her hands or control her. Well, except for telling her to lock the door behind him. He seemed to like her just as she was, a fresh experience for Elizabeth. She smiled to herself. It was refreshing and relaxing.

Somehow, she thought they'd just go along as they were. Forever hadn't entered her head; she was still trying to establish the new normal for herself and Timothy. Brendan had slipped into that normal, and it felt good.

But what felt good to her and to Timothy obviously was not shared by Brendan. He didn't find the same contentment in their being together. He wanted more.

Did she have more to give?

Chapter Ten

In Mexico

Alejandro and Sally pulled up to the gates. Rolling down his window, Alejandro identified himself. They heard a click, then the gates rolled back on themselves, letting them into the estate.

The drive meandered through the manicured gardens. Sally lost her slouch, her face changing from a sulk to calculated interest.

"You didn't tell me you put Jordy in a place like this."

"All of my clients are wealthy," said Alejandro. "They could not afford our adoption fees otherwise."

Maybe this wouldn't be so bad after all, thought Sally. She could get used to living in a place like this, the sort of place she deserved. "A nanny is above the other staff, right? Kind of like a family friend?"

Alejandro looked at her, his brow wrinkled. "What would give you an idea like that? You're paid help."

Maybe not for long, Sally schemed. She could change her status. "What are their names again?"

"The child's name is Jordy," Alejandro reminded her. "You

named him, and Germaine and Emma decided it would be less confusing for the kid if they kept the name he was used to."

"Germaine and Emma," Sally repeated, to lock those names in her mind. She'd never been good with names.

"No. To you, they are Señor y Señora Molina."

Sally rolled her eyes. "Whatever."

Alejandro's voice became harsh. "I mean it. You will be polite and deferential to them and address them formally. You are not their friend. You are not here as a guest. You are a servant and will act accordingly."

"So, what are they going to do if I don't? They're not about to throw a four-year-old out on his ear."

"No, but they might throw you out." How could she be so oblivious to the ways of the world? Alejandro didn't know why he'd been lured in by her potential. Rarely did he read people wrong. "Señor Molina will be quick to report to me if you don't work out." He put the car into park and turned off the ignition. Turning, he draped one arm along the top of the seats. His fingers wrapped around Sally's neck. "If you don't please Señor and Señora Molina, you're out. And I don't mean just out of this mansion, but out of my organization. You screw up and you're on your own." He gave her neck a squeeze, hard enough that Sally tried to pull away. "Comprende?"

When she didn't speak, his grip tightened, and he waggled her neck back and forth.

"Yeah, I get it. Enough already. Let go." Inwardly she seethed. How dare he treat her like this, as if she was some underling, some hired help?

Their staring contest ended as they heard the front door open. A woman clad entirely in black, save for the stark, white apron over her dress, stood in the doorway, expressionless, watching them.

His expression changing instantly, Alejandro leapt from the car, hurrying around to open the passenger door for Sally, his face beaming with cheer and good will.

"Señor Ramon?" The woman's tone was neutral.

"Si," replied Alejandro. With a hand under Sally's elbow, he escorted her up the wide terrazzo steps to the front door. "And this is Sally."

Leaning a hip on the doorframe, Cynthia surveyed the scene in her dining room with satisfaction. This was working well. Although the girls were over two years apart in age, Natalie and Bonnie had forged a bond of sorts. While neither trusted easily, their friendship was coming, she believed. This would make their re-entrance into the school system easier, Cynthia was sure. She was pleased with the efforts Natalie made. Bonnie was more reticent, but then she had good reason to give her trust sparingly after what she'd been through. Cynthia went to check on the brownies baking in the oven; the girls deserved a treat.

In the kitchen's corner, Blitz dozed on his dog bed. Dogs were tough. He seemed close to his old self after his hurt foot.

Usually a gentle wee dog, Blitz had become a dervish, whirling, growling, and warning the world to back off when the vet attempted to examine his paw. Only once the tranquilizer took effect were they able to inspect his paw. The verdict was that his claw was broken off internally. The pain would be intense with each step. Left untreated, this would be the little dog's life. The vet asked Amy to step into the outer room and choose a treat for her pet, with the receptionist's help. In her absence, the vet explained what needed to be done. With a hard tug, his instrument pulled out the offending digit. Swabbing and applying antiseptic to the wound, he explained that the opening might just heal over, and Blitz would be minus one claw, or he might grow a replacement one. His paw would be sensitive for a while, then he should be back to his old self.

The vet trimmed Blitz's other nails as a precaution. Sometimes dogs caught a claw on a root or in carpet fibers, causing the digit to break. Or the cause could have been something else.

Although still limping slightly, Blitz was almost back to normal. The one difference was his avoidance of any proximity to Natalie. Dogs often felt that way about veterinarians, as well. Even though they helped heal them, the dog associated their pain with that person. Poor Natalie, thought Cynthia. That really wasn't fair. She vowed to work at Blitz, being more accepting of her second student.

The girls worked quietly in their notebooks at the dining room table. Cynthia glanced in from time to time as she chopped vegetables to add to a stew. She was glad she'd agreed to supervise Natalie's independent study schooling. Not only did it get her one step closer to returning to the teaching profession, but she was helping these girls. That felt good.

Both girls had suffered. Bonnie had lived a thankless, parentified life, being the primary caregiver for her two younger brothers. Even worse, only her foster mother, Anna's, intervention had saved her from being kidnapped and sold into a life too frightening to contemplate. She was safely back home now, living with Anna and Murph. Returning to school would be in her future next fall.

Natalie had her own trauma. Victimized in her previous school and neighborhood, she suffered bullying and malicious accusations and isolation.

Bonnie tried to ignore Natalie's stare. She pretended to concentrate fiercely on her math questions. She'd seen that look on Natalie's face before, and nothing good came of it. A quick glance up told Bonnie that Cynthia was still in the other room. Used to managing for herself, Bonnie resigned herself to doing so again. But something was coming, she knew.

Natalie opened her eyes wide and smiled at Bonnie. She had practiced this look in the mirror and knew how adults responded to it. It served her well. "Bonnie, your hair is so pretty."

Bonnie looked up. Her eyes met Natalie's, then slid away. "Thanks." She returned to her work, happier when no one noticed her, especially Natalie.

Natalie studied the younger girl, assessing. "Would you like me to braid your hair?"

Cynthia came in and heard this offer. "How nice of you, Natalie. I think you'd look lovely in braids, Bonnie."

"No, thanks." Bonnie's response was hardly audible. Into the silence she added, "I have to finish this."

"Nonsense," said Cynthia. "You've worked hard this afternoon; both of you have. You deserve a break."

"No," Bonnie started, but Cynthia didn't hear. She'd left the room to set up a high stool in the living room.

"Come on, girls." She set the stool in front of the full-length mirror. "There. Now you can watch how Natalie does it, Bonnie." What a bonding activity. It was nice to see these girls acting like typical teens after the rough times they'd been through. When Bonnie didn't budge from her chair, Cynthia reached across the table, gently shutting Bonnie's book. "It'll be fun. We'll surprise Anna when she picks you up."

The gleam of victory shone in Natalie's eyes, but only Bonnie saw it. Natalie slung an arm around Bonnie's neck. "Yeah, it'll be fun. I'm great at this." She gave a squeeze, and then let go as Bonnie climbed onto the high stool.

While Cynthia watched, Natalie carefully brushed Bonnie's hair with long, gentle strokes. Cynthia smiled to see the care Natalie took with her young friend. She thought of her own best friend from middle school. They'd spent every possible second together until Sarah had moved away with her family. The girls swore that they'd remain best friends forever, but slowly their emails and text messages had dwindled to nothing. Maybe Natalie and Bonnie would maintain their connection. Having a trusted friend made weathering life's storm easier. Smiling to herself, Cynthia returned to the kitchen, content to listen to the girls' conversation.

Well, it wasn't really a conversation. Bonnie rarely spoke, but Natalie chatted away. She talked about the last Game of Thrones episodes she'd watched and her admiration for powerful women who knew what they wanted, and got things done.

Once Cynthia left the room, the brush came down on Bonnie's head harder. Each stroke pulled Bonnie's head back. Although tears sprung in Bonnie's eyes, she determinately didn't allow them to fall, nor would she utter a sound. She would not give Natalie the satisfaction. It became a contest of wills.

Cynthia called from the kitchen, "What kind of braids will you make?"

"I think we'll do a four-strand French braid, don't you think?" Natalie hung on to a lock of Bonnie's hair and gave it a tug, turning Bonnie's face toward hers. Her knowing eyes met Bonnie's. She pulled Bonnie's head up and down. Whispering, she said, "Tell Cynthia how much you'll like that."

Bonnie scrunched her eyes shut. She'd withstood more things than Natalie could throw at her.

Pretending she was unfazed by Bonnie's lack of response, Natalie began dividing the younger girl's hair into sections. "Cynthia," she called. "Any chance that you could help hold on to some of these sections?" As Cynthia's steps approached, she changed tactic. "I'm sorry, Cynthia. I know that you have better things to do than stand here while we do girl stuff. But would you have any clips or bobby pins I could use? I'll do a better job with something to hold sections in place as I work."

"Of course, my dear. I'll be right back." Cynthia smiled at the girls as she went to her bedroom for clips. Returning, she said, "Be careful with this one. It always snags in my hair, pulling it. The others are all right, though."

As soon as Cynthia left, Natalie picked up the clip they'd been warned about. She twisted a clump of hair near Bonnie's temple, wound it tightly, then clamped it as if welded to the scalp. She smiled in satisfaction as she watched the younger girl's eyes water. Bonnie was so easy to manipulate. That she wouldn't talk was a bonus.

Slowly, painstakingly, Natalie worked tiny sections of hair at a time, pulling them so tightly that Bonnie's scalp showed between each twist of the plait. Bonnie uttered not a word.

Cynthia checked in with them. "How lovely! Natalie, you're doing such a good job. Look at how even those rows are." She gave Bonnie's shoulder a squeeze. "Nice to have such a talented friend, willing to do this for you, isn't it?"

Natalie smiled in triumph, her eyes meeting Bonnie's in the mirror. Cynthia was lame. How could adults be so gullible? This was no challenge at all.

Chapter Eleven

In Mexico

Alejandro's rented hybrid Prius pulled to a silent halt in the portico covering the entrance to the mansion. The imposing entrance gates impressed Sally's avarice, but once inside the grounds, her head could not stop swiveling around.

The doorbell's deep tones reverberated through the air. Seconds later, the arched double doors opened.

Sally instantly labelled this woman the penguin lady who opened the door. Who would allow themselves to be dressed like that? No way was she *wearing any such uniform.*

The penguin lady took a step back and darned if she didn't bow her head as a man and woman approached.

Ignoring the women, Germaine headed straight for Alejandro with his hand extended. "Alejandro, my man. Thanks for coming so quickly and arranging this."

"Anytime. You know that my agency and I are here for you." He shook Germaine's hand, covering their joined hands with his left and giving a squeeze. "And for the child, of course. We want only happy

placements." He released Germaine's hand and turned to Emma. "Señora Molina. You're looking beautiful, as always. I trust that motherhood is agreeing with you."

"I'm sure it will now that you've brought us your hand-picked nanny." The smile she gave Sally was tentative.

Alejandro wrapped a firm hand around Sally's arm. "Señor and Señora Molina, I'd like to present to you Ms. Sally Ramirez. She comes to you with over a dozen years of experience with children."

Sally tried to pull away from the appendage grasping her arm. No luck, he wasn't budging. "It's not been that many years," she said, looking directly at Señor Molina. "I'm not that old."

"Don't be bashful, Sally. It's all right in front of these people. They need to know just how many years you've been looking after children."

From farther back in the house came screeching. Sally's heart sank. She recognized that uproar and had spent years trying to avoid it. Where was Bonnie when you needed her?

The wails grew louder, and soon a young woman appeared at the top of the lush, carpeted stairs, holding the hand of a screaming child. Snot formed a channel between his nostrils and his lips, then dipped into his mouth. The child wiped his face on the young woman's clothes - clothes that mimicked those of the penguin lady. She looked horror-struck at the smeared mucus marring the pristine state of her starched white pinafore. Muffling her distaste, she led the child by the hand down the stairs.

His howls lessened to sniffs as he caught the glare of his new papa, Señor Molina. Two nights without supper had taught him that silence was best in this man's presence.

Looking beyond the austere Señor Molina were a man and woman. Usually, he tried to ignore the annoying people in this environment, but something about the lady... It twigged. Yanking his hand from that of his current keeper, he barreled down the stairway. "Momma!"

Señora Molina was shaken. "He never calls me Momma or

Mama. We've told him to, but he just won't. He doesn't call me anything."

Sally wanted to tell her she wasn't missing much, but a glare from Alejandro told her to keep her mouth shut.

By then Jordy reached the group of adults. He latched on to Sally's legs and peered behind her. "Bonnie?" He looked behind Alejandro and to the open door. Dashing out, he called, "Bonnie!" Head swiveling to all sides, he searched for his favorite person in the entire world. Where was she?

"There's that name again," said Emma Molina. "He's always calling for some Bonnie." Turning to Alejandro, she asked, "Any idea who that is?"

"You never know with kids," came his reply. He shrugged.

Addressing Sally, Emma said, "And he called you momma."

"Kids," said Alejandro. "When they're that young, they have generic labels for everything. Not much vocabulary development at this age, is there, Sally?"

She needed a nudge to respond. "That's right. Maybe every woman looks like a mother to him."

"But he never calls me that." Bitter disappointment laced Emma's words.

"He will," assured Alejandro. "And that word meant nothing. Look how he raced right on by Sally."

"True," admitted Emma. "He is a hard child to understand." To Sally, she said, "We are so grateful to have you here. I'm sure you will work miracles with this little boy, where others have failed."

The adults gravitated out the door and now watched Jordy race about the yard, as if playing hide-and-seek all by himself. Emma continued. "He's so young. Children are malleable. I'm sure that with your help he'll fit into our household in no time." She thought a few seconds, irked by Jordy's spontaneous word 'Momma.' "We should establish some ground rules. Even though he called you that name, it is not to be repeated. He can call you Sally or Nanny. But I am his mother now, and he will call no one but me Mama."

Alejandro pasted on his warmest smile; one he had practiced in front of the bathroom mirror since he was young. He knew how others, especially women, responded to it. "Of course not. That is a special name reserved for that one woman in his life - you." Cupping Sally's arm again, and giving it a squeeze, he added, "I'm sure Sally has no intention of usurping your role." He gave the arm he held another pinch.

Sally got the hint and spoke with all honesty. "No, I definitely have no desire to be a mother to this child." That's why I gave him up. Looking at Alejandro, she knew he understood. They were like that, the two of them. That's why she'd believed they'd be perfect business partners.

Mostly satisfied, Emma still had one concern. "I wish we knew who this Bonnie person was."

Germaine's one weakness was his wife. Any length to make her happy was never too much. Favoring Alejandro with the intensity of his gaze, he said, "Let's leave that with Alejandro, shall we? He'll get to the bottom of this for us and, if necessary, produce this Bonnie. Right?"

"Absolutely," agreed Alejandro. "This child's well-being is our goal." Stepping to Germaine's side, he turned his back to the women. "But there might be additional expenses involved."

Chapter Twelve

It was Saturday. Howard escaped the house, calling one of his new work mates to join him in a golf game. He'd never say so, but he was avoiding being home with his daughter. Coward.

Natalie was in one of *those* moods.

It was a teen thing; Barbara was sure of that. Still, some days it was hard to take.

An hour or so ago, she had seen Cynthia's car pull into her driveway. Maybe her neighbor was up for some company. Before she could think of all the reasons she should not impose, Natalie cranked her music up more decibels than any sound box should go without bursting.

Securing the slumbering Liam in his stroller, Barbara hollered up the stairs to let Natalie know where she was going, but stopped. What's the use? She knew she could never raise her voice to be heard above that racket. She settled for leaving a note on the kitchen table.

It took a while for Cynthia to respond to the doorbell,

giving Barbara ample time to rethink her impulsive decision. She'd turned the stroller around to head back home when the door opened.

"Sorry it took me a while. I was out back with the kids and wasn't sure if I heard the bell or not." She opened the door wider. "Come on in." She glanced behind Barbara. "Are you alone?"

"Yes. Well, not entirely alone." She nodded at her son.

"Come on back and we can visit. Timothy's here playing with Amy. It'll be nice to have another grownup to talk to."

Barbara's shoulders sank with relief. Grateful for Cynthia's ready acceptance, she could relate to the desire for adult conversation.

The afternoon was warm, with just the right amount of breeze blowing the sweet-incense fragrance of the nearby Jeffrey pines, Catalina currants, and musk sage. That was one thing Barbara appreciated about their new home - the evidence of nature nearby. She hoped Liam might take an interest in such things; Natalie certainly didn't.

Natalie. Was she ever not in Barbara's mind? Yes, for brief periods now, ever since she'd began spending school days with Cynthia. "I can't tell you how much we appreciate your willingness to teach Natalie. It's made such a big difference in our lives." In more ways than one, she didn't add.

"We're enjoying having her. She and Bonnie have developed a friendship. The other day she was so sweet to Bonnie, offering to do her hair for her."

That warmed Barbara's heart and brought a sheen of tears to her eyes. "You're the only one who's said anything like that in, well, in years." If ever, she thought.

Cynthia cocked her head and looked at Barbara through slightly narrowed eyes. "Why would you say that?"

"Because it's true." She tried not to let the bitterness enter her voice. "You do not know the hell we've been through. These last few years it got especially worse."

"Adolescence can be tough."

Barbara shook her head. "It was more than that." How much to say? "It started with bullying. At first, we thought it was just kid stuff, you know? It'd pass, and she'd toughen up. But it didn't pass; it got worse. Natalie said she didn't care, but she must. Every kid wants to have friends, right?"

Cynthia nodded, watching the closeness between Amy and her neighbor, Timothy. She was grateful they had their friendship.

"We put her in Brownies, then Girl Scouts. She didn't care about earning badges, although she was quite capable of doing any of the tasks. She seemed indifferent toward the other girls in her pack."

"Some of us are more social than others," said Cynthia.

Barbara shook her head. "It's more than that. They went camping one summer, and the rumors started. The leader said she saw Natalie hold a child's head under water and not let her up. Natalie said she was just playing, but the other child was crying. Howard said that the other girl was probably a wimp, afraid of the water."

Cynthia poured them some more coffee from the insulated carafe.

"On that same camping trip, some of the girls said they saw Natalie catching butterflies and moths and," she could hardly go on, "and pulling off their wings."

Cynthia looked at her sharply.

"Back home, stuff started happening more and more at

school. We'd get a call from the principal telling us that Natalie had pushed a kid or tripped a younger student. We were sure that she was defending herself or acting out against the ostracizing and bullying she suffered."

"Could be. If she felt powerless against her peers, she might take it out on someone smaller than herself."

That evoked fears in Barbara's mind about Liam. Sometimes she wondered if it was safe to leave her son alone with their daughter. In those moments, she'd be ashamed of herself. How could she think ill of the child they'd shared a home with for a dozen years?

"Then other stuff started happening." It was all spilling out now. "At first it was small stuff like gecko tails left on our neighbor's porches." She looked at Cynthia through tears. "They blamed it on Natalie." She swiped the back of her hand across her eyes. "A dog lost the tip of his tail. It was cut clean off. A cat went missing. Cats do that, though, don't they? How could anyone think our daughter had anything to do with it?"

Good question, thought Cynthia.

"A paper bag filled with newspapers was lit near a neighbor's garage. It started raining, one of those flash things, and put it out before any damage was done. Another time, a garden shed on the street behind us did burn down." There was an upside to this story. "We, of course, with everyone else, went to see what was happening when we heard the fire engine's siren. Natalie was the most animated we'd seen her in a long time. She watched everything the firefighters did so intently. We think that was what sparked her interest in entering that profession."

"I didn't know that was her goal."

"Well, you know how teens are. One day they want to

be an astronaut, the next a firefighter." She sipped her coffee, cradling it in her hands. "For a while, we thought she might want to be a vet. She took such an interest in the neighbor's pets. It's too bad Howard has such allergies; I think it would have been good for her if we had a dog or cat. But she spent hours with the neighbor's animals, patiently coaxing them to come to her." They'd been proud of their daughter's patience. "That stopped though when a woman accused her of breaking her dog's toe."

Cynthia got why school curriculums changed. She really did, but it made things harder for teachers. Yes, keeping up with the times was crucial for modern education, but revamping a subject's curriculum meant considerable new learning for the instructor.

The math curricula had been rejuvenated two years ago; it had been eight years since Cynthia last taught and she was playing catch-up now, trying to stay even just a few steps ahead of the girls as she taught them. Math was math, sure, but the way problems and calculations were explained and approached had changed. She so did not want to make a mistake and put Bonnie or Natalie even further behind when they returned to the classroom.

She spent much of her evenings studying and planning the next lessons. A classroom teacher would grapple with one grade's curriculum; Cynthia was learning what was required for Bonnie's grade, plus, since Natalie was three grades ahead but had missed so much class time, she also had to learn what made up the grades seven, eight, and nine coursework.

Normally, Cynthia didn't mind math, the way numbers fit together, the logic to the patterns. They were something you could count on. As long as those numbers weren't budget-related, she thought.

Bonnie grasped the math concepts easily enough, especially considering the amount of school that she had missed. Natalie did not have the same natural bent for the subject. Or perhaps it just didn't interest her. While Bonnie strove to please the adults in her life, Natalie seemed indifferent to their approval.

Now, where did that thought come from? Cynthia chided herself. That was an unkind thought about a young girl, especially one who was her student. Natalie had been through a lot. It was understandable that she might hold herself aloof and don some armor in self-protection; she'd been hurt in the past. In anyone should know what that was like, it was Cynthia.

Natalie waited patiently, her eyes wide and trusting, watching Cynthia.

"What was your question again, please?" Cynthia stalled for time, since she was unsure how to answer.

"Is this formula similar to what I did last year?"

"I'm sorry, dear. You'll have to give me a few minutes to search through the curriculum you took last year. It's changed since I was last in the classroom, and I don't want to steer you wrong."

"That's all right." Natalie gave a saccharine smile. She tilted her head to one side as she observed Cynthia. "You're not very good at this, are you?"

Cynthia's eyes widened. Had she heard that right?

Bonnie's head jerked up; she looked from Natalie to Cynthia and back again.

Reaching over, Natalie patted Cynthia's hand, then gave

it a squeeze. "That's all right. You can practice on us. Bonnie and I don't mind, do we, Bonnie?"

Standing at the gas pump, Howard drummed the fingers of his left hand on his car roof as he filled his truck with fuel. Idly glancing around, he squinted at a man getting out of white SUV. Did that guy have a common face, or had he seen him somewhere before?

The fellow turned around as he inserted the nozzle into his gas tank.

The cogs turned and meshed in Howard's brain. Yes! It was him. A little older, a little heavier, (who wasn't?) but it was the same guy. It had been over a dozen years, but Howard knew that face, the one that changed their lives forever.

The nozzle clicked beneath his hand. Hanging up the hose, and replacing his gas cap, Howard locked the car, then headed for the man.

"Al. Is that really you? Alejandro Ramon?"

The man turned, a question in his gaze. "Do I know you?"

Howard held out his hand. "No reason that you'd remember me, but I certainly remember you. You gave my wife and I the greatest gift possible. Twelve years ago."

Shaking hands, Alejandro asked, "An adoption?"

"Yep, Natalie. You said that the kid had a rough start, been in several placements, but you thought we might be her forever home. You were right."

Alejandro returned Howard's smile. "How old is she now? How is she doing?"

"She'll be sixteen her next birthday. She's a beautiful

girl. We're so proud of her." His face clouded. "She had some trouble at her last school - bullying, you know." He shook his head. "Mean girls and all that. But we're proud of how she's come through it. She's a strong kid."

"Glad to hear it."

"Say, why don't you come meet her?"

"I'm not sure…"

"Wait right here. I'll just pay for my gas, then be back."

Inside, Howard paid his bill and pointed out the window toward Alejandro, who was hanging up his hose. "And I'll pay for that guy's fill as well."

Leaving the building, Howard met Alejandro, who was on his way in. Taking Alejandro's arm, Howard turned him around. "All taken care of," he said. "My treat. Now, have you got a few minutes? Come on over to the house to meet Natalie. And Barbara would love to see you again."

In Cynthia's dining room, Bonnie pretended to be intent on her work, trying to ignore the looks Natalie shot her way.

Studying some of the curricular outcomes, Cynthia was planning next week's lessons for the girls.

"Do you ever feel like you don't belong?" Natalie's question fell into a void.

Cynthia found her voice. "Natalie! What do you mean?"

"Well, Bonnie's a foster kid. She's not with her real parents. They didn't want her."

"Natalie!" Sheesh, this kid. "You can't know that."

"Well, why isn't she with her parents then?"

Silence.

Trying to find where to prod next, Natalie tried a different route, directing this question to Cynthia. "Don't people get paid to take in foster kids? Do they make good money off of her?"

Before Cynthia could think of a suitable retort, Natalie turned to the stone-faced Bonnie. "I don't mean anything by it. I'm just curious."

No reaction from Bonnie.

"It's the same with me, you know." Natalie made her eyes open wide with frankness. "I'm not with my real parents either. I've no idea who they were. I'm adopted."

Trying to smooth things over, Cynthia said, "Being adopted means you were chosen. Barbara and Howard picked you out of all the babies they could have had to be their daughter."

Natalie just looked at her, thinking, are you for real? "Adoption is about loss, and how can loss be good? No one comes out of it whole when they have to have new mothers." She looked at Bonnie. "No one."

"That's not true. That can't be true," countered Cynthia. "Lots of good things come out of adoptive and foster homes." She squeezed Bonnie's hand. "It delighted Anna and Murph to have Bonnie in their lives."

"Spoken like someone who doesn't know loss."

Did she really need to defend herself to this girl? Looking at Bonnie, who watched the interchange with glistening eyes, Cynthia knew she had to try. "Yes, I've known loss. Amy's father, my husband, died."

Natalie looked at her curiously. "What was that like?"

Cynthia's brows knit together. Awful! About as awful as it gets. "What do you mean, what was it like?"

"Was it like an accident? Was he killed?"

"No. He got cancer, was sick, then died."

"Did it take him like a long time to die? Did he suffer?"

What was with this kid? "Yes! Yes, he suffered. He suffered horribly and so did we."

"Was that it? I mean, was that it for losses for you?"

Okay, deep breath, Cynthia. You're the adult here. Remember that. She consciously released her fingernails from the gouges they made in her clenched palms. She let her shoulders sag. Okay, relax. Take control. You're a teacher; act like one.

Obviously, Natalie was a troubled child. She needed to talk. She trusted the people in this room. So, we'll let her talk, but steer the conversation into a little less volatile area.

"Yes, I've been through other losses. I was an army brat."

"What's that?" Natalie looked to Bonnie, but she didn't know either.

"It means that my father was in the military. Service men get moved around a lot, and often their families move with them. So, every few years, sometimes more than that, we'd have to pack up and move. You know what moving is like."

"Where'd you move to?"

"Sometimes a different city or a different state. Sometimes a different country."

"Why?"

"That was my dad's job, and when you're in the service, you go where you're needed. And, we went with him, my mom and me."

"Did you like that? Was it exciting always seeing new places?"

"No, it wasn't exciting. It was hard." She was the new kid everywhere she went, picked on and alone. She sympathized with the bullying Natalie had suffered. "We never made friends, or at least had friends for very long. My mom and I were close because we were the only ones always around."

"That would suck to be only friends with your mom."

Poor Barbara, thought Cynthia. She couldn't remember feeling that way about her own mom when she was a teen. But then, her circumstances were certainly not the norm.

Maybe Natalie was simply reaffirming that she was not alone in suffering hard times.

Chapter Thirteen

"Hey, babe!" Howard yelled into the house. "Look who I ran into."

Hearing two deep voices, then that male-bonding laughter, Barbara picked up her freshly diapered son and descended the stairs. In their kitchen, she found her husband cracking open a beer for his guest.

"Barb, you won't believe this. Remember this guy?"

Alejandro set his beer bottle on the counter and approached Barbara with his hand extended. "Good to see you again. I'm Al, Alejandro Ramon. It's been so long; you likely don't remember me."

"This is the guy who arranged the adoption."

Ah, now Barbara remembered. "Hi! Nice to see you. Thanks again for all your help when we first got Natalie. We appreciated you didn't just bring us our child but checked up on how we were doing."

"This is a human being we're talking about. My agency makes sure that we have a suitable match. You can't be too careful for the child's sake, you know." Looking around, he nodded his approval. "Looks like she landed in a good place."

"We've only been here a few weeks and are still getting organized," explained Barbara. "But we like it, and the neighbors are good."

Neighbors? Trying not to appear too interested, he asked, "Neighbors? You've met them already?"

"That's where Nat is right now," said Howard. "The woman two doors down is a teacher, so she's homeschooling Natalie and another girl for the rest of this year. Couldn't have worked out better for us."

Or for me, thought Alejandro.

Finishing his beer, Howard placed his bottle in the recycling bin, checking his watch. "Say, why don't you come meet Natalie. School's almost over for the day, so we won't be intruding."

"You'll stay for supper, of course," added Barbara.

The doorbell rang just in time. Grateful for the interruption, Cynthia excused herself. Outside the dining room, she took a second to rest her back against the hallway wall. Tilting her head back and closing her eyes, she told herself that Natalie was just a child, a child who meant well and was trying, in that awkward, teenager way, to be kind. To Cynthia's wobbly self-confidence, it was hard to remember to be the grownup in the situation.

The bell pealed again. Pushing off from the wall, Cynthia checked the peephole. On the other side of the door stood Natalie's father, with another man.

Unlocking the door, she welcomed Howard in.

"Hey, Cynthia. Hope we're not interrupting. I have a

special friend here I wanted to meet Natalie." Howard tipped his head in her direction. "And you, of course. I'd like you to meet Al Ramon. He runs the adoption agency that brought us Natalie."

Cynthia squirmed as Alejandro's appreciative gaze swept over her and he clasped her hand in both of his.

"I see why Howard likes this neighborhood so much," Alejandro said.

Pulling her hand away, Cynthia conjured up a fake smile. Something about this guy rubbed her the wrong way. Maybe it was the obvious way he checked her out, or the gleam in his eye. She had to see past his ogling; if he was a friend of Barb and Howard's, he must be okay. Striving for a neutral tone, she tried to be charitable. "You must be proud of the work your agency does." Over her shoulder, she called to Natalie, asking her to come.

"Yes. We're in the business of making lives better. Sadly, there is always a need, always parents looking to enrich their family lives and children needing homes. It's a win-win for everyone."

With narrowed eyes, Natalie approached.

Her dad reached out, putting his arm around her shoulders and pulling her close. "And this, this is our little girl. Bet you'd never recognize her as the screaming three-year-old you brought us all those years ago."

"True, so true. She's grown into a beautiful young lady." Alejandro assessed Natalie, from the way she stood in her father's embrace, to the judging way she returned his gaze.

Turning to his daughter, Howard explained. "This is Alejandro Ramon. Al runs the adoption agency that brought you to us." He gave her shoulders a squeeze. "Our happiest day ever."

Natalie didn't smile. "I thought your happiest day was when your son was born."

"That was a good day, too, but you are the one who started our dream of having a family. You'll always be our little girl, our princess."

"Then why don't you treat me like one?"

Alejandro wouldn't have caught Natalie's remark if he hadn't been standing too close.

Howard threw back his head and laughed. To Alejandro he said, "Don't you just love this kid? She can dead-pan the right interjection into any conversation. Witty, isn't she?"

Witty, or truthful, wondered Alejandro.

The stove timer sounded. "Excuse me," said Cynthia. "I need to get those cookies out of the oven. Want to try some?"

Natalie, Howard, and Alejandro trailed behind her.

Passing the door to the dining room, Howard noticed Bonnie. "Hey, there. How's it going?"

Bonnie nodded at him, a small smile on her lips.

Releasing his daughter, Howard put his hand on Alejandro's shoulder. He didn't notice the change in Bonnie's demeanor.

From her seat on the opposite side of the dining room table, Bonnie's twelve-year-old body seemed to shrink into herself. Her eyes larger than the china plates in the cabinet behind her, she stared at the man beside Howard, the man of her nightmares, the devil who tore apart her family. Her trembling began in her fisted hands, then traveled up her arms, until it felt like her whole body convulsed with each pounding heartbeat.

Well, well, thought Alejandro. Could this day get any better?

"Al," said Howard. "This is Bonnie Ramirez. She's the

other student here studying with Nat. Bonnie, this is Al Ramon. He runs an agency that connects needy kids with new homes."

A whimper escaped Bonnie's throat. Visions played in her mind, movie loops she could neither forget nor control. Like those nightmares you could never wake up from, the ones where you knew what would happen next but were powerless to change how it would play out, or to halt the action.

Eyes darting, cataloging all potential escape routes. Her breath came in short, shallow pants.

Synapses firing, her brain flashed images about, pictures of her little brother Benjie in all his cuteness, stretching his arms for her to pick him up. Jordy when he first came home from the hospital, how their mother was too tired to care for him and this infant so trustingly relied on eight-year-old Bonnie to be his everything. The unconditional love the little boys gave her until this man took them away.

From the kitchen, Cynthia called, "Natalie, would you grab an oven mitt and give me a hand, please?"

Howard, nose in the air and sniffing, shepherded his daughter toward the delicious odors.

Leaning against the doorjamb, Alejandro crossed his arms and smirked. "Well, well. Fancy seeing you again. How's things?"

The whites of Bonnie's eyes shone starkly in contrast to the sudden pallor of her face.

He narrowed his obsidian eyes and thrust out his chin. "Miss me?" he asked. "What? Cat got your tongue?" Alejandro laughed. "That's right. Your mother said how stubborn you were, refusing to talk when you didn't want to." He shifted position, entering the room. Placing both hands on the back of a dining room chair across from Bonnie, he leaned forward, angling his body towards the frozen girl. "Speaking of mothers, I saw yours the other day." Satisfied with Bonnie's reaction to that news, he left it for now. Let her wonder. Let her beg for answers. And remind her that this wasn't over. "I had plans for you. Still do."

Bonnie, her eyes never leaving the face of this devil, picked up her pencil, the only weapon near enough to clutch in her fist. Could she kill him? *Should* she kill him? She could not let him harm Cynthia. From the kitchen, she heard Cynthia's laughter in response to something Howard said. Cynthia was oblivious to the danger in her house.

Amy! Amy would be home from school soon. There was no way Bonnie was letting Alejandro have Amy. He would not take her the way he'd snatched her brothers and tried to take her.

Memories flooded her brain. Her joy at seeing her little brothers again. Her flicker of jealousy at seeing their mom lead the boys to a helicopter. How come *they* got to have a ride, and she didn't? Watching the big man in the chopper give the boys some red juice, then seeing the toddlers slump over, asleep. Then they were gone. Forever.

Howard's voice was overly loud in this charged atmosphere.

"Later," Alejandro mouthed, laying his index finger against his lips in a "shh" motion. "Or else," he added. He cocked his thumb and fingers into a pistol shape and pointed it at Bonnie.

Neither Howard nor Cynthia seemed to sense

anything amiss in the dining room, although Natalie looked between Alejandro and Bonnie. Had she picked up on the vibes?

Natalie moved closer to Alejandro, ostensibly to make room for Cynthia to lay the platter of gooey, warm chocolate chip cookies in the middle of the dining room table. Alejandro was cool, in an old man sort of way, thought Natalie. He might break up the tedium of the days. No way was Bonnie laying claim to him. If anyone was getting the attention of this new person, it was Natalie.

Bonnie stood, keeping her chair and the table between herself and this intruder that Howard had helped invade the house. While Alejandro's attention remained fixed on the cookies, she edged around the table toward the doorway.

Making herself as tiny as possible, she rounded the doorway and was out. Three steps took her to the kitchen, where Cynthia was putting the baking pans in the sink. Bonnie grabbed Cynthia's left hand and pulled her toward the back door.

Cynthia resisted, reclaiming her hand. "What's got into you?"

Bonnie opened her mouth, her eyes darting to the dining room. She tried, oh she really did, but the words just would not come out. In her mind they ricocheted, tumbling round and round. Run! Danger! He's a bad man. He took Jordy and Benjie. He hurt Anna. Let's get Amy and get out of here.

Her eyes signaled her frantic thoughts, but no words escaped her lips. She stood there, never more frustrated or ashamed of her failures. She had been unable to protect her little brothers. Now, would others she loved, Amy and Cynthia, be harmed, too?

She tried again to take Cynthia's arm and push her out of the house.

"Bonnie! We have guests. What are you doing?" Without waiting for an answer, Cynthia joined the others in the dining room.

A part, the primal part of Bonnie, sprinted for the back door. But the rational part of her mind stopped her. Could she leave? Could she save herself without at least trying to protect Cynthia? Amy would be home soon. Could she leave her vulnerable to Alejandro?

Shrinking in on herself, Bonnie decided. She could not. From the safer corner of the kitchen doorway, she watched the scene unrolling in the dining room.

The doorbell chimed not just once, but in that pattern of two long, then three short bursts that only Amy would use. "Excuse me," said Cynthia. Checking through the peephole, she saw Keira rolling her eyes and snatching Amy's hand away from the doorbell to prevent her from repeating her warning to her mother that they were home.

Cynthia unlocked and opened the door. Three small bodies pushed by. For a few minutes, Cynthia had forgotten that Keira's son Daniel, and Elizabeth's son, Timothy, were coming for a play date after school. "Wash your hands, then cookies are on the dining room table," she called to the kids. To Keira she said, "Thanks for bringing them home from school. Do you want to come in for a while? Natalie's father's here and brought over a friend."

"No thanks. Gotta get some stuff done. I'll be back in two hours to get Daniel. Thanks for letting him play here. He's been looking forward to it all week."

Amy, Daniel, and Timothy all washed their hands in a

remarkably short time in the half-bath off the hallway. Then Amy squealed, "Bonnie's still here!" The three children raced around the dining room table, agilely skirting chairs, and adults to reach the young almost-teen that they adored.

Bonnie's speed matched that of the younger kids as she shoved her body in between the kids and the men, gathering the children to her, then behind her. Pushing the chair against the table and lining up its partner beside it, she created a physical barrier between Alejandro and this brood of children. No way was he getting them.

Alejandro smirked, not trying to hide his mocking laugh.

Misinterpreting, Howard clapped him on the shoulder. "They're something, aren't they? Makes it feel like there's a lot more than four of them here." He smiled at his daughter. "Not like my Natalie here. She's grown out of those stages. Now she has the poise of a young lady." He wrapped one arm around her shoulders and bowed his head to kiss the top of her hair. Natalie did an eye-roll that only hours of practice could perfect.

Cynthia sorted out plates and napkins for the three new arrivals, who eagerly awaited their cookies. Only Bonnie noticed how Alejandro's eyes raked Natalie from head to toe.

Bonnie's hopes rose when she heard Keira's voice. Keira and Elizabeth had met Alejandro once when he threatened Anna as she and Bonnie packed things up to move into Murph's house. Brendan had arrived just as the women prepared to defend their friend. The police presence had persuaded Alejandro to leave, but not for good.

If Keira saw this man here in Cynthia's house, she'd raise the alarm and they'd all be safe. But she left. Without even coming in.

Something inside Bonnie died. She was no good. As

hard as she had tried for years, she'd not been able to keep her family together. She missed Carl, her mother's husband, although she didn't miss Archie, the mean man her mother used to replace Carl.

She missed her mother, of course she did. Girls were supposed to love their mothers. But most of all, she missed her little brothers. There must have been a good reason for her mother to place her brothers in a helicopter and let them be taken away. Anna promised that Brendan and Jake were working on trying to figure out where Jordy and Benjie were, and how they could get them back.

Bonnie's eyes narrowed, and she turned the intensity of her glare onto Alejandro. She bet *he* knew where they were. She could ask him...

The balloon inside her chest cavity deflated, and she shrank into herself. No, she couldn't. The words wouldn't come; she couldn't speak. Oh, the words were there all right; they reverberated inside her head, filling up all the empty spaces, tumbling over and over each other until she could not tell them apart, could not pick which ones to utter first, convinced that they would make no sense to anyone else, that they'd think her an idiot and she'd fail again.

If only she could call out to Keira. If only she could explain to Cynthia. But she couldn't. Ensnared in this prison of anxiety, she just couldn't.

She heard Cynthia and Keira exchange goodbyes and the front door close. Keira was gone and with her all hope.

Chapter Fourteen

"Hi, Cynthia. It's Anna."

After chatting about their kids for a few minutes, Anna got to the reason for her phone call. "I was just talking to a colleague in the break room. His wife's a teacher, but she doesn't have a regular contract. He said she doesn't want to be committed long-term, but enjoys working with kids, so she's a substitute teacher. It's a separate application process from applying for a teaching position. The school district maintains a list of sub teachers, then calls them when a teacher's away sick, at a conference or takes a leave. His wife ends up working about half-time, but sometimes for a few weeks at a time to cover a leave. She also turns down jobs if she doesn't want to work that day."

"Sounds interesting, but I'm going to need to make regular income next year."

"His wife says that subbing is a good way to end up with a permanent teaching contract. They get to know your work and administrators request the subs they like. Then, when a vacancy comes up, they already know you and want you."

"Hmmm. Appealing. But I'm already committed to you and to Natalie's parents for this school year."

"The girls are old enough to be left to work independently some days. Murph and I certainly won't mind if you're away subbing some days. I bet Barbara would say it's okay, too."

"I'll give it some thought. Thanks for letting me know."

All her life, Cynthia had just let things happen. She went to college because her friends were. It seemed the thing to do. She chose her major because two friends were going into teaching. Why not take classes alongside them? The world always needed teachers, right?

Then, it turned out she was good at it.

The same with Hugh, her husband. He had pursued her at college. It was easy to just go along with his invitations. Why not? And it had worked out. That is, until he died.

Starting up her computer, Cynthia brought up the school district's website. Yes, there it was - a separate area for substitute teaching. Why had she never noticed this before? Scrolling through the requirements and the application process, she thought she met the criteria. This might get her foot in the door.

She picked up her phone to call Barbara. No, she might better do this in person, so she could judge her neighbor's reaction to the proposal.

"Would that mean that on those days Natalie would stay at home here?" That was Barbara's first question.

"That's an option, but she and Bonnie are welcome to

spend the day working at my house. They're both familiar with where things are and can make themselves at home."

Barbara tried to hide her relief. She loved her daughter, she truly did, but sometimes life was easier when they spent more time apart.

The bell over the door tinkled as Natalie preceded Alejandro into the bakery. Barbara and Howard were so pleased at Alejandro's interest in getting to know Natalie. He explained that he liked to check up on his adoptees whenever possible. Besides, it got Natalie out of the house for a while.

Alejandro's gaze swept the interior of the bakery.

"Yeah, I know, it's not much," explained Natalie. "But it's close, and the food is pretty decent."

From behind the counter, Jeff scowled at her.

As Alejandro headed to a table, Natalie stopped him. "You have to place your order at the counter first." Surveying the menu board, she asked, "Are we on a budget?"

"No." Alejandro grinned. "Go wild, and order whatever you like."

Natalie rolled her eyes. "My parents *never* say that."

Jeff regarded them as he took their orders. His eyes shifted between the young girl and this man she was with.

Alejandro settled into a corner table, choosing the chair that faced the door. "Your parents don't let you order what you want?" he asked.

Natalie shook her head. "Hardly ever. We're on a

budget, they say. They don't get that I'm not a budget kind of girl."

That made Alejandro smile. "I hear ya."

Warming to her subject, Natalie continued. "They don't get me. It's like we're from different worlds and I don't want to be a part of theirs."

The aromas came first, wafting from the kitchen. As interesting as Natalie's words were, the smells snagged Alejandro's attention.

Jeff appeared at the table with a tray containing a warm pastrami on rye panini, a chocolate eclair, a mocha latte, and an Americano coffee. After arranging their orders on the table, Jeff was in no hurry to leave. Facing Natalie, he asked, "Who's this guy?"

Natalie's eyebrows formed a straight line. Her mouth twisted, "None of your..."

Alejandro's shoe tapped her foot. Interrupting, he stood and held out his hand to Jeff. "Hi. I'm Al Ramon, a friend of her parents. I've known Howard and Barbara since before Natalie can even remember."

Jeff shook his hand, then recoiled when Alejandro brought his other hand up to cover Jeff's. Pulling away from the contact, Jeff asked Natalie, "Do your parents know you're here?"

Alejandro answered for her. "Of course, they do. We just came from there. I thought I'd take Nat out for a treat, and they recommended this place."

"Well, I'll be watching. Let me know if you need anything else." Jeff backed away, going into the kitchen to confer with Ellie, his boss, and friend. There was something about Alejandro that didn't sit well with him.

"That was a little intrusive," said Alejandro. "But it's nice that there are people looking out for you."

Natalie tossed her hair over her shoulder. "That's just it. I don't need anyone looking out for me. I can take care of myself."

"I'm getting that sense from you."

"Well, I can. I don't need other people to do it for me." She blew on the foam covering her latte. "I tell my parents that all the time, but they still try to give me rules and impose their ideas on me."

"Isn't that what parents do?"

"Not to me they shouldn't. I'm not like other kids."

The corners of Alejandro's lips curled up. "I can see that." He leaned back in his chair, stretching out his legs. "How are you different?"

"I'm not needy the way most kids my age are." She warmed to her subject. "I don't need their approval or anyone else's.

Alejandro nodded. He could relate.

"If I want something, I go after it."

This girl was intriguing, thought Alejandro. He studied her face, cataloguing her features. I wonder...

"Alejandro! Why have you not been returning my calls?" Sally's screeching came over his voice mail. For the fifth time, each time more strident than the one before.

Alejandro hated that shrill tone in anyone's voice, but it was especially grating coming from Sally. What had possessed him to hook up with her in the first place? Yeah, she had charms, but they were fading, and fast. He had believed that she could be useful, plus she brought along three kids as assets to their business venture.

And look how *that* had worked out. They'd lost Bonnie, no thanks to Anna and her meddling. The police had shut down his main stable, the place where he stashed young women who supplied the babies for his adoption agency - a win-win, he believed, for both him and the women. Almost like a community service.

Now Sally's second kid was proving to be a problem. Alejandro's business could not afford unhappy customers, not in the circle in which they operated. Placing Sally with the kid as his nanny was supposed to take care of the problem. Obviously not.

Well, he couldn't ignore Sally forever, not if he wanted to keep Germaine and Emma happy.

Sally was a loose cannon. Why he'd thought he could rely on her was a mystery. Usually, his business acumen stood him in good stead. He'd gotten too cocky with the success of his stables. Who would have thought that someone like Anna could bring him down?

Anna. He was not done with her yet. But harming her would not be enough. No, never. She'd been willing to sacrifice herself for Bonnie, a kid she'd only known for a few months. They weren't even related.

No, Anna was best got at through her friends, those she cared about. If her friends or their children were harmed, Anna would torture herself with guilt forever. Good.

Anna's friends formed a tight circle. It had not been difficult to follow some of them home from Anna's house, Anna, and that Murphy guy she shacked up with.

Anna's new friends had kids, young, vulnerable kids. That's why Alejandro had been watching the street where two of them lived. What luck that he'd run into Howard and gained legitimate entry into their street. He had not yet formed his plan, but soon...

"Sally, querida. How are things?" He knew to hold the earpiece away from his head, anticipated the decibels of her reply.

He was not wrong. He rarely was.

"I've been calling you for weeks! Why didn't you get back to me? You have to get me out of here!"

"Why? Your job is to keep Germaine and Emma happy. To do that, you must keep your kid happy. How hard can that be?"

"Hard? You just try it! Try to be around that whiny kid all day who does nothing but scream and ask for Bonnie. Bonnie, this, Bonnie, that. You'd think *she* was his mother."

Well, thought Alejandro. She was likely more of a mother than you ever were. He'd been around enough women like Sally to know when to keep some thoughts to himself.

"Look. Germaine is an important client. He runs in influential circles. A word from him could ruin future business for me." He remembered he needed to keep Sally reeled in. "For us. If he puts out the word that he's unhappy with our services or that we provide defective goods, it can be all over."

Sally, never swift on the uptake, pondered the meaning of 'defective goods' and if she should be insulted. "But..."

"You're aware of how much we got paid for the adoption transaction. You enjoyed the bounty of that. Do you want wells like that to run dry?"

"But it's not helping me now." This came out like a whine.

"No? You're living in a mansion. You're paid an exorbitant salary for someone uneducated and untrained. The Molinas bought the resume I made up for you." He touched the speaker icon for his phone and set it on his desk. This conversation might take more than the two minutes he'd hoped. "This is your kid we're talking about. Can't you turn him into a cheerful boy, living the life with his mommy by his side?"

"I'm not *that* kind of mother, and you know it. I'm meant for better things."

"How is Emma feeling about things?"

"She thinks they may have made a mistake."

Not good. Not good at all.

"She thinks he screams less now. But he's not cuddly with her." Sally lowered her voice. "He's never really been cuddly with anyone but Bonnie. And maybe Carl. Besides, he's always so grubby and has that dirty little boy smell."

Was there any point in reminding her that as a nanny, it was her job to keep him clean, to wash away that dirt smell?

"I'd better touch base with Germaine." Alejandro's brain schemed the next steps. "Why don't you go do something motherly for once?"

"Bonnie! Why aren't you dressed?" Strange, thought Anna. Usually Bonnie was so responsible; they never had to prod her about getting ready in the morning. "I just have time to drop you at Cynthia's before I go to work."

Bonnie shook her head.

Murph turned from filling his travel mug with coffee. "What do you mean, Bonnie? Are you not feeling well?"

"Not going." Those were the only words she uttered.

Anna and Murph looked at each other. "Bonnie, we need to leave in fifteen minutes." Anna and Murph retired to their bedroom to finish getting ready for work. "What's going on with her?" Murph asked.

"No idea. Today should be a simple day. Cynthia won't be there; she has a subbing job at the school today. It's just Natalie and Bonnie together, and Cynthia left the work for them to complete."

"Cynthia's reports don't suggest that Bonnie's having any difficulty with the academics. In fact, just the opposite. I wonder what's going on?"

When they returned to the kitchen, Bonnie was indeed dressed, but her hair unbrushed, and her toast was half-eaten on a plate in front of her. Circling her plate were books and notebooks, the contents of Bonnie's backpack. She had a pencil in one hand, making notes in her book. Her gaze remained firmly on her schoolwork, despite being aware of her foster parents' presence.

"Bonnie?" asked Anna.

"Staying here." It wasn't a question; Bonnie stated a fact.

Murph and Anna had a conversation with their eyes. Bonnie was almost thirteen, and often babysat the younger kids. They were not worried about leaving her at home. But why did she not want to spend the day with Natalie? You'd think that two young girls would relish the time adult-free and together.

"You're sure?"

Bonnie nodded. This time her eyes met Anna, communicating her determination.

"Okay. We'll lock up and set the alarm when we leave. Don't open the door for anyone but us. Call us if there's any problem."

Bonnie rolled her eyes. Sweet as she was, that teen attitude was creeping in. Or maybe she'd picked that up from Natalie, who had the roll down perfectly.

"If you change your mind, I can come home at noon, and take you to Cynthia's if you'd like."

"No. I'm fine here." Those were quite a few words in a row for Bonnie. She meant this.

They each kissed the top of her head, gathered their briefcases, and went out the door to the garage. Standing beside their cars, Murph asked, "What do you think that's about?"

"You don't think it has something to do with Natalie, do you?"

Anna used her car's Bluetooth to call Cynthia. "Morning. I'll be fast since I know you're getting ready for work. Bonnie says that she'd rather stay home to work today. When I left, she already had her books on the table and was writing in her notebook."

"That's fine. She knows what she needs to do today. I had thought that she and Natalie might enjoy hanging out together though."

"Bonnie was adamant about not leaving the house. Funny, it's the first time she's done that."

Cynthia worried. "Maybe it's the change in routine. This will be the first day I'm away subbing, so perhaps she's not happy with me."

"No, I didn't get the sense that was the problem." Anna turned on the flicker to turn into the parking lot of the courthouse that housed her office. "Have a good day teaching."

"Amy," Cynthia called. "Go knock on Timothy's door and tell them we're ready to leave." It was Cynthia's turn to get the kids to and from school this week. Luckily, she was subbing at their school today.

As she gathered Amy's backpack, plus her own lunch kit and bag, the doorbell rang. Admitting Natalie inside, Cynthia wondered how Natalie would react to her solitary day. "Morning, Natalie. Make yourself at home. Snacks are on the kitchen counter, drinks in the fridge. You're on your own today; Bonnie decided to work from her home." She watched the emotions play over Natalie's face as her eyes squinted and her mouth pursed, then her facial muscles relaxed, and she turned on a smile. She'd had some plans for Bonnie, but maybe this was better. She'd have the run of Cynthia's house all to herself. She wondered what secrets she might find…

Chapter Fifteen

Cynthia watched Natalie and Bonnie closely. As far as she could see, nothing differed about them as they sat at her dining room table, doing their schoolwork. Bonnie was always willing to attack whichever task she assigned; Natalie more reluctant, but that hadn't changed. Natalie, although bright enough, was not motivated by academics.

With just the two of them, Cynthia was able to adapt lessons and alter assignments on the fly to make them suit something that might spark Natalie's interest. But how would that work in a regular classroom? Teachers didn't have the luxury of creating different assignments and differing expectations for every child in the room. Sometimes a student had to just suck it up and do the assigned work. She was not at all sure how Natalie would fare in a large group situation.

Maybe Natalie had become used to doing what she wanted in the time she'd been away from the demands of a formal classroom. Cynthia wasn't sure. There was something about this girl...

Since Barbara's confessions about some of the problem situations Natalie had been in, Cynthia was less and less sure about things. Had she misread this child?

Kids were kids and all deserved a chance. Or a second chance. That was why the McDaw family moved here, to give their daughter a fresh start.

That's what Cynthia would do, too. Natalie was a fifteen-year-old girl, a victim, who had had nasty innuendoes and accusations made against her. What kid wouldn't be prickly in those circumstances? The things they'd said about her didn't fit with the young girl Cynthia saw five days a week.

Besides, wouldn't Bonnie have said something if there were things going on behind Cynthia's back?

Cynthia's musings were broken by the ring tone on her cell phone. "Excuse me, girls. I'll be right back."

"Hey, Cynthia. It's Elizabeth. I wonder…" Her voice trailed off. Taking a deep breath, she started again. It was so hard for her to ask for help. She absolutely hated coming across as needy. "I'm at the bakery. Is there any chance that you could join me here?" She rushed on as Cynthia hesitated. "I mean you and the girls. I know that you're teaching them right now. But the bakery is empty. They could do their work here. Surely you don't lecture them every minute?"

This was a new Elizabeth, a tone that Cynthia had not heard before. Other than swapping babysitting or something to do with their kids, she could not think of when Elizabeth had asked anything of her in the past year.

"Sure. Save us a table. Or tables. The girls will bring their work."

When she was a young teen, she'd have been all over the opportunity to do homework at a bakery with its yummy drinks and treats. But Bonnie and Natalie weren't like other kids. She's forgotten that.

"Hey, guys," she said. "Pack up your things and bring your books. We're going to the bakery to finish up our lessons this afternoon."

Silence met her cheerful pronouncement. Stony silence.

Bonnie's body tensed. She seemed to shrink in on herself, and her breathing became rapid and shallow.

What an idiot I am, thought Cynthia. You know about Bonnie's anxiety and how she doesn't react well to the unexpected. What surprised her was Natalie.

Natalie's brows lowered, and her eyes narrowed. Instead of shrinking like Bonnie, her chest seemed to puff out. She raised her chin and put her shoulders back.

Yep, this could have been handled better, Cynthia thought. Just about any way other than this announcement would have been an improvement. But she'd done it now. To recant would mean losing control, something not conducive to a good teaching situation.

Cynthia let out a breath slowly. She deliberately relaxed her shoulders and her facial muscles. Don't show fear, she told herself. You've done this with a room of seventh graders and come out on top. You can handle two girls.

"You've been working hard, both of you. You deserve a break - *we* deserve a break."

Bonnie looked down at the open notebook in front of her.

"Don't worry, you'll still be doing your assignments. It'll just be a change of venue."

Neither girl's stance relented.

"You've both been to the bakery before. The walk there will do us good. Think of it as a P.E. period."

Nope, they looked unconvinced. Turning to Bonnie, she thought she'd approach the more malleable of the two first. "Bonnie, Elizabeth is there. She wants some company."

"Oh, I get it," said Natalie, sarcasm dripping in her tone. "You want to go hang out with your friend, rather than teach us the way you're paid to do."

Bonnie elbowed the older girl. While she'd put up with a lot on her own account, she fiercely defended those important to her.

Cynthia studied the objects in her china cabinet while she counted to ten. Forwards, then backwards. "You're right. I want to talk to my friend. But we can combine that with your work. You both have your assignments to carry you through to the end of the school day. This is simply a change of venue." Straightening her shoulders, she looked Natalie directly in the eye. This child would not cow her. "When you're in school, you move room to room throughout the day. Think of going to the bakery as moving to another room. It's good for you to get used to concentrating in different places. After all, not all classrooms will be as geared to your studies as is this dining room. Besides," she added. "I already rang your mom and told her where we'd be. She said she might walk down with Liam when he wakes up from his nap."

Natalie rolled her eyes.

Cynthia was not sure that last bit was an inducement for Natalie. Well, straight bribery might work. "You girls can have the beverage and treat of your choice when we get there. I know that you both like their baked goods."

"The stupid place isn't even licensed."

Natalie's protest stopped Cynthia.

Bonnie stood up, pushing her chair in, then gathering up her books. Cynthia knew that this was a big move for Bonnie. Her anxiety made it hard for her to accept new or unexpected situations. Cynthia regretted not preparing her better for this.

Natalie's crossed arms showed she was still not on board with this.

Standing with her books clasped to her chest, Bonnie tried. "It's nice at the bakery," her small voice said.

"Yeah, if you're a dweeb."

"Natalie!" Cynthia's voice was sharp with a reprimand.

Instead of flinching, Bonnie approached Natalie and put a hand on her shoulder. "It'll be all right," she whispered. "You'll like it."

Call to Mexico

"Senor Molina. This is Alejandro Ramon. I'm calling to check on how things are going with your son. Is the new nanny working out?"

"Better than the last one, at least. The last two, actually. Can't say that the boy has really bonded with her, but that might be a good thing. My Emma was starting to think it was just her that the child doesn't warm up to. But now she's realizing that's just the way he is with everyone."

Not good news, thought Alejandro.

"Do you think there's something wrong with the child? I assure you that the pediatrician gave him a clean bill of health before the adoption."

"Physically, he seems healthy. He's just not what we expected."

"In what way?"

"We thought that a four-year-old would be thrilled with all the toys he has. Kids that age are happy and love to play. Not so much this boy. We made sure to have a nanny and other help available, fearing he'd be too demanding of Emma's attention. But he mostly ignores her. He ignores everyone. It takes a lot to coax even a smile out of him."

Alejandro ground his back teeth together. Not good. He consciously relaxed his grip on his phone, released the breath he'd been holding and opened his throat so his voice would come across as relaxed. He hated to do this, but his reputation was about all he had left, that and a few assets he was nurturing carefully. He allowed himself a couple more seconds to consider, then knew what he had to do. "Do you remember the adoption contract you signed? It came with a one-year guarantee. If you and Señora Molina are not satisfied, we will come for this child and find you another, more suitable son or daughter."

The relief in Germaine's voice was tangible. "I'm so glad you're honoring your contract. Emma and I've talked about this endlessly these past months. At first, we believed that he'd settle down once everything wasn't so new and strange. But it's not happening. Other people we know who've adopted children have them fitting in as part of the family in far less time than we've given this."

"All right. Give me a week or so, then I'll be in touch. We'll pick up this boy, then talk to you later about your options." One of his options was not a refund on the fifty grand he'd paid. That money was already spent. Since his stable was no longer in place, he had no steady stream of income.

"Emma wonders if we made a mistake in the child's age we specified. And maybe the sex. She now thinks that a little girl might have been better and one a little older. Maybe six or seven, one who will be in school during the day."

Instantly, an image came to Alejandro's mind. The daughter of Howard and Barbara's neighbor was about that age. She was a perky little thing from what he'd observed. Plus, the mother was a friend of Anna's. Two birds with one stone...

He hung up, then dialed Sally's mobile phone.

Alejandro met them at the private airport. He watched as the child hovered at the top of the stairways, unsure if he should brave the steps or seek refuge back inside the small jet he'd just emerged from. Sally appeared on the landing and urged Jordy forward. He clung to the handrail. Impatience plain in her every movement, Sally clasped him around the upper arm and jerked him towards the open stairs. He had no choice but to follow on his feet or be dragged down to the tarmac.

Alejandro had the trunk open, ready to receive their suitcases as his employee packed them away. With a nod, Alejandro got behind the wheel, only to notice the kid standing beside the car. Sally was in the passenger seat, her seatbelt in place. "What about the boy?" he asked her.

"Oh, for god's sake. Can't the kid even get into a car on his own?" Sighing, she undid her belt and opened her door.

"Get in there," she hollered at her son. When he didn't move, she shoved him into the back seat.

Jordy landed with a heap, then righted himself without a word. His eyes met Alejandro's in the rear-view mirror. He understood the warning in that glance. Without a word, he watched the sky go by, the only thing he could see when his head barely came to the bottom of the side window.

"Al."

Alejandro knew that whine. What had he ever seen in Sally? "What is it this time?" He'd installed Sally and her kid in the same hotel where he and Sally had stayed before, even in the same suite. That way, she and the brat had separate bedrooms. And, when he himself wanted to visit Sally, they had some privacy. She had all the room service she wished, and the kid had his toys. He stuck to himself, anyway. So what was Sally whining about?

"I can't do this anymore." Sally was firm. "You either get this kid out of here or you look after him yourself."

Right. Like *that* would ever happen. She had the kid; why should she kick up a stink about looking after him for a few days?

Alejandro had spent the past week going over his adoptive parent applications. Keeping these parents happy was key to his reputation. While he didn't give a rat's ass what anyone thought about him, people's opinions and word of mouth meant something to his business. He needed satisfied, wealthy clients who would tell others in their circle about his adoption agency. Discreetly, of course, as was the wont with people of this class.

Try as he might, he couldn't see how this kid, this Jordy,

would match the criteria any of his clients sought. Sure, he was the right age and sex for some, but the kid's temperament just wouldn't cut it. His best bet had been with that last placement, and that hadn't worked at all.

Alejandro was not heartless. He could not just off a kid, even an annoying kid. No, a better plan was taking shape.

Anna. She filled his heart with a blackness he'd never felt for anyone before. This was personal. He'd given her everything, she had wanted for nothing. And yet, she'd thrown it back in his face. All he'd asked of her was that she produce a kid. Not every year, although that would have been nice, but sometimes. She messed that up so that she could have no more children. What use was she then?

He'd been willing to still provide for her, move her into a new position, looking after the other girls. But no, she'd chosen to leave. Huh. She'd even thought she had a home to go back to in California. Had she really known so little of her parents?

He'd expected Anna to come crawling back to him. After all, she had no experience in this world, other than to be looked after by her stepfather, then by him. But she hadn't. She had more of a backbone than he expected and made it on her own.

She owed him, though. He'd paid her way for years. He wrote off her stepfather's debt for her. Then look how she repaid him? He'd offered her a job, a far better paying job than she'd managed to find for herself, and still she refused him. People didn't turn down Alejandro Ramon.

Then, before he'd exacted his revenge, she turned the tables on him. She single-handedly ruined his business, or a good portion of it. His stable of brood women vanished overnight. He'd lost Bonnie, who would have brought in a good chunk of change in her pre-pubescent state. There were clients who would have paid plenty for her.

Anna would pay for thwarting his plans.

In the meantime, he'd hurt her little by little. Death by a thousand cuts. And he knew just what would get to her.

———

"You're right, it's almost time," Alejandro soothed Sally. "Let's dump the kid on Anna."

"Anna? Why Anna?" The wheels turned. "Oooo. I get it. She'll know that you're around."

"Soon."

Chapter Sixteen

Cynthia settled Natalie and Bonnie at a table near the wall, where there would be fewer distractions if the bakery got busy. Bonnie left her books in a neat pile before heading to the counter to place her order.

Watching Bonnie's back, Natalie spread her belongings out in three sections, taking up most of the tabletop, then trailed joined Bonnie and Cynthia at the bakery's display case. "You said we could have anything we want, right?" She checked with Cynthia.

"Yes, you may."

Using her shoulder, Natalie's slight nudge pushed Bonnie to the side. "You don't need to hog the entire space," she told the younger girl.

Bonnie's face colored. Looking at her sandals, Bonnie murmured, "Sorry."

From behind the counter, Jeff watched their interactions. Even though Natalie had placed herself in front, he ignored her. "Bonnie, would you point out what you'd like, please?"

Without meeting his gaze, Bonnie knelt and pointed at a cinnamon bun.

"Excellent choice. We just brought them out of the oven," said Jeff. The aroma of warm dough, cinnamon, and brown sugar filled the room. "I'll give you this one instead. It's bigger." Using tongs, he placed the largest, gooiest bun on a plate, along with a knife and fork.

"Hey! That's the one *I* wanted," complained Natalie. "How come she's special?"

Ignoring her comment, Jeff stood, ready to take her order.

"Those look too fattening, anyway. You might want to watch that," she told Bonnie. Facing the counter, she told Jeff, "I'll have a chocolate eclair, an apple rose cupcake, and a piece of strawberry cheesecake."

"All at once?"

"You can bring them to me as I finish the previous one." Accepting the eclair plate from Jeff, she instructed him, "And don't forget extra whipped cream on my mocha latte." Her lips curled into a bright smile. "Please."

Over her head, Cynthia's eyes met Jeff's and winced. "Sorry," she mouthed.

Jeff just shook his head as he prepared their drinks.

Elizabeth fiddled with her napkin, crumbling the remains of her carrot cake muffin into tiny bits. When Cynthia joined her, she asked in a low voice, "Is she like that always?"

Cynthia shook her head. "This is the first time I've seen anything like that from her." Her charitable side came out. "Maybe she's just disgruntled. She didn't want to come. Although she seems confident, she's even more stuck in her routine than Bonnie. Bonnie got over the funk about coming here and even tried to help Natalie."

"She's a good kid." She frowned. "You might want to watch the other one, though. I wouldn't want her to hurt Bonnie." She remembered Timothy's reluctance to go to Cynthia's the other evening when Natalie babysat the kids. He seemed all right when she picked him up. The kids were all quiet, but it was getting near their bedtimes. "Did Amy say anything about the other night when Natalie babysat them?"

"Not really, just that Natalie was on the computer doing homework, and left them alone."

Alone. That brought Elizabeth back to the reason she'd wanted to talk with her friend. Sheesh, this was hard. Her mother's words rang in her mind - "You keep yourself to yourself." True, but over the last year or so, Elizabeth had learned the value of friendships, of having people to lean on. Still, confessing personal stuff was hard.

"Brendan's ticked with me." There. She'd said it.

"How so?" That sounded odd to Cynthia. She'd seen Brendan and Elizabeth together often. They seemed to get along well, and Brendan acted like he thought the world of Elizabeth and Timothy. She said so.

"That's the problem," said Elizabeth. "He says he wants more."

Puzzled, Cynthia asked, "And that's a bad thing?"

"Yes! No., I mean sort of. I thought we were fine. He's great with Timothy and we have a good time together. I've been content." She stirred her now cooling coffee. "But he's not. I had no idea until he blew up at me the other night."

Cynthia could hardly see Brendan blowing up. "What for?"

"Timothy had glommed onto him, wanting to play with

Brendan during his bath, then getting him to read to him before bed. This was after Bren had spent much of the evening on the floor building with him." Her face coloring, Elizabeth looked at her friend. "I apologized to him for Timothy monopolizing his time and said that he didn't have to agree when Timothy wanted his attention." She let out a sigh. "That's when he got mad. He said he wants to be with Timothy. What he doesn't like is having to leave every night."

Not sure what to say, Cynthia glanced at the girls. Bonnie had her books stacked on top of each other, taking up as little room as possible on their shared table. As she tried setting her cup down after taking a sip, Natalie shoved the table, causing Bonnie's cup to spill over the sides and onto her book. Judging by the napkins lying around, and the state of Bonnie's notebook, this was not the first time such a mishap occurred.

Jeff was there before she could say anything. With a fresh batch of napkins in hand, he picked up Bonnie's things. "Come with me," he told her. "One table is too small for the two of you. You sit over here, Bonnie."

Gratefully, Bonnie smiled at him, moving her cup and plate to the separate table Jeff indicated.

"I'll move, too. This table is too tippy." Natalie piled her books together to move to Bonnie's new table.

"No." Jeff's voice was firm. "Here, I'll show you some-thing." He moved Natalie's things onto the chair vacated by Bonnie. Flipping the table onto its side, he motioned for Natalie to get on the floor with him. "See these things?" He pointed to the round disks on the bottom of the table's legs. "They're levelers. You turn them in or out to adjust the height of each leg. This is an old building and the floor-boards have warped over time. I have each table perfectly levelled. But," his look was direct, "you moved the table. If you're going to do that, you need to level it."

Despite herself, this interested Natalie. She felt the empty table behind her, testing to see if it wobbled. It didn't.

Jeff set her table upright again. "Here. Try it to see which leg you need to adjust."

Natalie did as he instructed, then altered the legs until the table sat perfectly stable. Despite herself, she smiled at Jeff. "Thanks." She *liked* feeling competent.

Jeff nodded, then returned to his kitchen.

Her mind only half on watching this interaction, Cynthia debated on what to say. Just be blunt, she told herself. This is your friend you're talking to, and she's asked for help. "Did he ask you to marry him?"

Elizabeth's eyes grew round, and she sat back in her chair. "No!" Then, more quietly, "I mean no, we've never talked about anything like that. I *was* married less than two years ago and look how that turned out."

"Brendan is nothing like Jackson was."

"So true." She smiled. "My taste in men has improved. But I am just getting used to being single, to being my own person, rather than living for some man. I never want to be swallowed up by a man again."

"Do you feel Brendan is trying to do that to you?"

Elizabeth shook her head. "No, I never get anything like that from him. He's independent and seems to like that I have a brain as well. He doesn't try to make me do things his way, and he doesn't intrude."

"So what's the problem? Is he pushing you into something you're not ready for?"

"Not really. He says he knows that it's too soon for me. But he wants some sign that I will eventually get there." Her voice caught in her throat. "He said that he doesn't want me to string him along." Using a napkin, she swiped under one eye. "I'd never do that to him. *Never*. He's a good man and Timothy loves him."

"Maybe it's not just Timothy's love that he wants."

Hidden behind a fistful of napkins, her voice was so low Cynthia had to lean closer to hear. "I know. And I do. Maybe." Elizabeth clenched and unclenched her fists. Get it together, she told herself. You cannot make a spectacle of yourself in public. "I feel so selfish. Here I've been going along, just enjoying what we have. I thought we were fine. I took his presence for granted, never thinking about what our relationship was doing to him." Her watery eyes met Cynthia's. "If he hadn't said something the other night, I think I'd have been content to go on as we are forever."

"And now?"

"Now, he's made me think. It feels like he's forced me out of my little bubble, and I hate that." More fiercely, "I hate I was *in* a bubble. That's what I did with Jackson, spinning my version of the reality I wanted to, what I thought was real. I was wrong. Our lives were not the picture of marital bliss I fooled myself into believing. He was not happy with me.

"Now here I am, doing it again. I thought that both Brendan and I were happy, but I was wrong. *I* was happy, but he isn't. Am I going down that same road again? God, I thought that after everything with Jackson, I'd never live with blinders on again. And look, the first relationship I'm in after my disastrous marriage, here I am doing the same thing."

"Things aren't always what they seem."

"No kidding!"

"I see a difference there, though. While your former

husband didn't talk to you about what he was feeling, Brendan has. Doesn't that show he trusts you? Isn't that what you'd want in a relationship?" Allowing Elizabeth time to compose herself, Cynthia watched the girls. Natalie was playing on her phone. She'd consumed her first pastry, played with the second, but the third was untouched. That was fine; she could take it home with her.

Bonnie hunched over her notebook, writing furiously. Her shiny, dark hair hid her face from view. So much about Bonnie was hidden. Who knew what her earlier life had been like? From age eight on, she spent much of her time caring for her little brothers, even frequently missing school to tend to them. Her life was easier now that she lived with Anna and Murph. While her anxiety and selective mutism had certainly not worsened, she still struggled to express her thoughts orally. The writing exercises were helping, at least somewhat. There was so much that went on behind those dark, doe-like eyes, so much trapped inside that little mind that Bonnie could not get out. Although she seemed a happier kid these days, the traumas and losses she'd suffered had to play a big role in how she responded to the world.

Mostly, she'd seemed to be getting better, acting more like a twelve-year-old girl. That is, until the last week or so. Somehow, Bonnie seemed to shrink into herself more. That constantly troubled expression was back on her face, the wariness in her eyes.

Yes, things were not always as they seemed.

Chapter Seventeen

"Bonnie, you seem quiet lately. Is something wrong?" Anna worried. It was so hard to tell with a child who had selective mutism. They had to rely on body language much of the time.

Despite her challenges with oral communication, Bonnie had become a warm, happy child, smiling and affectionate. She seemed to enjoy her life here with Anna and Murph. Until lately, that is. She and Murph had talked about it again last night, and neither could put their finger on when they felt the change started, but they both felt the difference in the child now.

Considering all the losses Bonnie had suffered, yeah, she could be mourning. Her little brothers meant the world to her, and now they were gone. Who knows where? Thankfully, Bonnie's imagination didn't stretch to the sort of circumstances Anna feared for the boys.

Then there was the loss of her mother, such as Sally was in the mothering department. She'd still been a constant in

Bonnie's life. Now she was gone, too. And how did a kid process the reality that her mother had appeared to send her children away?

The other loss was Carl, her stepfather. Perhaps ineffectual, he'd at least been there for a chunk of Bonnie's life. At least he'd been kind to her. Although he lived in the same city, he'd made no attempt to visit Bonnie, nor had he responded to Anna and Murph's invitations to get together. Those were four people Bonnie had lost. Who knew how many others there had been in her young life?

Bonnie had bi-weekly sessions with a therapist. Since talk therapy was out of the question, they focused on art and play therapy. So far, Bonnie created scenes from past years, mostly things with her little brothers. There had been nothing yet of the trauma of seeing a battered Anna tied up, of Sally luring Bonnie to Alejandro's car, of seeing her mom lead her little brothers to a helicopter, and watching it fly away, of she and Anna walking through the dark forest at night, fleeing Alejandro's compound.

Yeah, that was a lot for any kid to process.

Bonnie trembled inside. When Anna looked at her with those concerned eyes, she wanted to blurt out all that was inside her, the growing fears, the frustration, the utter blindness of the adults around her.

But she couldn't.

When she tried, the panic rose. It started in her belly, this roiling, churning mass that grew and gained momentum as it filled the void in her abdominal cavity. In Health, Bonnie studied the human body, so she knew just where the organs were located, knew about the spaces between them, so could picture the mass seeping into all those crevasses and crannies, pushing against the organs, crowding them out, until there was no room, no room for her lungs to expand to take another breath.

She had seen the devil.

She'd seen what he did to Anna, her beloved Anna, the kindest person imaginable. She'd seen his influence over her mother, making her mom send her little brothers away in that chopper.

Bonnie had thought never to see that man again, that devil. Then he appeared suddenly at Cynthia's.

Cynthia's home had become a second refuge for Bonnie, second only to the haven she'd found with Anna and Murph.

Bonnie enjoyed learning, although the prospect of sitting in a classroom with other kids, when the teacher might call on her and try to make her talk, was terrifying. What if she said the wrong thing? What if everyone laughed at her?

But with Cynthia as her teacher, it didn't matter. Cynthia understood and didn't try to force her to speak. She said some words when she could, but Cynthia didn't judge her.

Bonnie knew she disappointed Anna and Murph when she didn't talk. They pretended it was okay, but she knew it wasn't. They wanted her to talk the way other kids did - easily, without thinking. Bonnie didn't know how they did it.

There were so many variables. Words could get mixed up. You never knew how what you said might come across. People interpreted things differently. She had tried so often with her mother, saying what she thought was right, an okay thing, only to have her mother scream at her what a stupid, wicked child she was. It was safer to not say anything.

Then it became harder to open her mouth. Even when the words were there, words she was pretty sure were right, that broiling, churning mass would burble up from her belly, stifling her breathing, filling her throat until there was no room for words to come out. No room for anything.

Chapter Eighteen

While Cynthia went to the other tables to check first on Natalie, then on Bonnie's progress, Elizabeth composed herself. Enough being maudlin, she could almost hear her mother chiding her. You're in public, put on your public face. So she did.

The women finished their coffee talking about everyday things, the emotional stuff stored in a compartment that may or may not be opened again.

The bell over the bakery door tinkled, and Keira held the door open for her son Daniel, Timothy, and Amy. It was Keira's turn to bring the kids home from school.

With barely a hug for their mothers, and a greeting to Bonnie, the three children splayed their hands on the glass display case to make their selection from today's assortment of goodies.

A tsunami of expressions washed over Natalie's face. Hurt at the snub. Then anger. What was she, chopped liver? Finally, a mask of indifference. Not one of those ungrateful brats paid her any attention.

Catching Natalie's expressions, Cynthia's heart clenched for the young girl. How many times in her life had she felt overlooked or ignored? "Kids," she called. "Come back here." Reluctantly, they abandoned their inspection of delectable eats ad clustered around Amy's mother. "You forgot something." The kids looked confused. "You didn't say hello to Natalie."

No one said anything.

"Timothy, where are your manners?" prodded Elizabeth.

He gave a quick glance Natalie's way and waved one hand. Daniel copied the gesture.

Eyes on her toes, Amy said, "Hi."

Natalie rose from her chair, approached, and crouched beside the kids. Pasting on her brightest smile, she said, "Hey, kids. Good to see you. How are things?"

"Fine," muttered Amy, still taking a great interest in her shoes.

Clasping Timothy's limp hand in hers, and placing a palm on Daniel's back, Natalie stood, saying, "Let's go inspect your choices," shepherding the children back to the bakery's counter. Squatting, she animatedly discussed the offerings with her young charges.

"Well, that was awkward," whispered Keira. "I wonder what got into the kids? Did they not notice her there?"

"Poor Natalie. I fear that she's experienced a lot of this in her life. Her mom says she was excluded and picked on by mean girls at her last school."

"Girls can be the worst," agreed Keira. With her spiky, blue-toned hair, she did not look the picture of someone trying to fit in, but she could relate to being excluded.

Timothy and Daniel took their plates to Bonnie's table. When Amy started to follow, Natalie put an arm around her shoulders. "Why don't you share my table with me?"

Glancing at her mother, Amy knew she had no choice. Silently she allowed herself to be led by Natalie, who seated the girl with her back to her friends and their mothers.

From Cynthia's chair, she could see the animated efforts Natalie was going to, to engage Amy in conversation. No, life had not been fair to Natalie.

Cynthia's cell phone pinged an incoming text message. It was from Barbara. She, Howard, and their kids were going out for supper with a family friend. Howard had to work late, and Barbara was running behind schedule because of Liam. So, their friend, Mr. Ramon, would meet Natalie at the bakery, then take her to the restaurant in a while. Barbara texted Natalie as well.

Cynthia approached the small table shared by Natalie and Amy. "Your mom says Mr. Ramon will meet you here and take you to the restaurant to meet your parents. Is that all right with you?"

"Yeah, of course, Uncle Al. He's an old friend of my parents. You met him when my dad brought him to your place."

"Right. I thought that was his name. Just wanted to make sure you're fine with it."

"He's cool. It'll be quieter riding to the restaurant with him. Liam squawks so much lately."

Returning to her table, Cynthia conveyed the gist of the message to Keira and Elizabeth.

"Ramon." Elizabeth thought for a moment. "Isn't that the name of Anna's ex?"

"I think so," said Keira. "But it's also the surname of about a million other people as well."

Downing the dregs of her coffee, Keira rose and called to Daniel. "We have to get going. See you later."

As they took their leave, Elizabeth gathered her purse and her son. "We need to head home, as well."

As they left, Cynthia motioned to Bonnie to join her. They had a few minutes before Anna or Murph arrived at Cynthia's home to collect Bonnie. She didn't feel right leaving Natalie here all alone; hopefully Mr. Ramon would arrive soon.

Natalie rolled her eyes. "I'm fine. Sheesh. It's not like I'm a child. I'm almost sixteen. I know this guy; he's a friend of my parents. I'm supposed to call him uncle. And I'm not alone." She gestured toward the counter. "That Jeff guys hovers around, watching, and Ellie is in the back."

"True, true, I know. I just don't feel like I can abandon you here, though. We'll wait with you a while longer. Your mom said your Uncle Al was coming soon."

Amy slid her chair to the side so that she and Bonnie had good eye contact. The two of them made faces at each other, giggling at the other's antics. Natalie pretended such games were far beneath her. Cynthia checked her phone for any more messages from Barbara.

The bell over the door tinkled. Natalie sat up straighter, a welcoming smile lighting her face.

Turning in her chair, Cynthia saw the man Howard had brought to her house last week, Al Ramon. Collecting her purse, she told Amy to finish up her Italian soda, and Bonnie to gather up her books. Rising, she turned to the man approaching their table. "Al, good to see you again." The pair shook hands. Bonnie, her back to the door, froze and the mention of that name. Cynthia's attention was

147

otherwise engaged; she did not see the visceral reaction Bonnie had to the presence of that man.

After greeting Natalie, Al made small talk with Cynthia for a moment, asking to be reminded of who the lovely young women were at Cynthia's table. Bonnie's face and shoulders remained a block of ice. Amy gave her usual elf grin and stood to shake the man's extended hand. He grinned effusively in return. Even the gap in her front teeth was appealing. This kid had potential.

Cynthia's Fitbit vibrated, the sound barely audible to those near her. Glancing at her wrist, she saw it was her reminder. "Time to go, kids. Anna will be at the house to pick up Bonnie soon."

Carefully avoiding the gleam in Alejandro's eyes, Bonnie was the first one out the door and starting down the street.

"Hey, Bonnie. Wait up," called Amy. She skipped after her friend.

Cynthia trailed after the girls. As she walked, she sent a text to Barbara, letting her know Alejandro had arrived and was with Natalie. She felt uneasy leaving the young girl alone with a strange man. But he was only a stranger, really only a semi-stranger, to her. After all, he was a family friend of Barbara and Howard, and Natalie seemed eager to chat with him.

She did not know what caused her misgiving. Maybe it was all the nasty stuff that had happened to her friends a year ago. Or maybe she was just a nervous Nelly. Still, she wished he'd arrived a few minutes earlier. Elizabeth and Keira might have had opinions.

"Quieter now that they're gone, isn't it?" Alejandro took an initial sip of his coffee. Not bad, not bad at all, he thought. Better than he'd expected from a little neighborhood place.

"Especially with Amy out of here. That kid rarely shuts up." One side of her mouth quirked up. "They're a weird little bunch. Bonnie and the boys hardly say a word, just the opposite of Amy."

"And what about you? What were you like at her age?"

"Me? I don't think I rambled on about anything and everything."

"Your mom complained that sometimes you give them the silent treatment."

"Well, who wouldn't? They are so hard to take sometimes. It's like we're a different species." She noted the merriment on Alejandro's face. "Yeah, I get it. That's what all teenagers say, but it's different." She leaned forward in her chair. "It really is different with me."

"How so?" Glancing at this watch, he saw they had another half hour before they needed to be at the restaurant. Alejandro sat back in his chair, ready to listen.

"You really want to know?" It wasn't often she had an adult inviting her to tell her story, an adult who wasn't condescending.

Alejandro nodded, wrapping both hands around his mug.

"When I was little, they'd buy me stuff. I know they were trying hard, but what they'd get was so lame. They thought little girls should love things like that. Maybe some did, but not me. Why would I want to spend my day dressing some doll in stupid clothes?"

"What did you prefer doing?"

"I liked nature and science stuff."

"Ah, so did I when I was a kid." Calculating, he asked a question casually. "Ever play with bugs?"

"Yes!" Natalie pounced on that. "Insects were endlessly fascinating to me. They were everywhere. It wasn't hard to catch them."

Alejandro nodded encouragement.

"I did experiments, you know, like the scientific method and all that. We had a lot of grasshoppers one summer. I watched how they moved, how they jumped. I had a ruler and measured how far they'd jump." She warmed to her subject, remembering her excitement at discovering fascinating things about those grasshoppers. "Once released from their tin, some would hop immediately. Others would sort of rest for a while before attempting to get away." She smiled to herself. "They might have thought they were getting away, but they could only do that when I let them."

"You like being in control?"

She nodded. "Mostly." Well, that wasn't quite true - she liked being in control all the time. "I tried to figure out how their joints moved, how their legs worked. How did they get the power to jump so many times their body height?" She checked so see that she had his attention. "Their limbs aren't like ours, you know."

"True, but I wouldn't have expected a small child to think about things like that."

Natalie shrugged, a half-hidden smile showing she was inwardly pleased. "The next summer I stepped up my experiments. Trying to figure out what part of their legs gave them this enormous power, I'd remove part of the leg. With some, it was just the bit that touched the ground. With others, it was at their ankle joint, or then their knee joint. Did you know," she asked, "that even with an entire leg missing, a grasshopper will still try to jump?" She snickered. "Not very well, though. But they still try."

Alejandro gave an encouraging smile and nod.

"I liked that, that kind of determination. They were sort of like me."

"And me, too," said Alejandro.

"I experimented on moths and butterflies, too. I know they don't hop," she added, "but I needed to see what made them fly. Did they need all four wings to fly? What would happen if I removed the back one on just one side? Could they learn to compensate? Could they still fly?"

"Could they?"

"Not very well. It just sort of flopped to the ground and maybe buzzed in a circle." This guy didn't seem grossed out by what she was saying. Dare she say more? It was so refreshing to talk to an adult who didn't get all bent out of shape about little things.

"My parents weren't interested in my experiments at all. In fact," she peered across the table at Alejandro, trying to gauge his reaction. "They acted like it grossed them out. My dad went into a rant about what kind of kid spent her days pulling wings off a butterfly. He didn't get it."

"Not everyone does."

True, thought Natalie. Good answer. "I had to become secretive about my experiments after that. The sun here gets pretty strong. I broke a glass beer bottle of dad's, smashing it with a hammer so I could use the bottom. The glass was thick and about the right size to hold. I experimented with catching sun rays with it, trying to melt plastic."

"How did that work for you?"

"Not very well. But then I found a magnifying glass. There was a little one in the first aid kit. That worked better. I could light small bits of paper on fire with it." Her eyes gleamed. "Once I collected a pile of dead leaves and set them under a bush beside the house. It took a while to get the angle just right, but I was patient and I got them to light up." Her face showed disappointment. "I didn't have enough leaves though to really make a fire."

"Is that a good thing or a bad thing?"

"My lame parents would say it was a good thing, but they don't get it." She leaned forward, elbows on the table, fists framing her chin. "Do you have any idea what it's like to be patient, waiting for just the right direction, just the right ray? Then to finally see that tiny wisp of smoke, just a faint tendril that you might miss if you weren't watching as closely as I was. Then you need to keep the magnifying glass just so, while gently blowing on the smoke. If you blow too hard, it's all over and you need to start again. But when you get it just right, that smoke tendril becomes a tiny flame, then a bigger one and bigger."

"Have you ever seen a large fire?"

Eyes flashing excitement, "Once, just once. And it wasn't a huge fire, nothing really major."

"Where was it?"

"It was just a shed in a neighbor's yard. It didn't light very well."

Alejandro looked at Natalie speculatively and urged her to go on.

"By then I'd learned that leaves aren't the best things to burn. They produce inconsistent results. Newspapers work better."

"Definitely."

"And mom started a new hobby, a really lame one. Embroidery. But her eyesight isn't very good, she's pretty old, you know. So, she got this giant magnifying glass that she'd wear on a rope around her neck, and it rested on her chest. She looked like a read dweeb with it, but when she wasn't using it, it made a brilliant device to gather and point light. Getting flames going was way easier with it."

He knew there was more to this story. "And then?"

"Everyone made such a big deal out of it. It was just an old, wooden shed. They just had some crap in it, nothing worth anything, just stuff like an ancient lawnmower, a rake, and junk like that. And the fire didn't even make it along the fence. It was nowhere near their house, but you'd think it was the end of the world. The neighbors yelled, my parents yelled, the police came, the fire department came."

"Sounds exciting."

"Oh, it was. You should have seen it. The flames form such pretty colors and they dance all around. You'd be surprised how much heat they spread, too. Crap, it was fine. No one was getting hurt if they'd just stood back and watched it. It wasn't a big deal, but they made it into one."

"They?"

"Everyone. The neighbors, my parents, the cops, the firefighters. Then I had to go for counseling. Can you believe how lame that was?"

Yeah, actually he could.

Glancing at his watch, he finished up the last of his coffee, pushing back his chair. "We'd better get going or your parents will be waiting for us." Following Natalie out of the bakery, he watched the set of her shoulders, the way she held her head. Somewhere deep inside, her movements struck a chord.

Chapter Nineteen

Some of the easy camaraderie between herself and Brendan had fled. Elizabeth missed it, missed never having to think before she spoke, never having to consider a gesture or a touch before she did it, never having to wonder how her action might be interpreted.

It put her on edge. This was the first relationship she'd had with a man where she felt she could simply be herself, and that was enough. Now, though, she second-guessed everything.

Oh, they still talked every day, but maybe not for as long. They still spent time together, but it was no longer the relaxing highlight of her day.

"Look, this isn't working, is it?" Brendan slouched on her couch. It was just the two of them now that Timothy was in bed.

Elizabeth's heart sank. *He's breaking up with me. He can't take it anymore. I'm not enough for him.*

Her mother's training came in handy. School your expression. Shoulders back, chin up, never, ever wear your heart on your sleeve. Think about the image you must project to the world.

Brendan ran his hand over his face. "I'm sorry. I cocked this up, didn't I?"

Huh?

"We had a good thing going and because I couldn't keep my big mouth shut, now you're uncomfortable with me."

Well, that last part was true, for sure. She studied the teacup in her hands.

"Can we roll this back and try again?" Brendan sat up. Turning, he took Elizabeth's hand. It lay limp in his grasp as he massaged her fingers, trying to squeeze some warmth back into their relationship. "I get it," he said. "I pushed too soon. I know you're not ready for anything more."

Turning slightly, Elizabeth watched as he ran his other hand through his hair, leaving it in unkempt spikes. His strands were never the kind to fall naturally into place. She rather liked that about him. He never strove for perfection in his appearance. He was what he was. She'd miss that, oh how she'd miss him.

"Look, this is driving me nuts." Brendan let go of her hand and stood to pace. "Do you want me out of here?" He stopped in front of her. "You are ever so polite, but I notice that you're not yourself with me anymore. The casualness has disappeared, and you're on edge. Are you trying to find a nice way to tell me to get lost?"

Get lost! How could he ever think that? "No!" It burst from her before she could carefully form a proper response.

"No? Then what? What gives?"

She thought it was supposed to be women who wanted

to talk about their relationship, or at least that's what happened in books. But not in her family. Definitely not. Unpleasant and uncomfortable things were not talked about.

With a quick glance at his face, she realized Brendan was waiting for an answer. What gives? How to answer that? She'd better try. For this man, she'd try. "It feels different now."

"No kidding!" He resumed his pacing. "Sorry, sorry. I'll shut up and let you talk."

Composing herself, Elizabeth tried. "I liked what we had. It was fun and easy." She checked to see how he was taking this, but his face was partially hidden as he leaned his head on his arm that was propped along her mantel edge. He seemed to take an inordinate interest in the photos she had arranged there - many of Timothy, but some included Brendan, as well.

She continued. "That's about as far ahead as I thought. It was good. We'd come to rely on you, and it felt right that you were here." That was safe enough to say, and certainly true. "It felt like you were part of our lives - a good part. An important part."

His eyes met hers. Was that hope she saw in them?

Okay, confession time. She was not used to baring her soul, but if that was what this man needed, she owed it to him to try.

"I'm not sure you would have liked me if you'd met me a few years ago." She held up a hand to stop his interruption. Now that she'd started, she needed to get through it. "I'm different now. Back then, I was all about pleasing others. My parents had certain standards I had to meet. Mostly, it was all about pleasing Daddy. Then, when I met Jackson, it was all about keeping him happy as well." She looked down at the hands she was wringing together. "Guess I didn't do as good a job with that as I'd thought." Her mother's voice in her ear, she folded her hands in her lap, forcing them to keep still. "After everything that happened, the abductions, finding out that Jackson wanted me killed, I vowed 'Never again'. I was done living my life for other people, for men."

"Is that what you think I'm doing to you?"

"You? Never! You're the first man who doesn't need me to be something, some image he has in his mind. You seemed to think I'm all right just as I am."

"Damned right I do."

Okay. This living in limbo was not good. Out with it. He could either accept her feelings or not. "But that night, after hearing everything you said, realizing how you felt, all the old stuff came rolling back. While I had thought that things were fine, they weren't for you. When you said you wanted more, it felt like you wanted me to be different than I was. That just me, like this, wasn't enough."

In a second, he was there in front of her, bending onto one knee, taking her hands in his. "No! You've got that wrong. You're perfect as you are." He hung his head. "I guess it was *my* insecurities. I wanted some kind of commitment from you, some assurance that the greatest thing to ever enter my life wouldn't go away." He grimaced. "I hate sounding so needy."

Elizabeth wound her arms around his neck and pulled him closer. "Yes."

"Yes, I'm sounding needy?"

She laughed. "I'm needy for you, too. Yes, to wanting to be with you. I can't imagine our lives without you."

Brendan's eyes met hers. "You mean it?"

Elizabeth nodded. "But can we still go slow? I'm new to

this standing-on-my-own-feet thing. I'm getting the hang of it, but for a minute there I had the feeling that another man was trying to take over my life."

Brendan pulled out of her embrace and held up his hands. "No! That's not what I'm trying to do. I just want to be a part of your lives."

"You are. You're such an important part of us."

"Thank god. I feared I had chased you away."

Elizabeth hesitated, hating to admit that for a bit, when she felt threatened by his words, she had withdrawn.

He caught her look. "So I guess you don't want me to make any wedding announcement just yet."

She tried to disguise the instant horror that flooded her eyes.

He caught it but laughed. "It's okay. I get it. Marriage didn't work out well for you the last time." He squeezed her hands. "But I can guarantee it will be better this time." He sealed his promise with a kiss. "I can wait, though. As long as I know it will come sometime, I'm good with being patient."

Elizabeth sank into his embrace, her lips conveying what her words couldn't say.

It became a regular thing. Wednesdays after Natalie's school day was over, she and Alejandro walked down to the bakery, loitered a while, then returned home where Alejandro stayed for supper with Howard and Barbara and their kids. Although Elizabeth's home was three doors down from that of Natalie's family, Alejandro appreciated the good planning that Elizabeth, the only one on the street who might recognize him from a year ago, lived in the opposite direction of the bakery. He was careful to keep a baseball cap low over his face when he entered or left Howard's home, just in case.

Having few acquaintances of their own yet, Howard and Barbara were glad for this trusted friend, willing to spend time with their daughter.

"Do you ever get tired of people trying to make you something you aren't?" Natalie enjoyed the time she spent with Uncle Al, although she found it lame that her parents insisted she call him that. For once, here was an adult she could talk to, one who didn't give her those judging looks. And he listened; he listened as if he cared. She didn't have to decide what she should hide and what was all right to say. She didn't think he'd use what she said against her, the way therapists and counselors had in the past.

"Yeah, I have. That happened to me when I was younger. Don't worry. It gets better when you're a grownup. Then you get to make your own mold, instead of anyone trying to force you into theirs."

Natalie tilted her head to the side and studied her companion. This was interesting. No one had ever talked to her this way. "Who tried to make you into something?"

A disgusted expression flitted over Al's face. "Who didn't? Too many people to remember them all."

Natalie waited.

"My mother, for one. She was religious and so hoped I would be, too. She'd have loved a son who went into the priesthood. Hah! As if that was the life for me."

"Why not?"

"A life of poverty? A vow of servitude? No, I had better things to do."

"Who else then?"

"The priest, for sure. Mom made me meet with him often. He tried to talk to me about God's will, and do unto others."

"How'd you handle it?" She really needed to know because she was so sick of others trying to bend her will to theirs.

"I learned to read people. It's not hard when you try. Just use your imagination and put yourself inside their head. Figure out what they want, then give it to them."

"But I don't want to give them what they want."

Alejandro laughed. "No, I don't mean really give them what they want. I learned to say what they wanted to hear or do some small thing that would please them. Then they think they've got you convinced, and they stay off your back."

Natalie's eyes gleamed. Maybe he was on to something. "That's not giving in?"

He shook his head. "Not at all. You're still in charge. You're choosing to act a certain way so that in the end you get what you want." He took a bite of his pastry. "It's a process." He remembered how he'd felt in his teen years. "It takes time to build the kind of world you want, but I know that it's hard to be patient."

Natalie's eyes narrowed. "Have you built the kind of world you want?"

Alejandro thought for a minute. Taking a sip of his coffee, he debated how much to disclose to this child. He assessed her. Was she actually a child? Maybe in chronological years, yes, but he saw so much of himself in her. At her age, he had been so much older, so much wiser than his peers. Even than the adults he knew. While they were on a treadmill of existence, he already had plans in place, plans that would elevate him far above anything they dreamed of. "Yeah, I did." He was not bragging, just stating a fact. But Natalie was sharp and caught the nuance. "Did?"

That pleased Alejandro. He liked this kid. "I had it. I had it all, and it was only going better. Then it got screwed up by a do-gooder, someone who should have known better than to mess with me."

Natalie leaned forward. "What are you doing about it now?" She knew he would not leave it like that.

Alejandro's lips curled. "I have plans."

"Need any help?"

His smile broadened. "I'll think about that. You just might be able to assist."

Alejandro stacked their dirty plates together on the table. Turning his back to the counter, he used a napkin to wrap around the spoon Natalie had used to eat her whipped cream and pocketed it.

Chapter Twenty

Cynthia noticed that Bonnie had switched spots. A creature of habit, Bonnie liked things the same - easier to manage her anxiety that way. But today, she sat at the far end of the table, the narrow end. And instead of keeping her belongings in one neat stack as usual, she had them spread around, almost like creating a visible barrier to her territory.

But Natalie had a question, so Cynthia thought no more about it. In fact, Natalie had lots of questions today. Somehow, needy was not an adjective she would have used to describe the older girl, but today, well… Come on, she told herself. Your job is to teach these students. She should be glad that Natalie felt free enough to ask questions. Still…

Although the girls brought lunches with them, Natalie always prepared something extra for them. Today, Natalie refused to eat with them. "I'm not hungry," she said. "Why should I have to eat when I don't feel like it?"

Okay, okay. It wasn't her job to make the kid eat,

Cynthia told herself. It felt weird, though, to eat in front of her. Well, they didn't exactly eat in front of her; Natalie refused to join her and Bonnie at the kitchen table for lunch. Instead, she remained in the dining room.

When Bonnie passed the doorway to the dining room on the way to the washroom, her eyes widened when she saw what Natalie was doing. Bonnie retraced her steps back to the kitchen, caught Cynthia's eye, then nodded her head toward the dining room.

Getting her meaning, Cynthia rose to check on Natalie. The student's fingers tapped away on Cynthia's laptop. Why would she be on that? "Natalie?"

Hastily, Natalie closed out of the incognito browser and pulled up the math homework site she'd opened, just in case. "Oh, hi," she said, her face all brightness and innocence. "I was stuck on this math problem and didn't want to disturb you during your lunch break. So, I borrowed your computer to look up how to do this." She turned the computer so Natalie could see the page. "Is that all right?"

"Of course, it is, but feel free to ask me anytime, lunch break or not. That's why I'm here."

They ended their lessons a bit early that afternoon, or at least Cynthia excused herself to get things ready. Barbara, Elizabeth, Keira, and Bonnie's foster mom, Anna, were stopping by for tea after school today.

When the women arrived, they took turns holding baby Liam, who was awake and eager for company. Natalie had met them all when they dropped off or picked up kids at Cynthia's. They rather disgusted her with the way they all made googly eyes at her little brother. Stepbrother, she reminded herself.

Not opposed to being by herself, Natalie hated feeling uncomfortable. She didn't want to sit and listen to the inane conversation her mother and these women exchanged. She'd rather stick a fork in her eye than ever become like them.

But she didn't want to hang with the little kids, either. They served a purpose sometimes, but they were so trying on her patience most of the time. Besides, their precious *Bonnie* was with them. The kids had totally ignored her when *she* walked nearby.

Even Blitz, their stupid little dog, wanted nothing to do with her. When Cynthia held the patio door open so he could come outside, he'd trotted out, then sniffed the air. His eyes turned to Natalie, then he'd made a wide circle around the patio chairs before running to where the children played on the swings and slide. Little snot.

She pretended to be engrossed in the math textbook she'd brought outside with her. At least she could have grabbed something halfway decent, but this had been on top of the stack. Usually, she planned better than that.

"You really like math?" asked Elizabeth.

"Not really. I need to get caught up, though."

"I used to think math sucked," said Keira, "until I got into high school and learned some of the applications. Some of the logic is helpful when coding."

One side of Natalie's lip curled up.

The women laughed. "You'll get it when you're older," said Keira.

Could these women be any more condescending?

A frown from Barbara told Natalie that she was letting her feelings show too much. How could her mother want her to live a lie? What kind of value was that to pass onto your kid? She could not wait until she was old enough to be out of here and on her own. Somehow, someday, she'd find people who got her.

Cynthia emerged from the house with a large tray in her hands. "Anyone want a snack?" she called. As one, the kids abandoned their games and raced toward the patio. They each inspected the decorated cupcakes before making their choice.

Natalie thought about the time Cynthia had spent first baking the things, then going to all that work making designs and smiley faces, each one different. And for what? She could have been devoting that time to helping Natalie. Wasn't that what Howard and Barbara paid her for? (Lately she had found it harder and harder to think of the couple as mom and dad. The older she got, the more her adoptive parents seemed foreign to her.)

The way these women gushed over the children was nauseating. It was as if these were the greatest kids in the world. Well, they weren't. Natalie had babysat them, so she knew. They were just kids, defective in some way, all of them. Three of the four couldn't talk, or hardly at all, and the fourth wouldn't shut up. Who needed kids like that around?

Enough. She needed to put a stop to this, or she really would throw up. Throwing up. Years of practice had made her good at acting. Her parents always believed her. She conjured up the feelings from the last time she'd barfed. That time she hadn't been faking, she really had the flu and badly. She pictured that queasy, tied-in-knots feeling in her stomach, the saliva pooling in her mouth, the instant just before she retched, and that acid-laced bolus spewed out of her mouth.

Barbara noticed and frowned. "Natalie, dear, are you feeling all right?"

All heads turned toward Natalie. She swallowed. Allowing a slight quaver into her voice, she said, "Sure, I'm fine, mom. I don't want to disturb your party. It's just my hypoglycemia, you know. I haven't had anything to eat yet today, and my blood sugar's wonky."

"Didn't you eat your lunch?" her mother asked.

Natalie shook her head. "I forgot it at home."

"You could have run home and got it."

"I know, but I had so many assignments to get through, I thought I should just keep working." She smiled shyly at Cynthia. "Don't want to disappoint my teacher, you know."

Cynthia's and Bonnie's eyes met. They remember Natalie's refusal to eat lunch with them. Bonnie knew that Natalie's lunch bag sat all day on the floor by Natalie's chair.

"Oh, you poor dear," said Elizabeth. "My mother had hypoglycemia. She felt really awful sometimes. Here." She shoved the plate of cupcakes in front of Natalie. "Have some before the kids take them all."

Natalie backed her chair away from the table, her eyes wide and moist. "Oh, I can't. If I have anything sweet on an empty stomach, I'll be ill. It's protein I need, not carbs."

Cynthia thought of the cheese, ham, and mushroom omelet she'd made for lunch, enough for the three of them to share. All eyes turned to her. "I'll go make you something," she offered.

Well, that was interesting, thought Anna as she and Bonnie drove home after leaving Cynthia's. Something about Natalie's story about experiencing hypoglycemia didn't ring true. She wasn't sure what felt wrong, but the glance Bonnie and Cynthia share confirmed her suspicions.

She looked at Bonnie out of the corner of her eye. The child watched the view go by, her face giving away nothing. It tempted Anna to ask Bonnie about the interchange, but that came dangerously close to gossiping about their friends. She couldn't subject a child to that. Besides, the odds of Bonnie saying anything were slim. She'd talk to Murph about it later, though.

"You're right, it seems odd." Anna and Murph were preparing supper while Bonnie did her homework in her room. "Couple that with Bonnie's reluctance to be around Natalie and it adds up to something wrong."

"I feel bad being suspicious of the girl. I'm not saying that Bonnie's always an angel, but we've never noticed her being anything but great around other kids."

"Bonnie might be the exception. Everyone responds to adversity differently, including kids. Bonnie has such a sweet nature, but not everyone would respond to her sort of life experiences the way she has."

Anna told Murph what Barbara had relayed to Cynthia about Natalie's earlier life.

"Sounds like she might have Reactive Attachment Disorder."

"What's that?"

"During the first year of life, a baby learns that if it cries, someone will come tend to it, giving it food, companionship, changing its diaper, those crucial things. The baby gets to trust the caregivers and bonds to them.

"But when a kid gets moved from home to home, especially when some of their basic needs aren't met in some of those environments, the baby never develops that feeling of trust, that others are to be relied on. Some kids become withdrawn. Some become clingy and needy, desperate to have their needs met. Many kids with RAD come across as manipulative as they get older. Their needs were never met in a typical way; they had to go to extraordinary methods to get the attention they required. It can compromise trust and empathy."

"Natalie does seem difficult to get close to."

They listened to the sounds of Bonnie moving around upstairs.

"Thank goodness Bonnie didn't respond that way, even though I'm not sure her early life was any easier than what Natalie experienced."

"Do events change you? Or do they just reveal who you really are, who you would have been all along?"

Bonnie entered the kitchen, smiling at Anna and Murph, her arms full of books. She crouched by the back door, placing her books in her backpack, ready for tomorrow. She put a hand on the doorknob, looking back at her foster parents.

"Sure, go on outside," said Anna. "The dogs are waiting for you."

"We'll call you for supper in about twenty minutes," added Murph.

Through the picture window, they watched Bonnie look for their dogs. Usually their German Shepherd, Sandy, and their Corgi, Morgan, were right by the door, waiting for Bonnie to appear. Today, though, the two raced toward Bonnie from the magnificent tree in the center of their field, looking back at the tree and barking. Sandy would go so far, then back to the tree, looking in Bonnie's direction. Odd.

Anna peered closer at the base of the tree.

"I'll get the binoculars," offered Murph. "There's something there."

"I'd better call Bonnie back in here."

Bonnie was almost half-way to the tree. She turned when she heard Anna's voice, but instead of obeying, she waved and kept going. So unlike Bonnie. Anna couldn't think of the last time she had been disobedient.

Murph was beside her and running after Bonnie. "Come on. It's a child."

When they got to the tree, Bonnie was sitting on the ground, her back against the trunk, with a little boy in her lap. The child's arms were around Bonnie's neck, as if permanently fused there. On either side of the kids, a dog stood guard. Sandy looked like he was saying, "Thank goodness you're here. Now someone can take charge."

It had been over a year since Anna had last seen this child. Her last glimpse of him had been as he and his younger brother were taken away from Alejandro's compound in a helicopter. Anna's mind wrestled with the possibility that this was indeed Bonnie's little brother.

Any doubt cleared up when Bonnie's gaze met hers over the child's head. "Jordy," she said.

Anna found the number in the contacts on her phone. "Judge Bursey?" she said when the call connected.

"Anna, what did I tell you? When we're not in court, call me Frank."

"Yes, Frank. But this call is professional, not personal."

Judge Bursey's demeanor changed. "Has something happened to Bonnie?" He was the one who had placed the girl in Anna and Murph's care. He was familiar with the foster girl's history and all that Anna and Bonnie had been through over a year ago.

"It's Jordy. Bonnie's brother. One of the two who were taken from the compound. He's back. He's here."

Chapter Twenty-One

Bonnie and Jordy played on the living room floor, within the careful sight of Anna.

After making sure that all doors and windows were locked and making the rounds of the house to insure there'd been no intruders, Murph phoned Brendan, and then Jake. They had no idea how Jordy had appeared on Murph and Anna's property, but they knew how he'd left the last time - taken by their mother, Sally, and Alejandro Ramon. If Jordy suddenly materialized, did that mean Alejandro was in the area?

Brendan and Jake were officers in the police department and part of the international team that had worked to track down and rescue Anna and Bonnie from Alejandro's compound in Mexico. Except the two had pretty much rescued themselves. But there'd been no sign of Alejandro, and none of the cooperating agencies had seen any sign of him since.

As Jordy climbed onto his big sister's lap, Bonnie heard

something crinkle. Inspecting Jordy's pockets, she found a folded, crumpled piece of paper. Smoothing it out, she read:

To whom it may concern,

This is Jordy Ramirez, brother to Bonnie.
His adoptive home didn't work out, and he needs a new place to live.

You're already looking after Bonnie. Jordy isn't much work. Bonnie will do most of the looking after.
I give him into your care.

Sally Ramirez Sykes

Bonnie set Jordy on the couch beside her and took the letter to Anna in the kitchen. She watched while Anna silently read the note, her face paling. Raising her head, she looked at Bonnie.

"Me. What about me?" the girl asked.

Anna knew what she meant. "Your mom already placed you in our care. She knew and approved and signed the papers authorizing us to be your foster parents." She pulled Bonnie to her for a hug and stroked her hair. "She knew you were safe with us and loved." She read the letter again. "Looks like now she wants the same thing for Jordy." Giving Bonnie another squeeze, she said, "I'm going to go show this to Murph. He's in the study. I'll be right back."

Murph was on the phone with Brendan, making arrangements. Jake was picking up Keira and Daniel and taking them to Elizabeth's house. He'd then escort Cynthia and Amy to Elizabeth's. Of all their houses, Elizabeth's had the most security. Brendan had already met with his captain, Evan Dulles. Captain Dulles notified the Violent Crimes Against Children International Task Force that they'd worked with when Bonnie and her brothers were abducted, as well as the Mexican federales they'd joined with in the rescue of Anna and Bonnie.

There were many people interested in Alejandro's whereabouts. Captain Dulles arranged for police to drive by Elizabeth's home and, later tonight, Murph and Anna's place. Once Jake had the women and kids safely stowed away at Elizabeth's, he'd join Brendan at Murph's.

"I'm different, you know." Natalie had gotten used to talking to Uncle Al during their visits to the bakery, really talking. Somehow, she didn't feel like she had to hide things from him. He didn't judge her, and she was pretty sure she was right about that, after a lifetime of people looking down their noses at her.

"How so?" He thought they had had this conversation before, but it was interesting to hear her take on things. She reminded him so much of himself at that age. Or younger. He thought he'd grown up faster than she had.

"The things that matter to other people don't matter to me."

"Like what?"

"Like being popular. Like caring what others think of me." She tossed her long, heavy, black hair over her shoulder. "Why would I give a rat's ass what other people think?"

She watched his face for a reaction to her language. There was none. Her mother would have been on her case, trying to make her apologize, thinking she had some sort of control over her. As if.

"What does matter to you?"

"Getting what I want." There was no hesitation in her reply.

"What about what they want?"

Natalie shrugged. "That's their problem. They need to look after themselves, like I need to look after me."

"What if everyone thought like that?" Alejandro asked, intrigued.

"That sounds like something my mother would say." She corrected herself. "My adopted mother, I mean. The woman who raised me." She stirred her hot chocolate, incorporating the cinnamon sprinkles and whipped cream into the mocha-colored drink. "Maybe if everyone looked after their own wants first, the world would be a more honest place."

Interesting, thought Alejandro. "But maybe a tougher place for people like you and I to get what we want."

Natalie thought about this. "You mean it would make it harder to bend them to our will?"

He nodded. "It might make them less predictable, harder to manipulate." He waited to see how she'd respond to his choice of word.

Natalie sat with her lips pursed to the side, her eyes looking up and to the left. "Maybe you're right. Now, people are often pitifully easy to manipulate. They're so predictable that it's boring."

They drank in silence for a few moments. Then Natalie continued. "Take Bonnie, for instance."

Oh, yes, I'd love to, thought Alejandro.

"She's just there, like a lump. Everyone loves her so much. I just don't see it, but she is so easy to play. She's predictable. Always miss goodie-goodie, putting everyone else first. Huh! Makes me wonder what she's hiding."

Should I tell her, wondered Alejandro. Maybe not yet. They ate and drank in companionable silence.

Natalie grew bolder. "I said I'm different, but you're different, too." There. How would he react?

Alejandro's face didn't change, but something flickered in his eyes. He waited.

"You're different from other adults, different from anyone I've talked to before. You don't seem shocked by the stuff I say."

"I'm not."

"I've seen counselors up the wazoo. My parents, I mean, Barbara and Howard, made me. Sometimes they made me just because, but sometimes I wasn't allowed back in school until some stupid counselor okayed it. Who wants to go to school, anyway? Mostly I just kept silent." She used her spoon to skim some of the whipped cream and cinnamon from the top of her hot chocolate. "I can see why that Bonnie chick refuses to talk. There's power in owning the silence, in having some adults contort themselves trying to make you speak. It was hard not to laugh much of the time when I watch them."

Alejandro raised one eyebrow. "School might help you get where you want to be."

Natalie shrugged. "I can get there other ways." She glared at him. "I'm not stupid, you know."

"Stupid is not a word I'd use to describe you."

She relaxed. "I'm ten times smarter than any of them. Twenty times."

Alejandro smiled. "I think you might be a chip off the old block."

"What's that supposed to mean?"

Alejandro pulled an envelope from his pocket and tapped it on the tabletop. "You know you're adopted."

Natalie nodded. "Of course. Howard and Barbara never made that a secret. They put this big spin on it that it means I'm special since I was 'chosen'." She rolled her eyes. "As if. I know how these things work. There are these kids that nobody wants. They're like advertised in a book and parents who want to adopt go shopping, browsing the catalog until they see a kid whose picture they like." She glanced at Alejandro under her lashes. "I would have stood out in that catalog. I was a cute kid." Defiantly, she looked at him. "I'm not bragging, it's just a fact."

"True. And you still are."

"I know."

"Your parents told you that I run the adoption agency." A fact, not a question.

Natalie nodded.

"Ever heard of the word surrogate?"

This time she shook her head. "What's that?"

"Sometimes a woman can't have a baby herself but wants one. She can hire a surrogate, a woman who can have babies. The surrogate goes through the pregnancy, then gives the baby to the woman who wants the baby."

Natalie's face scrunched up. "What's in it for her? Who'd want to be ugly and fat for nine months?"

"Money."

"How much?"

"Enough. Enough for their needs. Sometimes they also get looked after during their pregnancy, then get paid a fee for their trouble."

Natalie had a calculating look. "How do you fit in?"

He smiled. She was quick. "Ah, in several ways. I broker the deals. I hook up couples who want a baby but can't have one with those who can have a kid, but don't want to raise one. And I arrange the adoptions." He watched to see how she took this. He could read nothing but interest on her face. And maybe avarice. He kept going. "Sometimes there's a girl willing to be a surrogate but is not yet pregnant. She needs someone to get her that way."

"More coffee?" Jeff hovered at their table, a pot in his hand.

Alejandro waited until Jeff refilled his cup, then moved to customers three tables away. "Sometimes I oblige them."

He could see the wheels turning in Natalie's mind. He wasn't sure how naïve she was about such things, but he had an idea she wouldn't be overly sentimental about the sex act.

It clicked. "So, you fathered some of the babies who were adopted?"

He nodded. "I didn't want kids spawned by just anyone off the street. I only wanted healthy, good-looking babies. How could I offer guarantees to the adoptive couples if I wasn't sure of the parentage?"

This made sense to Natalie. She processed what he said and calculated possibilities. She studied the man sitting across from her, with direct eyes so like hers. Their skin tone, their hair, their attitude towards life. "You're my father." A statement, not a question.

"I wondered. A few weeks ago, I thought it was a possibility. Then I did this." He tapped the envelope. Time to tell her the rest. "I took the spoon you used one time we were here. You licked it enough that I thought it might hold enough DNA for a test. I was right." He shoved the envelope across the table to you. "Go on, take a look."

Quickly, she scanned the results. Not sure that she'd understood it all, she began reading again, this time more slowly. Her heart beat faster, and she consciously loosened her grip on the edges of the paper. She raised her eyes to Uncle Al. "Fifty percent of our DNA is the same. You're my father." This time, she said it with conviction.

Alejandro nodded. "I'm your biological father."

Natalie couldn't help it. A grin split her face. Finally. Someone she belonged with. Then she controlled her expression. How many times in her life had she been let down by someone? She'd not known this man for long. Just because they were related by blood meant nothing. It didn't have to, but maybe… "What does this mean for us?"

Alejandro's shoulders shrugged, and he looked away. "It means whatever we want it to mean."

"So, like, hi, nice knowing ya then you fade away, never to be seen again."

"It could go like that, especially if you want."

"And if I don't want?" Finally, finally someone who understood her, someone she could be herself with, and he might just disappear.

"We could hang out, just like we are now."

Somehow, she couldn't see that going on for long. "Or?"

"Or I don't know." He had some ideas, but would need to feel her out first. Just because she carried his genes and seemed to think like him, she was still a kid and maybe she'd been too brainwashed by the people who raised her. "I don't think we should tell you parents."

"Barbara and Howard, you mean. No, they don't need

to know." She'd hug this knowledge to herself. Another thought occurred to her. "Who's my mother?"

"Does it matter?" Although Natalie's stunning green eyes reminded him of someone he had bedded once upon a time or three. Or four or more.

"Not really."

Chapter Twenty-Two

Before Cynthia started this home teaching business, Elizabeth told her to trust her instincts. Well, she had. Cynthia's instincts said that the experience of teaching two young teens would look good on her resume. Her instinct told her she *had* been good at teaching. How hard could it be to work with two kids when she'd managed over two dozen easily? Maybe not easily, she thought to herself. There had been days, but mostly it had been good. So, two kids would be a breeze.

But it wasn't. Oh, the teaching part was; it all came back to her. Bonnie was easy, so willing to please, so quick to catch on.

Natalie caught on as well, but perhaps not as readily. Cynthia was unsure if that was ability, too many gaps in her education, or disinterest. The older girl was no scholar, always wanting to know why she had to do this. Fair enough. An inquisitive mind was a good thing. But what else went on in that mind?

At first, Cynthia thought that Bonnie's reticence to

interact with Natalie was either shyness or resentment about having to share her teacher's time and attention with someone else. But when had she ever noticed a jealous bone in Bonnie's body? When she was with the younger kids, Bonnie gave unselfishly of her time to them, always putting herself in the back, encouraging the little ones to take the limelight. It had been the same when observing Bonnie with her little stepbrothers.

Bonnie had experienced a lot in her brief thirteen years on this planet. Maybe she'd honed survival instincts Cynthia had never developed. Was it possible that Bonnie sensed something in Natalie, something Cynthia had failed to see?

She thought about the afternoon when all the mothers had gathered here and Natalie's story about hypoglycemia and not eating lunch. When Cynthia had gone back into the kitchen to prepare the girl some food, she'd glanced under the dining room table as she went by. Sure enough, there sat Natalie's lunch bag in its usual place on the floor near her chair. Feeling guilty at snooping, Cynthia silently crept around the table to reach for the lunch bag. Shielding it from view with her body, she unzipped the bag to glance inside. There rested a lettuce and egg salad sandwich on rye bread, an apple, some squares of cheese, and a juice box, along with a now-cooling ice pack.

The kid had lunch - two options for lunch, in fact. Why had she lied about not being able to eat at noon?

What game was she playing? What did she have to gain?

Cynthia thought about other incidents, small things. Like Bonnie not wanting to spend the days here working with Natalie when Cynthia was away subbing at schools. Like Amy not wanting Natalie to babysit her. Like Timothy giving his mom a hard time when she told him Natalie, not Bonnie, would babysit the kids. Like Amy claiming Natalie hurt her on the swings. Then there was Blitz. Blitz loved everyone and felt the need to greet each person in turn. Except for Natalie. He gave her a wide berth. Dogs knew things, didn't they?

It was Saturday. Howard was golfing. Again. Natalie was in her room, doing whatever she insisted required a closed and locked door.

Craving some adult company, Barbara strapped Liam in his stroller and walked to Cynthia's. She'd only stay a few minutes, maybe have just one cup of coffee.

Settling in on Cynthia's back patio, Barbara appreciated the faint Santa Ana breeze that kept the morning temperature pleasant.

"I can't thank you enough. You've made such a difference in our lives since you started teaching Natalie."

"You know, I was nervous about this before we started. The thought of exposing Natalie to another young girl had me in knots. She's had such a tough time with peers, and I feared what Bonnie might do to her. But Bonnie's a sweetheart. Natalie's not said one wrong thing about her."

Cautiously, Cynthia sought a reply. "Yes, Bonnie is a sweetheart."

"Maybe it's the atmosphere you create, but I've never seen Natalie happier, not in years."

Really? thought Cynthia. To her, Natalie came across as disgruntled.

"Yes, having Bonnie as a friend, and you on her side, has made a world of difference. Well, and having her Uncle Al now, too. It must have been hard for Nat when her world shrunk to just her father and me."

Since Barbara had confessed about some of the difficulties Natalie experienced in their old neighborhood, Cynthia did some online research. There were news stories about the fires. In other instances, in their neighborhood, animal protection had been involved, inspecting incidents in the area. Of course, the school files were closed. But knowing how teachers and administrators worked, Cynthia found it hard to believe that the adults in that building simply had it in for Natalie. It was rare for administrators to require a student to visit a counselor before being allowed back into classes. And that had happened repeatedly.

Cynthia thought of the way Bonnie interacted with Amy and the other young kids. She was open and caring, smiling and laughing. Had she ever seen Bonnie smile at Natalie? Share a secret grin? Nope. Of course, initially she'd not been paying attention, but over the last weeks she'd consciously tried to observe, and there was a definite chill between the two, mostly emanating from Bonnie. What did Bonnie know that she might have missed?

Chapter Twenty-Three

Barbara, usually well-groomed, had major hair frizz ends sticking up in all the wrong places. Something disgusting semi-dried on her left shoulder and down her back. When Alejandro gave her a partial hug in greeting, his nose wrinkled. The stain smelled suspiciously like baby vomit. Not that he'd ever been closer than this to the stuff, but he suspected the kid had puked on her. He got that babies, disgusting things that they were, sometimes did things like that. Who in their right mind wouldn't throw their shirt in the trash and clean themselves up after something like that happened?

Natalie was eager to get out of the house. She grabbed Alejandro's arm, giving a tug toward the door. Alejandro wasn't free to move as eight-month-old Liam had pulled himself up, clinging to Alejandro's pant leg. Al cringed at the ruination that grubby little hand was making of his pants' crisp crease.

He had some things he wanted to pass by Natalie today. He'd thought more about how she might be useful. He'd need to reel her in slowly, but he suspected it wouldn't take much.

In the meantime, he needed Barbara and Howard to continue to trust him. He spied the stroller parked in the hallway. "Has Liam had his nap?"

"No, sadly. He wouldn't settle down this afternoon. He's been fed and changed and is now raring to go, but not for sleep."

To Natalie, he said, "Instead of going to the bakery, why don't we take your brother with us and head to the park?"

Natalie gave her characteristic eye-roll.

Barbara's eagerness was palpable. "Would you?" She pulled herself back. "I mean, only if you'd enjoy it, too." She looked at her daughter. "Natalie knows how to look after him. But as soon as he goes for a stroller ride, he falls asleep. The motion, or something."

"Okay, we should be able to handle that, right, Natalie?"

"Whatever."

Before he could change his mind, Barbara scooped Liam up and strapped him into the stroller. She filled the attached carryall with a bottle of milk, one of water, two diapers, and baby wipes. Reading the alarm in Al's eyes, she explained, "Just in case. I doubt you'll need any of this."

Alejandro had no intentions of cleaning up a kid, no matter what he did. He'd return the kid fast if it did anything too repugnant. In the meantime, he hoped Barbara would take the opportunity to scrape herself off before he had to come back and suffer through a dinner with this family.

SHARON A. MITCHEL

"Why'd you have to do that, say we'd bring *him* along?" Natalie crinkled up her nose at the smiling baby in the stroller.

"Your mom looked like she needed a break."

"Don't call her that. We both know she's not my mother. She never used to look that bad, not before she had *him*." It ran through Natalie's mind the times when Barbara wore strain on her face, all those times when she and Howard were called into the principal's office over something Natalie had done, or not done. And Barbara's pinched face when meeting with counselors and psychologists and psychiatrists and when trying to explain to neighbors that they had the wrong take on incidents. That was Barbara's own fault if she let stuff get to her. "Anyway, who cares if she needs a break?"

"Sometimes you need to calculate things out. Maybe if I do something nice for her now, she'll feel indebted to me later. Maybe she'll remember that I was kind to her, that I understood. She'll think only good of me and defend me to others. That might come in handy one day. It's like putting coins in the bank for when you might need them later." He raised one eyebrow at Natalie. "You should try it someday."

Natalie shrugged. She got the point, though. It was about thinking it through, calculating what actions might pay off for you later.

"Want something?" Alejandro indicated the concession stand at the side of the park.

"Sure."

"I'll find us a bench to sit on while you go get what you want. Bring me a coffee, black." He handed her a twenty-dollar bill from his wallet.

Finding a bench shaded by some trees, he sat at one end, pushing the stroller back and forth in a way that

186

blocked the entire bench. He didn't want anyone else thinking they could sit down there.

Natalie returned with a tray containing two chocolate dipped ice cream cones, one coffee, a can of soda and a huge cone of candy floss. She didn't offer Al change, but he didn't expect any.

"Nothing for your little brother?"

"No, but I'll share with him." She broke off a piece of candy floss and shoved it toward the baby's face.

Liam fisted both hands in the sticky mass, pulling it toward his gaping mouth. As some made it onto his tongue, his eyes grew wide at the taste, and he coughed a little. The pale pink goop turned almost red as threads of it mixed with drool and stuck to his chin.

"He's going to be a mess."

"Yes." Natalie grinned.

"Just so long as I don't have to clean him up."

"Nope, that's Barbara's job." She tore off a larger chunk and held it out to Liam's grasping hands. "Since she got the afternoon off, let's give her something to do when we take the kid home."

Alejandro laughed. "See? Now you're calculating, not just reacting. It's all about planning."

"And you're always planning, right?"

"Most of the time, yeah. There's no choice when you have a business like mine."

"Tell me more about your business." She looked at him from beneath her lashes. "A girl should know what her father does for a living. Right?"

"One thing we do is help young girls. There are girls who get thrown out of their family homes when they become pregnant out of wedlock. Alone, pregnant and vulnerable, they don't last long on the streets. We have scouts who are on the watch for such girls. We offer them food and shelter while they decide what to do. If they want to stay with us, we put them up in our compounds. They're safe there, out in the country with plenty of fresh air and good food. We offer them medical treatment and to place their babies in suitable homes after the birth."

"Then what?"

"Some of the girls like the good life we give them and decide to stay, especially if they had an easy pregnancy and delivery. They're willing to get pregnant again, after a suitable time, of course, and produce another healthy baby for our adoption service. It's an easy life for them.

"But we don't keep them against their will. They have a choice. If they prefer to leave after the birth, we drive them back to their home. Or we help them find temporary shelter in a hostel and hook them up with employment services."

"You sound like a Good Samaritan."

"Just good business."

"So, that's it?"

She was with him so far. Now to press a little further, see how far she'd go with this. "There was one time when a business associate did some dumb things. Got himself in way over his head with gambling debts. Irritated the wrong people, dangerous people. He came to me for help. The amount of money he needed was outrageous, and I knew that he could never pay me back. So, we made a deal. He had a daughter, a daughter who was hanging around like an albatross around his neck. It was his step-daughter, and he wanted her out of the house. He showed me pictures, and she was a pretty thing, and healthy. Perfect breeding age. He assured me she was quiet and obedient.

"So, we made a deal. I'd pay off all of his gambling

debts. I'd also marry his daughter and take her off his hands. From his point of view, it was a win-win."

"And for you?"

"She was easy on the eyes. I was short on candidates to fill the needs of our adoption agency. If they had to wait too long for their baby, some potential parents went elsewhere with their wish list and their wallets. Anna's coloring and mine were the perfect mix for what many of the wealthy Mexican clients put in for."

"Anna? Common name, but I know an Anna."

Alejandro met her gaze but said nothing. Would she connect the dots?

"The Anna I know is Bonnie's foster mother. And she's a friend of my teacher, Cynthia's."

Alejandro regarded her levelly.

Natalie returned his look. Then her lips curved in a smile. "So, it wasn't just a coincidence that Howard ran into you, was it?"

Alejandro's smile neither confirmed nor denied.

Their conversation turned to other, more mundane matters. Liam kicked his feet and squirmed in his stroller. Natalie fed him more cotton candy, consuming almost none of it herself. The baby's movements became more frenetic.

"Do babies get hyper from too much sugar?"

"Beats me." She gave him some more.

Natalie shared some stories from her experiences at school with mean girls and with stupid girls. Some were so easy to set up; they just walked right into stuff. There was so much that happened that no one ever associated Natalie with. It was pleasant to stand back and watch the repercussions of plans she had set in motion.

Alejandro smiled at Natalie. It was a smile that said, "I see you. I understand". Natalie had never before experienced that. It felt good to have a dad.

The sudden cessation of movement in the stroller caught their attention. Rather than the frenetic arm and leg motions, Liam went still, intense concentration focusing his expression. Into the silence, noise erupted, suspicious noises signaling juicy expulsions as Liam filled his diaper. Startled, Natalie and Al looked at each other. As the sounds went on and on, they broke into laughter.

"How can something that small have so much shit?"

Liam's face told them he wondered about that, too.

"I think your mother put diapers in the back of the stroller."

"So? Are you going to do anything about it?"

"Not me. You?"

"No way! Ew, gross." So far, the stench had not penetrated the plastic casing of the diaper. But it would, Natalie knew. "Better get this kid back to Barbara."

Alejandro gathered up the remains of their snacks and threw them in a trash can.

As they walked, Natalie mulled over what Al had told her about Anna. "There's more to the story, isn't there?"

Pleased, Alejandro had hoped that Natalie would wonder about it and ask. She was sharp. "Yes, that wasn't the last of Anna and I." He moved to the other side of Natalie as she pushed the stroller. Good. Now he was upwind, so the grisly mess inside Liam's diaper no longer wafted toward him. "Over time, my stable in Mexico grew to meet the demand of the adoptive parents on our list. Having that many women in one house was challenging, even though the estate was huge. The women bickered and were restless. I had staff to do the cooking, cleaning, and gardening, but needed someone to manage the girls on a day-to-day basis. I thought of Anna. She was always calm and pleasant, but sympathetic. She knew the house and the grounds. She'd be ideal managing the women.

"So, I came back for her. I knew what she was doing now, and I could offer her double the salary, for far less work, and a beautiful place to live. She'd even have her own suite in the mansion. She should have jumped at the chance, but she didn't. She refused." His eyes regarded those of his newly discovered daughter. "People don't refuse me. It doesn't go well for them."

Natalie smiled. She got that.

Chapter Twenty-Four

After leaving Cynthia's Wednesday afternoon, Al and Natalie headed to the park rather than the bakery. Both sought more privacy for their conversations.

"What? No cotton candy this time?"

"No. I hate that stuff. I just bought it to see how Liam would react to it." Natalie grinned. "We saw and heard how *that* turned out."

"And smelled how that turned out." Alejandro had hidden his smile when Barbara picked up her malodorous son.

Natalie had questions. "Where do you live? I mean when you're not here."

"I used to live on my estate, when not traveling."

"Estate. Not like the dinky house Howard and Barbara have."

"No, I mean an estate. The house had ten bedrooms plus two suites, offices, and a full staff to look after things." He smiled. "I like to live in comfort. I also like beautiful things. High walls kept us safe from anything that might try to enter. Eight acres of gardens and lawns surrounded the house."

"I would like to have seen it."

"I'll rebuild, and maybe you'll come spend some time at the replacement estate."

For a while they amused themselves by making up stories about people in the park. Amazing that their minds easily travelled down the same paths.

Time to see just how in tune to him Natalie was. Casually, Alejandro asked, "What do you think of Bonnie?"

"That dweeb? She can't even talk, you know." Her lip curled. "But Cynthia loves her, anyway. Everyone dotes on her."

"Everyone?"

"Well, not everyone, obviously. Her mother dumped her, and there's no father claiming her either."

"What if I told you, I know her mother?"

Natalie turned to Alejandro, her eyes sparkling with interest. "You do? Tell me about her."

"I met her when I was watching Anna, finding a way to lure her to work for me. Sally pretty much plopped herself in my lap. She was looking for a job, a better way of life, so I decided she'd be easier to bring in to look after my girls than struggling with Anna."

"How'd that work out?"

This was the time to decide. Just how much should he divulge. His instincts said that this girl, his daughter, had all the right genes, a testament to her breeding.

He decided. Now was the time to see which side Natalie would fall on. If things didn't go as he hoped, well, he could disappear, at least for a while.

"Sally brought with her some other, ah, assets."

"She's built?" Natalie gave a knowing look.

"Yes, that too, but more. See, our adoption business developed some offshoots. Not everyone was looking for babies; some wanted older kids."

"For...?"

Alejandro held up his hands. "Not my business. They put in their request, and I try to fill the order. As long as they pay, and give me a good recommendation, that's all I care about."

"So, Sally...?"

"Sally was not mother material. She said so herself, and it was apparent. But she did like money, and she wanted a better lifestyle." Then he added, "Both for herself and for her kids."

Natalie regarded him out of the corner of her eye.

"She had a two-year-old and a three-year-old, as well as Bonnie. The younger two were boys. I had orders for toddlers; adoptive parents who wanted to skip the baby stage of diapers and bottles and sleepless nights.

"In exchange for a hefty sum of money and guarantees that her sons would wind up in wealthy homes, Sally was willing to make the exchange. She said she was ensuring a better life for the boys."

"And did she?"

He nodded. "But Sally wanted Bonnie, too. She needed Bonnie to look after the boys before their adoption. Sally wasn't keen on getting her hands dirty. Plus, we had buyers interested in a girl Bonnie's age."

Natalie looked off into the distance, contemplating this. Her imagination stretched as far as it could. She gave a sideways look at Alejandro. "What did Bonnie say about this?"

Then she covered her mouth with her hand. "Oops. I forgot. Bonnie wouldn't say anything, would she?"

Alejandro laughed. "No idea what was in that girl's head. The deal never had a chance to go through. Anna showed up and ruined it."

"Anna? Timid little Anna?"

"She might be little, and quiet, but she's not timid. Not when it comes to defending those she cares about." Despite how Anna thwarted his plan, a part of Alejandro admired her.

"Anna brought with her the police. She didn't bring them directly, but her friends, the cops who date Elizabeth and Keira, did. My compound got raided and shut down."

"Wow."

"Yeah, wow."

"I bet it ticked you off."

Alejandro narrowed his eyes. "Still am. I don't forget."

"Now what?"

"I have some plans."

"I just bet you do." Rather than fear or disgust, Natalie's eyes reflected amusement and excitement.

"I still have requests for older kids. One family in particular wants a girl. They want her to be bright, cute, and six or seven. Know anyone like that?"

"That brat, Amy." Facing Alejandro full on, she continued. "You know what that kid did to me? She told her mother that I hurt her. She tattled on me!"

"Did you hurt her?"

"Not really. It was nothing. Just teaching her a lesson." More poured out. "She had the nerve to tell her mother that she didn't want me to babysit her, that she wanted Bonnie instead. I heard her when they didn't know I was in the backyard. Bonnie, Bonnie, Bonnie. All I hear is Saint Bonnie."

"You'd like to see Bonnie go away?"

"Darned right I would. She doesn't deserve the elevated position everyone around here's put her on."

"Perhaps I can help you out with that. I'll think about it. First though, maybe you can help me with a little something."

Chapter Twenty-Five

"Are you sure you're okay with this?" asked Alejandro.

"Yeah, I've got this." Sheesh. Did he think she was a kid or something? They'd been over it a gazillion times.

Natalie entered the school. In the entryway, the scent of disinfectant mixed with sweaty feet assaulted her senses. She was so glad she did not have to be a part of this now. Maybe never again, if she had her way. And she usually did. She smiled to herself.

Pulling open the second set of doors, she oriented herself. The sign said the office was straight ahead. She and Alejandro had talked about this. They'd both rather that she went straight to Amy's classroom, avoiding the notice of any pesky administrators or secretaries.

Thankfully, the school placed name plaques on each door, making it plain which teacher belonged in which room. Amy was such a chatterbox that anyone who'd been in her presence longer than half-an-hour knew her teacher was Ms. Harriet.

Finding the correct room took less than a minute.

Natalie knew schools. She knew how to brazen her way around. Glancing at the hallway clock, she saw it was less than five minutes until school dismissal time. Good. They'd timed this perfectly.

Without hesitation, she rapped on the door. A ginger-haired boy answered. "May I speak to Ms. Harriet, please?"

The child retreated. An older woman replaced him; she must have been well over thirty, at least. "Yes, may I help you?"

Natalie put on her best teacher-pleasing smile. "Hi! I have this note for you." She extended the envelope with Ms. Harriet's name written in block letters on the outside. As the teacher tore open the letter, Natalie explained. "I'm here to collect Amy Blythe. Her mom, Cynthia, asked me to. This note is from her." Practicing her most guileless tone, "I'm Amy's babysitter and her neighbor. Her mom asked me to come get her from school today."

With her attention half on her restless students, Ms. Harriet hastily scanned the hand-written note. She glanced at the clock above her white board. "Class, get your things ready. It's home-time." She searched for Amy. "Amy, will you come here a second, please?"

Amy separated herself from her classmates. She seemed surprised to see Natalie standing in the doorway of her classroom. "Hi," she said, with a question in her voice.

Putting on her warmest expression, Natalie crouched down to be eye-level with Amy. "Change of plan today. Your mom asked me to come get you from school." She put her finger to her lips. "Shhh. It's a surprise. I'm not supposed to tell you about it."

"A surprise? For me?" Amy loved surprises. Her mom used to plan them for her all the time, but lately she'd been so busy.

Ms. Harriet wrapped an arm around Amy's shoulders and asked her, "Do you know this girl?"

"Sure. That's Natalie."

"How do you know her?"

"Lots of ways." Anyone who knew Amy knew they were in for a litany. "Sometimes she babysits me. Sometimes she babysits me and my friends. My mom teaches her, well, her and Bonnie together. My mom's a teacher like you, you know, and Bonnie and Natalie are on home study programs..."

"I get it," interrupted Ms. Harriet. "You know each other."

"That's not all," said Amy. She was hard to get stopped once on a roll. "She lives on my street. She's two houses down. Well, not just her, but her mom and her dad and her baby brother. His name is Liam."

"I see," said Ms. Harriet. Looking to Natalie added, "I guess she's given you your bona fides. You are who you say you are, and Amy knows you. We're not supposed to release a child into the custody of anyone who is not on the guardian's written list." She glanced at the note she'd skimmed. "But this is in writing and Amy most definitely knows you," she grinned, "... in lots of ways, apparently. So, it's fine."

As Amy returned with her backpack, Ms. Harriet gave her a quick hug and said to her retreating back, "Have fun."

"Oh, we will," assured Natalie. "We have lots of fun and games planned."

"This way." Natalie's firm hand on Amy's shoulder directed her around the corner from the school where Alejandro's car was parked.

"Our rides usually wait over there." Amy pointed to the line of cars along the curb in front of the school.

"Not today." Natalie opened the back door of the white SUV.

Amy balked. "Wait! I'm not supposed to get into a car with strangers."

Natalie looked helplessly through the side window at Alejandro. This was not part of the plan they'd worked out.

Draping his right arm across the back of the seats, Alejandro turned around, angling his face towards the open back door. "You're so right, Amy. Your mom taught you well. Never get in a car with strangers." He gave her his warmest smile. "But I'm not a stranger, am I?"

"Oh, I know you," said Amy. "You're the guy from the bakery. Mom introduced us. You're friends with Natalie's parents."

"That's right. Good memory," said Alejandro. To Natalie, he added, "Look at the brain on Amy."

Amy beamed.

Natalie scowled. She knew he was flattering Amy so that she'd get in the car without a fuss. But really, the kid was not a genius or anything. She was not nearly as savvy as Natalie had been at that age. "Hop in," she told the girl, giving her a small shove. "I'll help you with your seat belt."

"I don't need any help. I can do it myself. I tell my mom that all the time." She looked around. "Hey, no booster seat. Good. Those are for babies. I'm not a baby, even though my mom treats me like one sometimes." She was off on a rant about how ill-treated she was when her mother did not realize how many things she could do for herself.

Alejandro looked at Natalie, then jerked his head toward Amy, as if to say, "Keep her talking." He navigated away from the school grounds, heading in the opposite direction of Amy's home.

"Where's Amy?"

Timothy shrugged.

Elizabeth turned to Daniel. Same response. She blew out a breath. She understood the difficulties both boys had with expressive language, but you'd think at least one of them could talk when she really needed to know something.

They looked unconcerned. Well, that was a good thing. She scanned the playground and the school door exits, looking for Amy's pixie face. Usually, her mouth was in gear and you could hear her chatter before seeing her presence, and usually she was leading the boys, shepherding them where they needed to go. It was not like Amy to trail behind. Ever.

The playground crush was thinning out. There were few parent cars left. She checked her watch. Amy should definitely have been here by now, even if she forgot something in her classroom.

Checking that she secured both boys in their seats, Elizabeth gave orders. "Don't move. Don't you dare get out of your seats. I'm going to put the air conditioning on, then lock the doors. Do. Not. Move. I'm going to find Amy. Are we clear about this?" She waited until her son and Daniel both made eye contact with her and nodded.

She hit the key fob to lock the doors, then used her key fob to remote start the car and the air conditioning, ensuring that the boys would not swelter in the heat.

It was a small school, and she knew which classroom was Amy's. The door was open. There was only one small boy. He sat on the floor, tying up his shoelaces. His impatient mother shifted from one foot to the other, holding her son's backpack in one hand, her purse in the other.

The teacher was wiping off the white board.

"Excuse me, Ms. Harriet."

"Oh, hi. Timothy's mother, right?"

"Yes, I'm Elizabeth Whitmore. I'm here to pick up Amy, but she didn't come out to the car."

"There must be some mistake. Didn't Mrs. Blythe contact you?"

"Noooo."

"She sent a note along with the babysitter. She wanted the sitter to collect Amy."

Elizabeth narrowed her eyes at the woman.

Hastily, the teacher defended herself. "The note was quite clear. And Amy and the girl obviously knew each other. I even asked Amy how she knew her." She looked up and to the left, trying to remember the exact words. "I think she said that the girl was a neighbor, that she babysat her sometimes and that her mom taught the girl."

Elizabeth let out a breath. "Natalie."

"Yes! That's the name. Do you know her, too?"

"Yes, I do, and she's all the things you mentioned, but it's weird that Cynthia wouldn't have told me she asked Natalie to come for her. We spoke this morning, and she mentioned nothing about changing plans."

"Maybe something came up, and she forgot."

Possibly, but not likely. Maybe Elizabeth was paranoid, but after having her son snatched not just once, but twice, she took no chances with her son. On top of that, they had kidnapped Bonnie and her brothers last year. While Anna had helped to get Bonnie back, they still didn't know what had become of the little boys.

All of them were careful of their children. They allowed only designated people to pick up their kids from school. Although it might be innocent, something didn't sit right with Elizabeth.

The other mother clutched her son's hand and edged him out of the classroom. She wanted no part of this other than to get her little man home safely.

Elizabeth and the teacher ignored them.

Pulling out her cell phone, Elizabeth pressed the numbers for Cynthia. The phone went to voice mail.

Trusting her gut feeling, Elizabeth demanded. "We need to talk to the principal."

"I'll call and get her to come down."

"Do you have the note you said came from Amy's mother?"

Squatting down, Ms. Harriet began going through the garbage and lunch scraps and detritus of a classroom. "Good thing the janitor hasn't emptied the trash can yet."

Trying Cynthia's number again. This time they connected. "Hey, Cynthia. It's Elizabeth."

"Did you call a few minutes ago? Sorry I missed it. I was working out with my pole in the basement."

"Look, I don't mean to alarm you, but Amy didn't come out to the car with the boys. I'm here with her teacher and the teacher says that you sent a note saying Natalie would pick up Amy today."

She held the phone away from her ear. The teacher and principal could hear Cynthia's raised voice and emphatic denial. Elizabeth said, "Hold on. Don't panic. I'll give you to the teacher and she can tell you what happened. We can probably straighten this out in a few minutes." I hope, she told herself.

While the teacher repeated her story to Cynthia, under the watchful eye of her boss, Elizabeth said, "I need a phone, any phone. Do you have one I can use?"

The principal pulled one from her pocket and handed it over, her face pale.

Elizabeth strode out the door. As soon as they reached the hallway, she keyed in a number she knew by heart. "Brendan, I think we have a problem."

Chapter Twenty-Six

Keeping Amy talking was not hardship. In fact, her incessant chatter was getting on Alejandro and Natalie's nerves.

"All that talking must make her thirsty," he said to Natalie.

"Yeah, it is," chirped Amy from the back seat of Alejandro's SUV.

"We can't have that, can we?" Alejandro strove for his most jovial voice. "Nat, get her something to drink, will you? We've got that juice in the cooler."

With a secret smile, Natalie opened the small, insulated container at her feet. She withdrew the drink container from the pool of melting ice and flipped up the straw. She'd never seen this stuff in action, but trusted that Alejandro said it would work. He'd perfected the formula on other kids. "Here." She passed the beverage back to Amy.

"Thanks!" Greedily, Amy sipped away. "Mmm. This is good." Sweet drinks were her weakness, but her mom was stingy with them, saving such treats only for special occasions. "Mom *never* gives me stuff like this."

Alejandro and Natalie shared a smile. Within minutes, there was silence. Blessed silence.

Arriving at the hotel, Alejandro climbed to the fourth level of the parkade, pulling into a vacant spot near the elevator. Natalie waited in the car while Alejandro called up the elevator and made sure that it was empty. He waved Natalie over to hold open the door, while he hoisted the slumbering Amy over his shoulder. As they got off on the seventh floor, they met a bellhop waiting for the elevator.

Pasting on a smile, Alejandro cradled Amy's head with a protective hand, pressing her face into his neck. He smiled at the man in uniform. "Too much birthday partying," he said. "She passed right out on the drive home." He was thankful that both Amy's dark hair and Natalie's matched his own. They'd easily pass as his kids.

"Nice that she has a big sister to help," replied the bellhop.

Natalie rolled her eyes. "He *made* me."

The man laughed and got on the elevator.

Waiting until the doors closed fully, Alejandro headed for the stairs. He checked the stairwell was empty, then led them up one flight. Again, checking that the eighth-floor hallway was empty, then entered, stopping in front of the suite he'd booked for the week. Swiping the sensor with his key card, he entered.

"About time," Sally complained. "You've left me here all alone. What am I supposed to do with myself all day?" As Alejandro turned, she noticed the girl in his arms. "What?

We just got rid of the last kid. Now you've brought me another brat?"

"She's got that right," said Natalie. "Who is this?" she asked her father.

Sally's eyes widened. "*Two* brats?"

"Hey!" Alejandro's tone was sharp. "I won't have you talking that way about my daughter."

"Your daughter?" Sally looked between the sleeping child and the petulant teen. Which one?

Entering one of the bedrooms, Alejandro set Amy down on the bed, none too gently. She didn't stir.

"Wait," Sally said. "That's my room."

"It's whoever's room I say it is."

Sally took a step back. Why'd he use that tone with her? She deserved better than that. What new game was he up to?

Natalie smirked.

Alejandro put his arm around her shoulders. "Sally, I'd like you to meet my daughter, Natalie." He enjoyed the shock on Sally's face. There was something satisfying about keeping people off guard. He loved having the upper hand. "Natalie, I'd like you to meet Sally. She's Bonnie's mother." He waited for a reaction. There was no change in Natalie's expression. Good kid. She knew how to handle herself. She'd go far. "And I use the term 'mother' loosely."

Natalie's laugh matched his.

Sally could see the resemblance. "I didn't know you had a daughter."

"There's a lot you don't know."

Sally looked between the two of them. "Who's the other kid?"

"She's for our little venture. I've got an order for a girl

about that age. In fact, the family that couldn't stand *your* kid, wants one like *her*, instead."

"That wasn't my fault. The kid was stuck on Bonnie. Nothing anyone did would please him if he didn't have Bonnie."

"Well, he has her now." We'll see for how long, though. That part of the plan wasn't yet fully formed. But it would be, oh yes, it would be.

"No kidding, we have a problem," replied Brendan. "I was just about to call you. Get the women and kids and keep them with you, locked up in your house. I or Jake will be over as soon as we can. Alejandro's here."

"What?!" Elizabeth squawked.

"We assume it's Alejandro. Jordy, Bonnie's little brother showed up on Murph and Anna's property."

"Is he okay?"

"Yeah, he seems fine, but doctors have not yet checked him over." Brendan thought about what Elizabeth said. "Wait. You knew? That's the problem?"

Elizabeth shook her head, forgetting Brendan couldn't see her. "No. Amy's missing. I came to get her from school and the teacher says that Natalie took her. She had a note from Cynthia saying it was okay. But Cynthia denies writing any note."

Brendan ran his hands down his face. Oh, man. Then his cop brain kicked in. "Look, stay there. Bring Timothy and Daniel into the school with you, and don't let them out of your sight. Better yet, have someone walk to your car with you to get them. Less can happen with two adults. Jake will meet you there." He thought a moment more. "I'll send

Boyd and Hernandez to the school. You met them; they investigated Bonnie's disappearance. They're familiar with this Alejandro character, if it's actually him involved this time." Who knows? Maybe they were linking events that were simply coincidence. Yeah, right. His cop instinct sounded alarm bells. "Maybe this was something Natalie dreamt up all on her own and she's at the park with Amy, or on their way home. Nothing to do with Alejandro." As if he believed that.

They sat in the staff room, Elizabeth and the principal, silent and grim-faced. Across from them the teacher, Ms. Harriet, sat quietly sobbing. In the far corner, Timothy and Daniel silently played with building blocks, casting questioning glances at the adults.

The school was locked up tight, each door and window checked. A sign on the front door told anyone wanting access to the building to phone the office number, scribbled on the bottom on the notice.

Finally, finally, the call they'd been waiting for. Ms. Topor hurried to the phone. "No, Mrs. Richelieu, I'm sure it's all right that Joseph forgot his homework. No need to come back for it. I'll talk to his teacher, and we'll excuse it this time." She returned, shaking her head. "Hate to tie up the line for something like that."

It was four-and-a-half more minutes by Elizabeth's watch before the phone rang again. This time, the principal's side of the conversation sounded more hopeful. "Yes. I'll be right there to let you in." As she almost ran out of the room, she informed Elizabeth that the police were here.

Checking to see that Timothy and Daniel had not

moved from their play on the carpet, Elizabeth waited at the door. Within seconds, Keira enveloped her in a hug. Towering over her was Jake, who threw his arms around both of them at once. "The kids?" he asked.

Elizabeth nodded behind her.

Keeping his arm around Elizabeth's shoulders, Jake turned his back to the others and whispered in her ear. "Brendan said he mentioned to you that Jordy's back."

She nodded.

"Keep that to yourself for now. Don't tell anyone. Got it?"

Elizabeth nodded again, a question in her eyes. A big one.

Keira swept over to her son and Timothy. Jake followed, giving each boy a squeeze and a kiss on top of their heads, then turned back to the women he didn't know.

He held out his hand. "I'm Detective Jake Dean."

Jake continued. "I worked the case when Timothy..." He looked around to see if the kids were listening. They had their backs to the adults standing in the doorway. "When he went missing last year. And the incident the year before that." He added, "I also know Amy."

Ms. Topor introduced herself as principal, and Ms. Harriet, Amy's teacher.

Signaling to Keira to keep the boys in the room, Jake motioned for Elizabeth, the principal, and the teacher to join him in the hallway.

He pulled out his notebook. "Start from the beginning. Who first noticed that Amy was not where she was supposed to be?"

"That would be me," said Elizabeth, then repeated her story about Amy not coming out to the car with the boys.

"What did you do next?"

"I locked the boys in the car and went to Amy's class-room to see if she was there."

"And what did you find there?"

Ms. Harriet stifled her sniffling enough to take over the story from there. From her pocket, the same one that now contained moist, crumpled tissues, she pulled the note, in less than pristine shape.

"Sorry. We've all handled it," explained Ms. Topor. "We didn't think; we always handle notes parents send us." Trying to make up for their error, "Here." She handed over a folder. "We made photocopies of it in case that helps you. We also included Amy's latest school picture."

Producing an evidence bag from his pocket, Jake slid the original, now slightly moist note inside and sealed the bag. He took the folder to read the photocopied version.

"You weren't suspicious about this note?" he asked Ms. Harriet.

She shook her head. "We get notes from parents all the time about changes to their pickup instructions. I would not have let Amy go with that young girl without a note."

"Did you think…" No. Jake cut himself off. Now was not the time.

The phone in the office rang again. "That might be the officers," Jake said. "Wait here."

He strode to the front door. He undid the deadbolt lock to admit Officers Boyd and Hernandez, then led them to the women. After making the introductions, he brought them up to speed on what they knew so far.

"No one has reached this Natalie?" Boyd asked.

Elizabeth held out her mobile phone. "There's no answer on their home phone, but Barbara, Natalie's mom, often unplugs when she's trying to get their baby to sleep. Maybe she forgot to plug it back in.

"I've tried Natalie's mobile over and over, but the calls go straight to voicemail." At their questioning look, she explained. "Natalie has babysat for us, for all of us. I mean for Amy, Timothy, and Daniel together, so we all have her mobile number, and she has ours."

"Was there any problem when she babysat? Any concerns?"

"No, nothing." Elizabeth thought for a second. "The kids weren't as enthused at the prospect of her minding them as they were when they had another sitter. But then they were all used to the other girl and Natalie was newer to them." Since two of the kids were autistic and didn't appreciate change, that was understandable. Yes, that explained their reticence. Didn't it?

"Okay." Jake was in organizational mode. To the principal he asked, "Is everything locked up as I asked?"

She nodded. "I locked all the doors and made the rounds of each classroom to make sure that all the windows were latched as well."

"Please, would you all remain in the staff room? We'll search the building."

Boyd and Hernandez, armed with pictures of Amy, each took a wing of the school to search. Jake would take the common areas like the washrooms, library, gym, offices, and storage rooms. But first, he had a phone call to make.

"Hey, Cynthia. It's Jake." She must be going nuts, he thought. "Are you hanging in there?" He listened. "No, you're doing exactly the right thing. Stay home in case Amy comes walking through your door. She might have taken a walk, or maybe she and Natalie are off doing something and will be home soon. We don't want her to come to an empty house or a locked door."

"Here's the plan. We're searching the school right now -

myself and Officers Boyd and Hernandez. They're good. They were involved with Bonnie's case last year.

"If we don't find Amy hiding out someplace here, the officers will escort Keira and Elizabeth to your house. We'd like you to all stay together, preferably at Elizabeth's place. Leave a note on the doors for Amy, telling her where you are, just in case she makes it home on her own. Got that?"

"Where will you be?"

"I'll be with Brendan. We're working another angle, but we'll meet you at Elizabeth's later." He remembered something. "And pack a small bag for yourself and Amy. You may be at Elizabeth's a while."

Chapter Twenty-Seven

Barbara took another peek into the oven. Things were still okay, but any longer and they'd be beyond dried out. "Where are they?" she asked. "Alejandro always has Natalie back long before this. He's never late."

It had become a thing for Alejandro to pick Natalie up after school at Cynthia's every Wednesday, take her for a treat at the bakery, then join them here for supper.

"I chatted with Cynthia earlier this afternoon, and she said Nat and Al had just left. It was a few minutes after three then." It was now over an hour past the time they were usually back home here, and Howard was getting worried. He checked his watch. Again. "It's past closing time for the bakery. Doubt anyone is there now."

"Try anyway." Barbara jostled Liam over her shoulder, keeping up the motion to keep him quiet.

"Hey." He was relieved when the phone was picked up. "Is this, um…" He scrambled to think of the name of the guy who cooked there.

Barbara mouthed the word "Jeff".

"Right, Jeff. I doubt you'll remember me. My name's Howard McDaw. I've only been there a few times, but my daughter, Natalie, she's a regular. She comes in every Wednesday afternoon with her Uncle Al. Pretty teen, with long, straight, dark hair."

"I know her. I keep my eye on them when they're here."

Howard frowned at the phone. Well, he had more important things to worry about than that odd remark. "Usually, Nat and Al are back here for supper by six o'clock. It's after seven now and we've not seen or heard from them. Would you have any idea when they left the bakery?"

"They didn't come here today."

"What? Where'd they go?"

"I don't know about that. They don't fill me in on their plans."

"Right. Of course not. Well, thank you." He started to hang up but caught the frantic hand motions of his wife. "Wait a second, will ya?" Then he got what Barbara was saying. "If you see them, will you call me, please? Here's my number."

Howard picked up his shoes from the mat by the front door.

"Where are you going?" Barbara asked.

"To the park. That's where they went with Liam the other week. Maybe they went there instead of to the bakery. Maybe they lost track of time."

Barbara looked at the gathering dusk outside. How could they not notice that it was early evening now?

Liam gave a complaining wail, and Barbara jostled him faster, pacing the kitchen floor.

She tried Natalie's mobile phone again, for the umpteenth time. Her call went straight to voice mail.

Alejandro's. Why had she not thought to call his phone? Sheesh. She dialed. "This number has been disconnected or is no longer in service." Why? Why would that be? She knew she had texted him last week and received a reply. She searched her phone, then cursed herself for diligently keeping her message folder pristine, deleting all but this day's texts.

Was there a way that the phone company could access her deleted texts? But what good would that do if Alejandro's phone was no longer in service?

Why would that be? Maybe he lost his phone and got a new one, forgetting to tell them his new number. Yes, that was probably it. Had to be.

But why wasn't Natalie answering her phone? She was glued to the thing; it was never turned off.

As she paced her kitchen floor, trying to calm a restless Liam and her own panicking heart, there was a knock at the front door.

Finally! It had to be Natalie and Alejandro. Maybe Nat forgot her key. That's why they knocked.

Then the doorbell pealed. That kind of impatience likely meant it was Natalie. When she wanted something, she wanted it NOW.

Barbara went to the door and unlocked it without first checking through the peephole. There stood two police officers in uniform.

Oh, that couldn't be good. It was *never* good news when the cops showed up on your doorstep. What had Natalie done now? She silenced that thought. There'd been no trouble since they moved here. Maybe there'd been an accident. Oh, please, let her little girl be all right.

"Ma'am?"

The officers were probably waiting for her to close her gaping mouth. She jiggled her son again to quiet his cries.

"Are you Mrs. McDaw?"

Barbara nodded.

"May we come in? We have some questions for you about the whereabouts of your daughter, Natalie."

Relief filled Barbara. "Yes, certainly. Thank you for coming. Did my husband call you?"

The two men looked at each other. "No, we haven't heard from your husband."

"Oh." That was strange. "Howard's out looking for Natalie."

"Then she's not here? We'd like to speak with her."

Barbara shook her head. "No, she's not here. We don't know where she is. I thought you were here to help find her."

"We will certainly help find her. Some more information from you will help. May we come in?"

"Of course." Barbara stepped back and led the men into the living room.

Taking out cards and handing them to her, the first man said, "I'm Officer Boyd, and this is Officer Hernandez. Detective Brendan James brought us into this."

"Oh, Brendan. Yes, we know him." Thank goodness he was on the job.

Officer Boyd nodded. "Good. We were just at the school Amy Blythe, your neighbor's daughter, attends. Apparently, a couple of mothers take turns picking up their children after school."

Barbara nodded. "Yes, my neighbors, Cynthia and Elizabeth and their friend Keira take turns collecting the three kids."

"So, you're familiar with these families?"

"Definitely. We've visited fairly often since we moved here. They've been very welcoming."

Officer Boyd regarded her steadily. Officer Hernandez walked around the room, paying close attention to the photos on the wall and the mantel. He picked up one. "Is this Natalie?" He turned it so both Barbara and his partner could see.

"Yes, Howard took that last summer. Her hair's a somewhat longer now, but it's a good likeness." She set Liam down in his playpen. "Would you like me to make a photocopy for you?" Anything that would assist them in finding her daughter.

"That would be helpful, please." After exchanging a look, Officer Hernandez followed Barbara into the next room where the printer lived.

When the two returned with several color reproductions of the photo, Officer Boyd suggested they all sit down. "When was the last time you saw your daughter?"

"This morning, just before she went to school. Well, it's not really school. She and another student are on a home study program, working with Cynthia Blythe. She lives two doors that way," she nodded to the east, "and Cynthia's a teacher."

"Didn't Natalie come home after school?"

"She usually does, but not on Wednesdays. She has an outing with a family friend in the late afternoon, then they return here for supper."

"Who is the family friend?"

"Alejandro Ramon."

Both men sat at attention. Barbara was not prepared for the intensity of their stares.

While Hernandez scribbled away in his notebook, Boyd asked, "How do you know this Ramon gentleman?"

"He runs an adoption agency. He was instrumental in bringing Natalie to us. We adopted her when she was three, almost thirteen years ago. Why?"

"You've been in contact with him all along?"

She shook her head. "No, only recently. Howard ran into him at the gas station a few months ago and recognized him. He brought him back to the house for a visit. Al and Natalie really hit it off. She even calls him Uncle Al. We've seen him at least once a week since then."

The two men shared a look, and then Hernandez took over the questioning.

"Do you know your neighbor's child, Amy?"

"Sure. She's Cynthia's little girl. I've seen her lots, and Natalie's babysat her a few times, along with some other kids." She looked between the two men. "Why?"

Before they could respond, they heard a key turning in the front door. It opened, and a man called, "Nothing, honey. Has she come home?"

Barbara, along with the officers, rose to their feet.

Howard stopped in the archway to the living room, startled to find two uniformed me in his home. "Barbara? What's going on?" He looked between the men. "Has something happened to Natalie? Is she all right?" He put his arm around his wife's shoulders and glanced into the playpen to make sure their son was safe and sound.

Boyd spoke first. "I'm Officer Boyd and this is Officer Hernandez. We're investigated a suspected disappearance."

"You called the police?" Howard asked his wife.

"No. I thought you must have."

"Mr. McDaw," interrupted Officer Boyd. "When did you last see your daughter?"

He thought. "That would be last night, before bed. When I left for work this morning, she wasn't up yet."

"Was there anything unusual about her last night or lately?"

The side of Howard's mouth curled up. "Unusual. Well, if you knew Natalie, unusual would be a word you used."

"How so?"

"She's not your typical teenager. She's struggled, so it's made her different. She's been the victim of bullying and harassment for years, so she's now not your typical girl." He realized that wasn't what the officer had meant. "But as far as different from her usual self, no I noticed nothing." He looked at his wife to see if she had anything to add.

Barbara shook her head. "That's what I told them, too."

"This harassment. Where did it happen? Are there any records?" Boyd had his pencil and notebook ready.

"Are there records? Certainly. You have no idea how many meetings we had with her former school. Dozens and dozens, but they did nothing to help her."

Boyd took down the name of the school and the principal the McDaws had dealt with.

Hernandez asked, "Is there a way that we can speak with each of you separately?"

———————

Natalie wandered over to the couch and picked up the remote. Unmuting the show, she scowled in distaste and quickly scrolled the channels for something better.

"Hey! I was watching that." Sally went to snatch the remote from the girl's hand.

Natalie put the remote behind her back. "Who'd watch such drivel? Only old ladies like soap operas."

Sally opened her mouth to reply, but Alejandro didn't give her the chance. He had a job for her. "Go downstairs to the shops and buy Natalie some clothes. Some of everything, and make sure it's nice stuff."

Sally wrinkled her nose. "Why can't she do it herself? I'm busy."

Alejandro's eyes pierced hers. "Because I said. And no one is to know that she's here." He paused for emphasis. "No one."

"Oh." Now Sally got it. "She'll go with the other kid?" She jerked her head towards the room where Amy slept.

Alejandro's glare would have reduced a lesser woman to silence. He took a step closer. "This is my *daughter*. She stays with me."

Sally backed off. She snatched the credit card from Alejandro's hand and flounced out of the suite.

Chapter Twenty-Eight

Howard sat with Officer Hernandez at the kitchen table. "Why do you need to talk to me without my wife?"

"Standard procedure. We want each of your recollections, untouched by memories someone else might offer. When we put them together, we'll have a fuller picture."

"We appreciate how quickly you're getting on this. We're really worried about Natalie."

"It's not just Natalie we're concerned about." He checked his notes. "Do you know a neighbor's child named Amy Blythe?"

"Sure. That's Cynthia's little girl. Nat has babysat her a few times. Nat's at their house all the time; Cynthia supervises her homeschooling."

"Are you aware that Amy is missing?" He watched Howard closely.

"Missing? Wasn't she at school today? She's not homeschooled."

"Yes, she was at school. But after school, your daughter picked her up."

"Oh, well, maybe they had a babysitting thing arranged. You'll have to ask my wife about that - she keeps track of those sorts of things." He thought for a minute. "Is that where Nat is now? Funny. I talked to Cynthia earlier, and she said that Natalie left a little after three o'clock with her Uncle Al." Then, he added, "He's a family friend and they usually go for an outing on Wednesdays after school."

"Tell me more about this Al."

"Oh, he's a great guy. He's really taken an interest in our Natalie. It's good for her to have some attention from someone who's not her old mom and dad. I think she gets bored with us, you know."

"How do you know Al? What's his full name?"

"Alejandro Ramon. I don't know his middle name, though. We first met him years ago, maybe fourteen or fifteen. Could be, I don't exactly remember, but Barbara might. She keeps all our paperwork."

Officer Hernandez waited.

"Al ran the adoption agency we used. He brought us Natalie. That was a happy day for us, let me tell you."

"Where is the adoption agency located?"

"Gosh, I don't know if it's there still. We had our own little guy recently, so didn't need to adopt again. It was south of the border, in Ensenada, at that time."

"Do you have the adoption papers?"

"Likely. But as I say, my wife keeps track of stuff like that." He frowned. "But what does that have to do with finding Natalie? She's been with us for over thirteen years. Why do you want to know about this stuff? I just want my kid back home."

Shopping was one of Sally's favorite pastimes. For far too much of her life, she'd been forced to curtail this love due to lack of money. Since being with Alejandro, she was freer to indulge herself. And Alejandro liked to see her looking pretty.

In his enamorment with his daughter's presence, he must have forgotten that Sally already had a credit card, a business one, that he'd told her to use for expenses. Well, she'd save them; she was running close to its monthly limit, anyway.

Alejandro lately hadn't been nice to her. Nice, according to Sally, meant adoring her, taking her places, and buying her things. She sensed a cooling in Alejandro's ardor for her. She had experience with reading the signs; it had happened too many times during her life. Well, there was always another man where that one came from.

But for now, she'd enjoy this run as long as she could.

The hotel was chic. Of course it was. She could not imagine Alejandro staying anywhere but in a place like this. He must like it, as this was where they had stayed before they'd collected her children and taken them on their little trip.

The plush carpets muffled her footsteps. Music filtered softly from around the corner where a string quartet played in the lobby. Sally couldn't name the instruments they played, but she knew they were skilled musicians, even if classical wasn't really her taste in tunes.

A swanky hotel meant swanky shops, and the boutiques here didn't disappoint. Except, they were meant for women like her, women who were well-developed and appreciated the finer things in life. What did they have to offer a teenager? She sniffed.

But Alejandro said to get something nice for Natalie, so she would. But not before buying herself some duds. Maybe some lingerie that would lure Alejandro back into her sphere. She had charms no mere daughter could ever compete with. Blood was not the only thing that bound people together.

Victoria's Secret was her first stop. Sure, there were better, more exclusive lingerie shops, but she found VS to have the mix of lust-inducing apparel she could most make use of. More risqué stuff, she ordered off the internet, but VS offered just the right combination of sex and class. Rather like herself, Sally thought.

Mindful of Alejandro's instructions, she first shopped for underwear for Natalie. Surely the child couldn't be more than a B cup. She found the plainest panties, ones on sale, in a bundle of three. How many did the kid need? She could rinse them out each night herself if three was not sufficient. Unsure if they even carried such things as she'd never sought them out herself, Sally found socks for the girl. Plain, white, ankle things. Two pairs should do. No, maybe three to match the undies. Then a bathing suit - a plain, navy one piece with a racer-back style. Feeling generous, she threw in a headband and a bracelet. There. That ought to keep the brat happy.

Asking the clerk to keep these things on the counter for her, Sally perused the store with herself in mind. Herself and Alejandro, that is. Over the past year, she'd learned the sort of things that turned him on, although those times when he looked like he couldn't get enough of her were becoming farther apart. She'd fix that.

Sally knew just the cut of bra that showed off her assets the best. She picked up matching thongs and bikini panties.

On to the nightwear area. This is where Sally really

shone, and her instincts were sound. Three seemed her magic number today. She had several negligees in the closet upstairs, so increasing her nighttime wardrobe by three only seemed reasonable. Silk and satin were her preferred fabrics for peignoir sets.

Sally checked the credit card before she got to the register. Yep, it was in Alejandro's name. That meant she'd need to tap for these purchases, and she didn't know what the contactless payment limit was for this card. So she'd make a series of separate purchases. Pretending to be unsure, she put one set back on a rack, taking careful note where she put it. She took the other two up to the register.

"Ma'am, do you want these other things as well?"

Ma'am. When had she become a ma'am instead of a miss? Snot-nosed kids these days. "I'm still thinking about them. Just these for now, thanks." The machine accepted the credit card without hesitation. As the clerk wrapped her garments in tissue, Sally said, "I've changed my mind. May I take this as well?" She went back for the sleepwear set she'd hung on the rack. She snickered to herself. Hopefully she'd be getting little sleep once she put it on.

"Certainly." It rang through successfully.

"Oh, what the heck. I guess I'll take these as well." Sally showed the pile of garments she'd set aside for Natalie. If it was over the card's limit, she'd set some items back.

"Would you like them packaged all together?"

"No. Separately." Success! Now, on to the next shop.

Sally next stocked up on bath oils and moisturizers. As an afterthought, she bought a bath bomb for Natalie. Alejandro would be pleased that she'd thought of this non-essential for his all-important daughter.

While she would have liked to spend more time browsing, she finished her shopping quickly. A few things for

Natalie to wear tomorrow and more for herself. She needed to get back upstairs and figure out just what was going on with Alejandro.

A daughter. He'd never mentioned that before, although she suspected that he'd sired dozens of babies. What was so special about this one?

After peeking in the playpen to check that Liam was still sleeping, Barbara seated herself on the sofa across from Officer Boyd.

He had his pencil and notebook ready. "You mentioned you know Amy Blythe."

"Oh, yes. She's Cynthia's daughter, a sweet little thing. They live two doors down. Natalie's babysat Amy a few times, Amy and the other neighbor's son, Timothy."

"Timothy?"

"Timothy Whitmore. He lives with his mother, Elizabeth."

Boyd nodded. "When did you last see Amy?"

"Gosh, I don't know. We see her around the neighborhood often." Barbara thought. "Maybe the last time when I was at their place, having coffee with her mother on their patio." Barbara corrected herself. "No, maybe I didn't exactly see her. I could hear her voice. She was next door playing with Timothy in his backyard."

"How close would you say that your daughter was to Amy?"

"Close? Like in friends? Well, that's difficult when there's such an age difference. Natalie is almost sixteen, about double Amy's age. You have little in common at their ages, other than as a babysitter."

"So they didn't hang out?"

"No, not in the way that Amy and Timothy do." That was a strange question. "Why?"

"Mrs. McDaw, are you aware that the child, Amy Blythe, is missing?"

Barbara sat back. "Amy? No! What's happened to her?"

"That's what we're trying to figure out." He studied the woman across from him, ready to pick up on even her tiniest reaction. "The last person Amy was seen with was your daughter."

Chapter Twenty-Nine

She stood up from her sofa, glaring at the man across the coffee table from her. "What do you mean that the last person Amy was with was my Natalie?" This made no sense to Barbara.

Officer Boyd remained relaxed but alert. "Exactly what I said. Amy was last seen in the company of your daughter." He motioned with his hand. "Please sit back down, Mrs. McDaw."

"But how could that be? It makes no sense. Where were they? Where *are* they?"

"That's what a lot of people would like to know." Boyd pulled from his pocket a photocopy of the note Natalie had given to the teacher. "This is what your daughter gave to Amy's teacher."

Barbara took the paper and skimmed it. She gave a shaky laugh and slumped back against the couch cushions. "Oh, I get it." Relief filled her face. "Cynthia must have asked her to babysit."

Boyd was relentless. "No. Mrs. Blythe denies asking your

daughter to babysit or to pick up Amy from school." He paused for effect. "And, she denies having written that note."

This was more puzzling than upsetting. "I don't get it," said Barbara.

"Neither do we. But the fact is, Amy Blythe is missing. As is your daughter. And they were last seen leaving the school hallway together."

Barbara's mind whirled, trying to find answers. "Maybe they're still at the school. Maybe they got wrapped up in something and forgot the time. Yes, that's probably it. Did someone search the school? They might be getting nervous now that it's dark and don't know what to do. Maybe they're locked in the building."

Boyd shook his head as he waited for her to wind down. "The school staff searched the building. Then we did ourselves, along with Detective Dean."

"And?"

"No trace of them."

Barbara wrung her hands. "But where can they be?"

Before entering the suite, Sally rearranged her parcels in the bags. She squished her own things into one bag, cringing at how she was treating such delicate, provocative garments. She could always send them out to be cleaned. She didn't want it to be overly obvious that most of the purchases were not for Natalie. She fluffed up the girl's bag, letting some of the tissue peek out over the top. She put her ear to the door, but the thick paneling muted any conversation going on in the suite.

Composing herself and affixing her most charming

smile to her face, she swiped her room key over the sensor and swept inside.

Hastily stowing her own things behind the bedroom door, Sally gushed over the items she'd purchased for Natalie, holding them up one at a time.

Alejandro looked bored.

Natalie said, "Whatever," then resumed flipping through the satellite TV channels.

There was a thud from the bedroom, then the pad of little feet. A drowsy Amy poked her head around the door-frame. "I gotta pee."

"Sally, show her where the bathroom is," ordered Alejandro.

Sally stared at him. This was how he thanked her for spending the last hours searching for stuff with which to clothe his daughter? Catching the look in his eye, she knew that this was not the time to raise the issue. She'd lived with men long enough to know when to push and when to let them think they were having their way. "Come on." She pushed Amy's shoulder toward the ensuite's loo.

"Ow!" came from the child.

Alejandro rose. "Careful with the goods, Sally. This one's valuable."

"Yes, aren't all children precious?" Maybe that was laying it on a bit thick. Sally shut the bathroom, then bedroom doors. While the kid was using the bathroom, Sally would stash away her newest acquisitions.

"Hey, Sally," Alejandro called from the other room. "You bought some clothes for the kid, right?"

Sally froze. That had not entered her mind. How was she supposed to know both kids would stay here long enough to need changes of clothes? "Ah, no. I didn't know she needed anything. You didn't mention it."

"A little initiative would be nice in my employees. I expect them to be able to think for themselves, at least to a certain degree. Surely you're capable of at least that?"

Natalie snickered.

"Well, go back and buy the kid some clothes. Some everyday stuff, then something nice for when she's placed. The jet's tied up with other jobs, so it'll be a few days, at least."

Her narrowed eyes and pinched mouth spoke volumes about how Sally felt, but she knew how to bide her time. Now was not the moment to speak her mind. But oh, she'd not forget each and every slight.

"Wait," Alejandro said. "Before you go, order room service for all of us. Something good." He winked at Natalie. "All this work makes me hungry."

Cynthia lay on the unyielding futon in Elizabeth's office. Grateful for her friend's hospitality, she craved her own soft bed. She yearned to turn back the clock, to just one day ago. That would be enough. Twenty-four hours ago, Amy had rested safely tucked up in her canopied princess bed, fast asleep. How had Cynthia ever taken such things for granted? She had never spent a night apart from her daughter since Amy was born.

She heard footsteps in the hallway above her head. Throwing back the covers, Cynthia carefully made her way to the door. As quietly as possible, she turned the knob, opening the door just enough to peer out.

Near the top of the staircase, she could see Keira entering Timothy's bedroom, where he and Daniel slept. Soon Keira returned, her son in her arms. Shutting Timothy's door behind her, she carried Daniel into the room Elizabeth had given her for the night.

Sighing, Cynthia silently shut her door. She could not blame Keira for wanting her son close. She would, too, if only that were possible.

Back in her lumpy bed, Cynthia pulled the cover over her shoulders. Some small part of her heart shamed her. It was the part that resented her friends for having their children safe and nearby. Geez. What sort of person would wish the kind of pain she was experiencing on her friends? She didn't, she truly didn't. But she could not stomp down the feelings of jealousy for their good fortune.

As if her friends had not been through enough. While she, Cynthia, had had the pleasure of bringing new life into this world with the support and teamwork of the man she loved, Keira had experienced none of that. She'd done it all alone, caring for her child, an autistic child at that, with admirable strength and determination. Now Jake tried to shoulder some of the load, or at least as much as Keira would allow.

Then there was Elizabeth, a truly formidable woman, although she didn't think of herself that way. Of all of them, Elizabeth came the closest to knowing how Cynthia felt right now. Her son had been abducted, not once, but twice. The first time, they snatched Elizabeth with him.

Oh, if only that were the case now. Cynthia would give anything to be able to take Amy's place, or to at least be with her.

It was a parent's duty to protect their child. Right. What a lousy job Cynthia had done of that.

Amy had suffered the pain of losing her father. No four-year-old should have to experience death. But Amy had coped.

Then near financial ruin. Amy did not know the precarious state her mom had allowed their bank account to sink to. What kind of parent did that, especially one who had the sole responsibility for a child's well-being? Yet Cynthia had allowed that to happen. Mostly through negligence, just not paying attention, keeping her head in la-la land, hoping they could drift forever the way they were. Well, the world didn't work like that. Ever.

Struggling to reclaim their money situation, Cynthia had agreed to tutor Natalie to bring in some cash and to jump-start her return to the teaching profession.

She rolled over, turning her face into the pillow to stifle her sobs. Oh, Hugh. What a mess she'd made of things. What would he think of her? She could imagine his fine features filled with disappointment. How had she let him down so badly, when he'd entrusted his most precious gift, their little girl, into her hands?

And Anna. Anna had no children of her own to raise. To raise was the key point. While Anna had given birth years ago, the baby, no babies, were stolen from her, adopted out somewhere, never to be seen again. Cynthia could not imagine the pain of that. But Anna was strong; she had gotten away and built a new life for herself.

As if that wasn't horrid enough, Anna's pain rekindled last year. The man who'd stolen her babies all those years ago returned. He wanted Anna. When she refused, he snatched her foster daughter, Bonnie. He also abducted Bonnie's little stepbrothers, selling them to who knows where. Now, the older boy was back, dropped off alone and untended on Anna and Murph's property.

Who could have done that?

There was only one person who could tie that boy to Anna. Alejandro. And no one knew where in the world he was.

Chapter Thirty

"What's this about some note?" Howard charged into his living room, Officer Hernandez trailing behind. Hernandez exchanged a look and a nod with his partner.

Barbara still had it clutched in her hand. "Here. Look."

Howard sat close to his wife and skimmed the note. Then he read it again, more slowly. "Cynthia's lying," he said flatly. "She has to be. How else could you explain this?" He shook the note at Boyd.

"That's what we'd like to know." Boyd regarded Howard steadily.

Hernandez took up his position in the doorway, barring any exit from the living room.

Boyd summed things up for them. "Here's what we know. Three women take turns picking up their three children from school. Today it was Elizabeth Whitmore's turn. Usually, the three kids walk together from the school building to the waiting car. Today, only the two boys were there. No Amy." He consulted his notes. "Mrs. Whitmore then locked the boys into her car and entered the school to find Amy. When she questioned Amy's teacher, the teacher produced the note and described the teenage girl who gave it to her. The description matches that of your daughter."

Howard scoffed. "You have no proof that it was her."

"The teacher then brought Amy over. Amy called Natalie by name right away. She told the teacher how the two knew each other and said that Natalie sometimes babysat her. Then she went off with Natalie willingly, after the teacher explained the note that your daughter brought her." He paused. "No one has seen either girl since."

"But…" Howard's mind raced with thoughts, with likely explanations, with half-formed ideas, but none bubbled up to the surface. All he could do was sputter.

Then an idea struck him. "Al! Cynthia said that Nat left her house with Al as usual for a Wednesday. Where's Al? Ask him. *He'll* know where the girls are." He pulled out his mobile phone. "I'll call him right now."

Everyone waited while he made the call. They could clearly hear the recording that notified the caller that that number was no longer in service.

Barbara slipped her hand into his. "I already tried that. Over and over and got the same recording. And when I call Nat, it just goes to voice mail."

"Here, I'll try it. She never has her phone off for long." Slowly he lowered his arm as he got heard his daughter's voice instruct, "Leave a message. I'll get back to you. Or maybe not." His shoulders sagged. His whole body sagged. "What do we do?"

"This is great!" Amy swung her feet against the chair rung.

The rhythmic thunk, thunk, thunk got on Sally's nerves. None of the others seemed to notice, though.

"Mommy never lets me have all the pop I want. Thanks, guys!" She beamed at the three sharing the suite with her. Ketchup smeared her chin and her t-shirt, but she didn't notice. The bright red condiment lathered her fingers as well. Spying that, she wiped her hand on her shirt before diving in for more greasy fries.

Alejandro took a large bite of his steak sandwich. It was good, medium rare, the way he liked it.

Natalie picked at her shrimp tacos. They were a tad under-spiced for her taste.

Sally picked away at a mixed green salad with a vinai-grette. The smells from the meals of the other three drove her nuts. How could they eat whatever they wanted, when just sniffing the aroma of their meals would put pounds on her hips?

Thunk, thunk, thunk. "Where is mommy? When's she coming?"

Natalie jumped in quickly before Alejandro could swallow and compose his answer. "She asked me to pick you up, remember? She has some stuff to do and is going out with friends. She said you're to stay with me until she calls."

A frown creased Amy's brow, and she stopped eating. "Mommy always tells me stuff ahead of time."

"I know, but this came up suddenly. I was at her place, you know, so she asked me to babysit."

Amy's uncertainly twisted into disgust. "I hate that word. I'm *not* a baby."

"No, you certainly aren't," assured Alejandro. "That's why your mother thought you were a big enough girl to stay with us tonight. Maybe for a few days." At Amy's imminent protest, he added, "Until your mommy comes for you."

It came to Cynthia in the night. How could it have slipped her mind?

She stood up from her futon at Elizabeth's and quietly crept up the stairs. It was barely six in the morning. Dare she wake him up now? Brendan had been up late with Jake, working on finding Amy and Natalie. But he said to call him any time if anything occurred to her.

This was uncomfortable. She stood outside Elizabeth's bedroom door, where Brendan slept. Should she knock? Should she just open the door and peek in to make sure he was there? Sheesh. There was no protocol for this.

But this was her friend Elizabeth, her closest friend. No one would understand the way she would. Cynthia raised her hand and knocked softly. She did not want to awaken the rest of the household.

No answer. She knocked again and twisted the doorknob to open it a crack. "Brendan," she called. "Brendan, are you awake?"

"Yeah, I'm here. Just a sec."

She closed the door as she heard bed sheets rustling.

In less than a minute, Brendan stood on her side of the bedroom door, his hair mushed to one side of his head. His jeans were on and zipped, but not buttoned up. An unbuttoned denim shirt hung on his shoulders. "What's up? Did you hear something?"

Cynthia shook her head. "No, but I remembered something." She hesitated because it could mean nothing at all.

But they didn't have many straws to grasp onto. "For the last while, maybe a month or more, I've sometimes noticed this car parked on the street. It parks in different places and doesn't belong to anyone who lives in the neighborhood. I see it at odd times. The front windshield is tinted, so I never got a good look at who's behind the wheel. I'm pretty sure it's a man. Maybe with dark hair."

Brendan patted his pockets, searching for his notebook. He glanced back at the closed bedroom door.

Cynthia motioned for him to come down the stairs with her. She knew where Elizabeth kept stationery.

"Did you get a license number?"

"No." She was ashamed that she hadn't tried harder to look. "But I'm not sure, but maybe I saw the same car sitting in Barbara and Howard's driveway a couple of times." She qualified that. "I'm not positive, but it may have been similar, at least."

Back on the futon, Cynthia tried to get comfortable. But how did she deserve comfort when who knew what was happening to Amy?

A vast, expanding emptiness inside her swallowed Cynthia up. It was like Amy's absence was a void that expanded by the hour. Soon, that void would fill every crevasse in Cynthia's body, allowing no room for air, no room for anything. Without Amy, there was nothing.

She dozed. Not much, but a little. Everyone - Elizabeth, Brendan, Keira, and Jake, all told her she needed to eat, needed to sleep, needed to keep her strength up for Amy's sake. Amy might need her, so she had to be ready.

She would be. If there was anything, anything she could do to get her girl back, she'd do it. She'd give up her life for that child in a heartbeat.

Although her body was exhausted, her brain wouldn't shut down. Cynthia tossed, then got up and paced.

There must be something she could do. Her daughter needed her, and here Cynthia was, in the comfort of her friend's home, safe and sound.

A stray thought niggled at her brain, some little thread. But like an elusive, dropped dollar bill tossed about in a gusty breeze, she couldn't quite catch it.

Amy liked things just so. Before going to sleep, her stuffed animals had to be arranged just so around her. She needed her bedroom door left opened just the right amount. She always ate the same cereal before bed. Amy was a creature of habit. How would she be sleeping without the comfort of all that was familiar to her?

Habit. Was it only Amy who liked things the same way, got stuck on things? No, she'd noticed that about her friends, too. Especially Elizabeth. After all the trauma she and Timothy had been through, Elizabeth had created habits and patterns of how they did things. She said that it was easier for autistic kids that way, and Keira agreed. But Cynthia thought it was partly for Elizabeth's comfort as well.

Did that extend to other people?

By people, she meant Alejandro.

Never had Cynthia hated anyone. Even the childhood bullies who taunted her, never her father or his career that had forced them to move all over the place. Not even the cancer that took her husband's life, although there were moments. Hugh had helped her through those, helped her to accept the inevitable.

But *this* wasn't inevitable. Fate had permanently erased her husband from her life, but no one had the right to take her child from her as well. They could not; they would not.

She thought of the structure of their days, the things Amy enjoyed, the patterns and habits they created together.

Habits. Where had her foggy brain been going with that thought? She centered her mind on Alejandro, the source behind all her current misery. She was sure of it.

How had she allowed that snake into her home? How had she merrily allowed Natalie to go off with him, week after week?

Natalie. Realistically, Cynthia knew that she could have done nothing to stop Natalie from accompanying Alejandro. Natalie's parents sanctioned and even welcomed his presence.

Were they in on this, too?

No, Cynthia's gut told her no, even though she'd not talked to either of them since yesterday's nightmare began. Brendan told her not to, since Natalie might be a suspect.

Natalie. Her thoughts returned to the teen. Initially feeling sorry for her, Cynthia tried to like her, tried to make her feel welcome, despite that tiny part of her subconscious that had misgivings. Why hadn't she listened to that little voice? Even as her suspicions grew, why had she ignored her instincts?

Instincts. Habits. Alejandro. The thoughts swirled in her skull, tendrils gathering, cycloning down a funnel.

Habits. She knew the hotel where the police had concentrated on their efforts to locate Alejandro the last time, but he slipped out of their grasp. Was there any chance that the snake was a creature of habit? Would he return to the place where he had stayed before?

She dressed. After hastily scribbling a note for Elizabeth and Brendan, she reset the alarm code, then slipped out the door into the early morning light.

Chapter Thirty-One

In the hotel suite, Alejandro worked on his laptop. Yesterday he'd used his camera to snap a number of photos of Amy. Now, he uploaded them to his website on the dark web. He'd open this new collection to potential adoptive parents, ones who had already paid a hefty deposit. But first, he'd show them to Germaine and Emma Molina to see if Amy fit their requirements.

In another room in their hotel suite, Amy basked in the liberties. At home, she could never watch this much television, or to try out whichever channel she wished. Pointing the remote at the sixty-inch screen mounted on the wall, she sprawled on the bed with her shoes on. Her mom would have a fit.

Thoughts of that same mother tempered her glee at putting one over on her mom. Amy had never slept away from her mom before. Last night, she'd cried, just a bit, and told these people that she wanted her mother. Natalie gave her more of that yummy red juice, then she went to sleep.

Unlimited TV was great, but she was not used to staying

still for so long. She loved being outside and playing with Timothy. Maybe she could call him, and his mom would bring him here to do stuff with her.

She went into the main room of the suite. "Hey, Natalie, can Timothy come to play with me?"

Oh, wouldn't that be priceless, thought Alejandro? A coup! But his cautious nature prevailed. Better to snatch these kids one at a time - draw out the torture for Anna as one by one, her best friends lost their children, all thanks to her.

Alejandro looked pointedly at Sally. She was supposed to look after these brats until they were placed.

Sally roused from her task of painting her toenails. Alejandro ordered her to stick around, so she'd had to cancel her pedicure appointment. Pity. "Why don't you go watch some cartoons?"

"I already did that." A pout entered Amy's voice. Not usually a petulant kid, the excitement of being here was waning.

"What do you like to play with?" Alejandro asked.

Amy rattled off a list of toys.

Alejandro did not know what she was talking about during most of it. When Amy didn't seem about to wind down, he interrupted. "Sally, did you get that?"

"Get what?"

Inwardly, he sighed. He'd need to replace her soon. "Did you take note of what she said she likes?"

"No, I didn't take any notes. Can't you see? My hands are busy."

"Put that away and pay attention." He turned to Amy. "Can you go over that again? Sally will go get you your favorite things."

"Me? Why me?" Now it was Sally whose pout was evident.

Ignoring that interchange, Amy again recited her list of favorite toys.

"Sally, go buy her the stuff she wants. Oh, and pick up some clothes for her, too." He tossed Sally his car keys.

"Why can't *she* do it?" Sally pointed at Natalie.

"My daughter doesn't have her driver's license yet. And she can't be seen."

"What about me?"

"No one's looking for you."

———————

The bell over the bakery door tinkled. Jeff looked up, watching the approach of a large man in an ill-fitting suit, the sort worn by someone who'd shed some pounds, but not taken the time to buy new clothes yet.

The man pulled out a leather case. Flipping it open, he showed Jeff his badge. "I'm Detective Gordon Boyd." He handed Jeff his business card. "Have you ever seen this girl?" He brought out a picture of Natalie.

"Yes, she's in here fairly regularly."

"Who does she come in with?"

"Sometimes her teacher, Cynthia, and another girl. They're part of a homeschooling thing. Sometimes they meet other friends here."

"Which friends?"

"Some women and their kids."

"That's it?"

"She's been here with her parents a few times, I think. They have a kid in a stroller. And sometimes with her uncle."

"Have you seen her recently?"

Jeff shook his head.

"Thanks for your time." He tapped the business card now laying on the countertop. "Call me at this number if you see her."

"Has she done something?"

"Her parents reported her missing, and we'd like to speak with her."

Jeff's face darkened. "It probably has something to do with that guy."

"Which guy is that?"

"The one she comes in here with on Wednesdays for the past few months. Uncle Al, she calls him."

"Know anything about him?"

"He's a creep."

This got Boyd's attention. "What's he done?"

"Nothing," Jeff admitted. "But I don't like the guy. There's something about him. I keep my eye on them when they're here. The first few times I asked Natalie if she was all right, but she seemed to want to be with her '*uncle*'."

At Anna and Murph's house, the kids had not yet stirred. Anna opened Bonnie's bedroom door a crack to check on them. Two tousled heads faced other as Jordy slept on the trundle bed they'd set up beside Bonnie's. Bonnie's arm stretched out, her fingers touching her little brother.

They must have exhausted the two after all the emotions of yesterday. Being reunited might feel wonderful, but it was still a strain. Their home had been full of people last night.

Judge Bursey arrived with a social worker to interview Jordy. She got little from the child, who would not speak at all without holding his sister's hand. While the social worker tried her best to pull information from the four-year-old's memory, Judge Bursey wrote an order, giving Anna and Murph temporary custody until they learned more. Jake and Brendan hovered in the background, desperate to glean any scraps of details they could get that would help them figure out how Jordy got here, and if there was a connection to Alejandro.

Of course, there was, thought Anna as she cradled her coffee cup. Alejandro was behind everything. Would her life never be free of him?

Murph came up from behind, wrapping his arms around her and kissing the top of her head. She leaned into him, looking out the blinds that allowed them to see out, but prevented anyone outside from seeing in.

Together, they stood surveying the solitary tree in their field, the tree where Bonnie had discovered Jordy, the tree where Bonnie had hid over a year ago, only to be convinced by her mother to climb down and come away with her.

Last night, the only usable words they'd gotten from Jordy were "momma" and "plane ride". Was Sally involved in this? Was she still with Alejandro? He wasn't known for his loyalty.

As Anna knew from personal experience, he was known, though, for trafficking in children.

Sally was away shopping and Amy was drowsily watching television in one of the bedrooms.

While it was nice spending time with her father and ordering whatever she wanted from the room service menu, Natalie grew bored. "Any idea how long we're staying here?"

Alejandro turned away from his computer to regard his daughter. "Why?" What did she really want to know?

"What's going to happen to her?" She jerked her head toward the room where the television droned.

Alejandro had been expecting this question. "You know how you told me that Howard and Barbara kept to a budget and didn't buy you all the things that you'd like?"

Natalie nodded.

"Do you think Cynthia is wealthy? Do you think she has the money to provide Amy with everything she wants?"

"Doubt it. Her house looks no better than ours. And why would she be teaching Bonnie and me if she didn't need the money?" Maybe now was the time to let him in on something. "Besides, I looked at her bank accounts."

Alejandro raised his eyebrows.

"Her passwords are lame. It only took me a couple of tries and I was in. And she stupidly uses the same password for everything."

"And?" This might be useful information.

"She's broke, or almost broke. She has less in her savings account than I do."

"Do you think that's what Amy deserves?"

Natalie shrugged. She didn't really care about Amy, but that might not be the answer Al sought. "No. Probably not. I know *I* wouldn't want that."

"There are people with money, lots of money, who can't have kids of their own, but want a family. There's a couple right now looking for a child. They want a girl of seven or so. They want her to be cute, smart, and perky. Does that description fit anyone you know?"

Natalie got it.

"These people are wealthy beyond anything you could imagine. Any child of theirs would want for nothing."

"Are you sure it's not an almost-sixteen-year-old they're looking for?"

"Nice try, but no. You know those pictures I took of Amy yesterday? I've sent them to these people. If they like her looks, then I'll make a recording of her talking or playing, then send that."

"Why?"

"I need to make sure that they're a good fit. The parents need to be happy." Then he added, "And, of course, the child needs to be happy, too."

Natalie smirked, tossing her hair over one shoulder. "What do *you* get out of it?"

"A hefty finder's fee."

"What do you mean by hefty?"

"More than Howard makes in a year."

That caught Natalie's interest. "How often do you make these, ah, finds?"

"As often as I can. Last year I relocated at least one baby a month and had three finder's fees lined up. Anna messed that up, so I only completed one of those satisfactorily."

"Anna? She seems pretty meek to me."

"Don't let that fool you. Never underestimate the quiet ones."

Chapter Thirty-Two

It was not a lot to go on, thought Brendan, as he sat at his desk in the police station. How many white SUVs were there in this city? At least Cynthia had narrowed it down somewhat. She said it was neither the smallest size SUV, nor one of the monster ones built on a truck chassis. Scrolling through vehicle dealer websites, they'd limited the possibilities to three brands - a Honda Pilot, a Toyota Highlander, or a Ford Explorer.

That still didn't narrow things much but was a start. He pulled up the electronic files required to start an all-points bulletin. As he pecked away at his computer, he heard other police enter the area. Two were discussing their latest vehicle shopping efforts. Jeremy would consider nothing but Ford products, while his buddy tried to convince him of the merits of Japanese car makers. Neither would budge in their beliefs. They were loyal to their brands, and nothing would deter them.

Brand loyalty.

The last time they had their run-in with Alejandro, he'd

driven a rented Toyota. Was there a chance that this guy also had a brand preference? If so, that could narrow their search, even if ever so slightly. They needed any edge they could get.

And, if he had brand loyalty, might he also repeat himself in other ways? Someplace in his notes he had the name of the hotel the guy had stayed in. They'd searched the hotel parkade for his car but lost him.

It would be a stupid move to use the same place again, but the guy was cocky. A long shot, but what would it hurt to look there again?

———

Discouraged, Hernandez put in a call to Brendan. "We've searched every parking stall in the hotel's parkade. We found three SUVs that might match the description. One's a Ford, one's a Toyota, and one's a Hyundai. I know the latter wasn't on your list, but it's similar. We traced the ownership and they're all clean. None are Alejandro, nor seem to have any connection with him."

"Okay, thanks. It was a gamble, but it's not like we have a lot of other leads."

———

Her household stirred. Brendan must have left sometime while Elizabeth slept; his side of the bed was cold when she'd awakened.

Elizabeth pulled aside the kitchen curtain to check. Yes, a police car still parked across the street with a lone occupant behind the steering wheel. She'd take him out some coffee as soon as it was ready.

Keira appeared, hair tossed, hands reaching for a cup of caffeine. "Gimme," she pleaded.

Overhead came the sounds of two little boys moving, already pulling out toys.

"Should we try to keep them quiet so Cynthia can sleep in?"

"We can try, but unless we get them out of the house, it's going to be hard." Four little feet pounded down the stairs toward them.

"Food." Keira knew what they wanted. "Why don't I get them dressed while you fix breakfast?" She shepherded the little boys back upstairs, cautioning them to be quiet as Cynthia was still sleeping.

After feeding their sons, they accompanied them into the backyard to play, hoping to let Cynthia sleep some more. She needed to rest after the emotional exhaustion of yesterday. And, until Amy was found and returned home safely, the bad parts weren't over.

Three hours later, Elizabeth prepared lunch while Keira monitored the kids in the backyard.

She prepared a light meal and set it on a tray, along with coffee and whatever else she thought might appeal to Cynthia. Her friend might not feel hungry, but she needed to eat something.

Rapping softly on the door to the office, Elizabeth waited. After knocking again, she balanced the tray against her side and quietly turned the knob. If Cynthia was sleeping soundly, she'd back out and leave her bed.

Tangled sheets and comforter greeted Elizabeth, but no

response to her hello. Setting down the tray on the desk, Elizabeth looked around, as if Cynthia might hide somewhere in the small room.

Maybe she was in the bathroom. Yes, that was it. While Elizabeth had been in the kitchen, Cynthia's form had slipped by.

She checked the half-bath on the first floor, then the main bathroom upstairs, and finally the en suite attached to Elizabeth's bedroom. All were empty. She called. And again. Loud enough that Keira came running in to see what was wrong.

Elizabeth pointed at the now-open office door. Keira poked her head in. "Oh, good," she said. "Cynthia's up now."

"Yes, she's obviously up, but I'm not sure it's good."

Shooting Elizabeth a puzzled look, Keira noticed something. At first, the white stationery had blended in with the white pillowcase. Picking up the stationery, Keira read. "Oh, no." She passed the note to Elizabeth.

Elizabeth,

Thanks for your hospitality.

I can't stand sitting around here doing nothing. I've got an idea I need to check out. I'll be in touch.

Love,
Cynthia

"Oh, crap!" Keira's voice cracked. "What has she done?"

Elizabeth's thumbs rapidly composed a text to Brendan that said:

Cyn's gone. No idea when she left. Will send you pic of the note she left.

Quickly, she spread the note out on the desk and snapped a shot of it, attaching it to a message to Brendan. Within a minute, her phone rang.

Brendan wasted no time. "When did you last see her?"

"Before I went to bed last night."

"Not this morning?"

"We thought she was sleeping in, so kept the kids quiet so she could rest. I just made some lunch and was taking it in to her on a tray. Her bed was empty and there was this note." She listened for a few seconds. "Yes, of course. We searched the house. She's not here."

A hundred possibilities raced through Brendan's mind. The scariest was that someone could have gotten into the house and taken her. That also meant the Elizabeth and Timothy could have been at risk. Unthinkable. "Is the police car still sitting outside?"

Elizabeth walked to the front window and pulled back the drape. "Yes."

How'd she get by him? Oh, another scary thought. "Is your alarm system on?"

Checking the keypad, Elizabeth said, "Yes, it's set. We had the back door one off for a while as we were in the back with the kids."

"Does it look like there was a struggle?"

"No, just a restless sleep."

"Does Cynthia know your passcode? Could she have disabled the alarm to open the door, then reset it?"

"Yes, she knows how to use my system. We know each other's codes."

"One more thing. Does that note look like Cynthia wrote it? Does it sound like her? Is that her handwriting?"

Pondering, Elizabeth said, "Yeah, it could be something she'd say, but I don't know her handwriting. How often do you even write something by hand these days?"

Keira, unashamedly eavesdropped offering, "I could go next door to Cynthia's and find something in her writing. She's teaching the girls, so there's likely stuff lying around that we could compare the note to."

"Stop!" Brendan's command came through the phone. "No! Don't go over there on your own. Stay there. I'll talk to the cop out front." He hung up.

Minutes later, there was a knock on the front door. Checking through the peep hole, Elizabeth saw a man in uniform. She unlocked the two deadbolts but left the chain on. "May I see some ID, please?"

"Sure. Good idea, lady." He showed her his badge and passed a business card through the slot in the door.

Keira called out, "The police car's empty now." She let the drapes fall closed again.

Elizabeth's phone rang. Brendan. "The officer at your door should be Cal Olesky. Is that what his ID says?"

"Yes."

"He'll accompany you to Cynthia's. Don't go inside her house without him. Have Keira stay with the kids and lock up behind you. I'll stay on the line." Elizabeth opened the desk drawer where she stored the spare key to her neighbor's front door.

In less than ten minutes they were back, Cynthia's house once again locked and the alarm set. The dining room had plenty of evidence of schoolwork. In one corner sat a stack of notebooks labelled with the word Lesson Plans, then a subject. Opening the first few notebooks, Elizabeth tried comparing the handwriting to that of the note. To her, they looked pretty close. Officer Olesky suggested they take a few of these notebooks with them to have an expert compare the writing.

Chapter Thirty-Three

Jake checked the roster. Although Officer Olesky was in front of Elizabeth's house now, he'd only come on shift at nine o'clock when he took over from a guy named Butting. He looked up Butting's home number. Who cared if he woke the guy up?

"Butting. This is Detective Jake Dean. I see nothing unusual in your notes from your surveillance of 23 Longham Drive."

"No, no one tried to get in."

That was an odd way to put it. "What about out?"

"Yeah, a lady came out of the house and came right up to my car. Said she was going for groceries so they could make breakfast. Said her car was in the garage next door. Had the keys in her hand."

"What'd you do?"

"I accompanied her to the garage and made sure no one was in there. Then she drove off."

"What time was this?"

"Maybe a bit before eight."

"Why wasn't this in your notes?"

"I was told to watch for anyone trying to get in." Something almost like a defensive whine crept into his voice. "No one told me to prevent anyone from leaving."

Jake could see why, at fifty-two, this guy was still a beat cop. While he mostly admired the brotherhood he was a part of, sometimes...

———

While one police car had remained outside Elizabeth's house all night, another unmarked car parked down the street, watching the McDaw's home. A third officer patrolled the back alley.

Although Boyd and Hernandez's instincts told them that Howard and Barbara's concern over their daughter's disappearance was genuine, police work didn't run on gut feelings. Just in case these two were in on this and planned to rabbit, they'd be tailed. Maybe that would be a good thing, and they'd lead them to Amy.

But they didn't leave their home all night.

First thing the next morning, Boyd and Hernandez returned.

Howard opened the door for them, a mug of coffee in hand. "Come in," he said. "Barbara has the paper you wanted to see."

Neatly placed in a file folder was a copy of Natalie's adoption papers and the correspondence they had with Alejandro's agency prior to when they received Natalie.

Pay dirt! Hernandez tried to hide his excitement. "Is there anything else? Any records of payment, any other correspondence, any phone numbers?"

Barbara was the bookkeeper for the family. Her head

tipped back, and her eyes pointed toward her forehead. "That was thirteen years ago. Prior to our move, yes, I would have been able to find our bank statements and cancelled checks from then. Now?" She looked around at the unpacked boxes still littering their dining room. "I know it's been months, but we haven't fully moved in, getting everything in its proper place." Embarrassed at her lack of proficiency, she offered, "If you give me a few days, I can maybe come up with that."

"It's okay, honey." Howard gave her shoulders a squeeze. "The place looks great, especially considering you have a baby to take care of. Who knew you'd be asked to pull out bank records from more than a dozen years ago?"

"Even though I don't have proof of it right now, I remember the fees. We paid a $10,000 deposit with our adoption application, then a further $20,000 when we got Nat." She thought of something else. "Do you want the photocopies of our documents," she nodded at the folder in Boyd's hand, "or the originals? I have them in our desk."

"Originals, please."

Speaking by radio, Hernandez ensured that the officers watching the front and back of the McDaw home would remain where they were, awaiting further direction from the detectives in charge. Then he phoned Brendan. "I'm bringing in something you'll want to see."

Uniendo Familias. That was the name of Alejandro's agency, at least back when the McDaws adopted Natalie. It translated as Uniting Families. How ironic when Alejandro

260

stole from one family, destroying them, to create a new family, auctioning a kid to the highest bidder.

Nope. That would not happen to Amy; not gonna happen. Gritting his teeth, Jake plugged that name into their search engines and let the computer whirl on that.

Brendan called his Mexican counterpart. They'd worked together during Anna and Bonnie's rescue and kept in touch since then, both hoping to find something that would help them locate Alejandro Ramon and his operations.

It took time, time they didn't have. With every second passing that Amy was missing, the chances of finding her decreased. Brendan pushed that thought to the back of his mind. Not helpful now, when he needed a clear head.

His phone rang. A number from Mexico. His comrades south of the border were all over this.

"Giving us Uniendo Familias really helped," said Detective Martín Javier. "It's a name on our watch list, but so far we have nothing more than suspicions. Can't find any connection to an Alejandro Ramon, but the official documents show us the name of the CEO."

"Excellent. It would have been too simple for Ramon to use his own name. Who's running the show?"

"First name is Eduardo." He spelled it out. "And get this. Do you know what that name means? Prosperous guardian."

"Our Alejandro has a sense of humor."

"And his last name is Arturo, which means king."

Would he lose his man card if he did an eye roll, Brendan wondered?

"Sounds like something Alejandro would come up with. He thinks he's such a clever bastard."

"It looks like the adoption agency is the only sub-branch of the company licensed to operate now. At one time he dabbled in what's listed as stables, but no tax records were ever filed for those sidelines."

"Stables. Yeah, right. We know what *that* means. We'll get him this time though, eh, Martín?" They exchanged a few more details, then hung up for now.

Chapter Thirty-Four

Cynthia had guided Amy through the lingering illness and death of the child's father. She had done it even when her own heart was breaking, even with no one there to hold her hand when things were toughest. She'd trusted her instincts to know what was right for her daughter. And Amy had come through it.

She was a happy, confident, bright little girl who had her mother by her side. Yes, her mothering instincts were enough.

She ordered another coffee. Whoever had designed this coffee shop in the hotel's mezzanine did it with forethought. If you had to kill some time, this was not a bad spot. In the background, soft music played - classic oldies and show tunes, typical elevator music, but she didn't mind it.

The plush carpets hushed the footsteps from people coming and going in the lobby. Staff spoke in soft voices.

Even up here, in the eating area, the rich draperies and crisp table linens muted the noise. Nice. A little above the class where Cynthia usually hung out, but still nice. She cringed for a second to think of what her bill would come to if she had to spend many hours eating and drinking here. But this was for Amy. Without Amy, nothing mattered.

From her seat near the railing, Cynthia had a perfect location. She could watch the comings and goings of the lobby, entrance, and elevators perfectly.

So what? A part of her brain plagued her psyche with questions. So, she had no other ideas. She doubted she could waltz up to the registration desk and ask which room Alejandro Ramon was in. Or even if he was a guest there. No, privacy laws would not allow that, plus then the staff would regard her suspiciously. They might even ask her to leave.

No, here she'd remain, at least until she had a better plan.

She had nothing else. Her gut told her that Alejandro, cocky bastard that he was, might return to the same hotel he'd used previously. He'd gotten away just fine then, hadn't he?

They lay in bed together, neither asleep, just pretending for the other's sake. Howard reached over, linking his wife's fingers with his. "I can tell by your breathing you'll still awake."

"I can tell by the lack of sound of *your* breathing, too, that you're not asleep." She mimicked the low snoring sounds Howard made when snoozing.

"Yeah, right. I only make gentlemanly noises in my sleep."

Barbara snorted like a pig.

They were silent for a bit.

"Next week's her birthday."

"I know. I don't always remember such things, but she'll be sixteen. That's a biggie." Howard was awful about recalling the dates of special occasions. Barbara had learned to put them on the calendar, lest they both be disappointed by his omissions.

"You came up with a great present for her." Natalie was difficult to buy for. Other things that seemed to thrill girls her age were just meh to Natalie.

Howard reached over and opened the drawer of his nightstand, withdrawing a folder. "A dozen driving lessons. Learning how to drive is a rite of passage for kids this age."

"*I* certainly don't want to teach her."

"Me neither. She has this thing against us telling her what to do. Normal teenage stuff, I suppose. But instructions from someone else will be easier. Easier on all of us."

"She'll be over the moon at the chance to drive a car."

Cynthia wished she'd brought her laptop with her. At least that would give her something to do, something to make her long wait here look legitimate. But her instinct had been to get here. Civilized man didn't operate on instinct alone. She should have tempered that instinct with some logic.

For now, her phone would have to do.

She watched a family of three check in at the front desk. The mom looked tired; the dad determined. Their little girl hung off her mother's arm, twisting and twirling and demanding attention. She displayed about as much energy as Amy. If only Hugh was still here and they were a family of three, they would not be in this desperate situation. I'm sorry, Hugh, she said. I'm sorry I didn't take better care of our daughter. But I swear to you, I will from now on.

She waved over a server. "Is there any way that I could reserve this table for a few minutes? I need to go check in downstairs, but I'll return in as soon as I have my room key." As the server returned with a Reserved sign, Cynthia added. "May I have some more coffee, please? And a cinnamon bun as well? Thanks."

If she had a room here, that might legitimize her presence, in case anyone noticed her loitering around.

"Will this be just for one person?"

"No, my daughter will join me later. She's eight. I'll bring up my luggage later, thanks." With room key in hand, Cynthia returned to the upper mezzanine's eating area, feeling more like she belonged.

The cinnamon bun was passable, but not as good as Ellie's from the bakery. Not by far. When she got Amy back, she swore she'd take that kid to the bakery every day, plus buy extra treats to take home.

Wishing they'd provided her with a paper napkin instead of just cloth ones, Cynthia wiped her sticky fingers.

Wait! That woman, the one with the shopping bags, pushing the elevator button. Was that Sally? Cynthia stood to get a better view. She'd only seen the woman a few times, and that was well over a year ago. She couldn't be sure.

Cynthia watched her enter the elevator, its sole occupant. She'd already printed her room number on the bottom of the bill just in case she had to leave suddenly, so she trusted that the restaurant would charge her food and drink to her room.

Charging down the stairs with less dignity than a place like this required, Cynthia jabbed the button to call up another elevator and watched the floor number where Sally's ride stopped. The door to her own elevator opened immediately, and she was in, pressing the button for the eighth floor over and over.

When the door opened in the eighth-floor hallway, Cynthia hung back. She didn't think she wanted Sally to see her, hadn't thought far enough ahead to know what to do if she did.

Sally was slow leaving the elevator, hoisting her awkward bundles in her arms. With a sigh, she lumbered to the last door on the left, her stilettos making her gait uneven under her burdened arms. She heaved another sigh in front of the door. She tried juggling her load, but a box of Lego Friends Vet Clinic kit tumbled to the floor. It was too much work to put her parcels down, retrieve her card key from her purse, then pick everything back up again. She raised her toe and kicked at the door. When nothing happened right away, she kicked three times again, harder this time.

"All right." The door opened. "What's your problem?"

Cynthia recognized Natalie's voice. Bingo!

Cynthia let the elevator doors close, and the box began a silent ride downward. Pulling her phone from her pocket, she noticed the battery icon only showed a bit of white left. Damn. Why hadn't she thought to charge it overnight at Elizabeth's? She didn't even have a charger with her.

She sent a text to Brendan. "Found Natalie. She's with Sally." She hit send, just in case she didn't have enough juice to send much. At least that was the gist of it.

Her second text gave the room number to the suite Sally just entered.

If Amy was last seen with Natalie and Natalie was here, then Amy must be, too. Separated from her only by one closed door was her little girl.

Chapter Thirty-Five

Sure, technology was a grand thing and beat their methods from half a century ago, but sheesh. Couldn't they put more power behind these computer processors and make the spit out information faster? Most officers struggled with patience, especially when a child's life was at stake.

Jake refreshed his coffee for the umpteenth time, the initial sip turning sour in his gut. Searching for Alejandro Ramon brought up little other than decades old records and Anna's statements, but not really anything of use in finding him.

Boyd worked his way through the car rental agencies. Hernandez checked airport records, although they knew from the last time that this guy didn't fly public carriers. He had his own plane and didn't file the required flight records.

They built their present computer search around various combinations of the names Eduardo Arturo, Alejandro Ramon, Uniendo Familias, Ensenada, and Tijuana.

Brendan's phone chirped the tone for an incoming text message. "Hey, it's from Cynthia's number." It simply said,

"Found Natalie. She's with Sally."

Immediately Brendan's thumbs flew over his keyboard, replying, demanding more information from her. Then he waited. And waited.

Damn it! What did that mean? Why didn't she answer her phone? Had someone nabbed her? Had she dropped her phone? And where was she? "Get a trace on this number!"

Loitering seemed the thing she did most today. Cynthia waited on the stairwell landing, not sure what to do next. She'd let Brendan know that she'd found Natalie and Sally and given them the hotel name and room number. He'd be here with help soon.

The elevator pinged. The doors opened to reveal a woman in the hotel uniform, pushing a two tiered trolly with plates covered by white domes. There was a glass of milk, one of orange juice, a soda, a coffee carafe, and two glasses of red wine. The cutlery clattered as the woman pushed the cart over the elevator's threshold, then pointed it toward the left, following the path that Sally had taken.

Taking a deep breath, Cynthia let the stairwell door clang open. "Oops, sorry," she told the maid. "Didn't mean to make such a racket." She caught up to her and stopped in front of room 873. "Ah, you've brought our food. Thanks so much. It smells delicious." She opened her purse for a tip. The first thing her fingers snagged was a twenty. "Thank you for your trouble."

The bill disappeared into the woman's front pocket. "I'll bring it in and set it up for you."

Cynthia shook her head. "Thanks, but that's all right. Our daughter's sleeping and we don't want to wake her up."

She put one hand on the cart's handle, the other feeling in her pocket. "Darn, where'd I put that key card."

"Here, I'll get that for you." The woman reached past Cynthia and swiped her own card along the reader. With a click, Cynthia was in.

"Mommy!" Amy launched herself into Cynthia's arms.

Cynthia only had time for a quick hug, savoring the feel of the child's warm body against her, before shoving her daughter behind her.

Not fast enough. Alejandro was there, ignoring Amy, and grabbing Cynthia's arm, yanking her farther into the room, away from the door, slamming it shut with his foot. "How'd you get in here?"

"I brought food." Cynthia indicated the trolley beside her.

"Good. I'm starving!" Amy began lifting the lids off of the dishes, figuring which one was hers. "Here it is!" She lifted the platter containing the kids' meal.

Well, at least she was unhurt, thought Cynthia, and hadn't lost her appetite. Now what, though? She hadn't thought further than getting to her daughter.

"Take the kid into the other room," Alejandro ordered Sally.

"But I need to eat, too. I did all that shopping, then ordering. She can eat by herself." Sally was sick of being told what to do.

Alejandro's fist gripped Sally's upper arm in a way that no one could interpret as friendly. His expression was less harsh as he spoke to Amy. "Take your plate in the other room, kiddo. You can watch TV while you eat."

Amy dared not look at her mom in case Cynthia

forbade her to eat in front of the television, something she never got to do at home.

Alejandro's gaze penetrated Sally's. He gave her a warning shake. Then, with a flick of his muscles, he sent her teetering on her heels toward the first bedroom.

Sally grasped the door jamb, regretting her stylish high heels. She slammed the door behind her, closing herself in with Amy. She kicked off her shoes. Almost immediately, she reopened the door. With dignity, she swept over to the food trolley and snagged both a crystal flute, and the freshly chilled bottle of wine. She took them with her into the bedroom, using her hip to shut the door.

"Nat, get me a washcloth and the sashes from some bathrobes." Alejandro kept Cynthia pinned in place with his eyes.

Unlike Sally, Natalie knew when to shut up and do what she was told. Besides, she didn't like the way Cynthia looked at her. Leaving the room gave her some time to plan. Glad to have a task to do, she avoided meeting Cynthia's eyes. While Cynthia wasn't the brightest, she'd never actually been unkind to Natalie, unlike most other teachers. Still, she was pretty mundane, and Alejandro had plans, enticing plans. Cynthia was in the way.

"Mommy," called Amy.

"Tell her you need to talk to me," said Alejandro. "If not, the same thing that's happening to you will happen to her." He nodded at the rope substitutes in Natalie's hands.

"In a bit, baby. I need to talk out here for a while."

The robes in this suite were creamy white and plush, and the sashes extra-long. Plenty of length to tie each of Cynthia's arms and legs to a side of a chair. Alejandro stood in front of her with a washcloth aimed at her mouth.

Cynthia shook her head. "You don't need that. I won't scream. I don't want to frighten Amy."

That last part, Alejandro believed. "How'd you find us?"

"I guessed. This is where you stayed last time."

Alejandro frowned.

Natalie glared at him. *This* was planning? *These* were calculated moves?

Okay, one mistake, thought Alejandro. One minor mistake. Everything else would fall into place.

From her side pocket, Cynthia's cell phone chirped.

"What's that?" Alejandro asked.

"That's my cell. It's the low battery warning." Now why did I add that, she thought?

"Nat, bring it to me."

Natalie reached into Cynthia's pocket and retrieved the phone. She'd used it before, during their lessons, when her own battery had died, and she needed to look something up on the internet. She began scrolling. Alarmed, she turned the screen toward Alejandro. "Look what it says."

"Found Natalie. She's with Sally."

Then the next text gave their hotel name and room number.

"*Who* did you send this to?"

Cynthia said nothing.

Natalie touched the little *i* for information on the contact. "They went to Brendan James. That's Elizabeth's boyfriend. He's a cop."

"I know who James is." Alejandro ran his hand down his face. He still didn't get it. The pieces weren't connecting. "This is a big place," he told Cynthia. "How did you know which room we were in?"

Involuntarily, Cynthia's gaze drifted toward the closed bedroom door that hid her daughter and Sally.

Sally. Of course. Disgusted with both himself and her, Alejandro paced. Sloppy. He was getting sloppy.

"How long ago did she send those texts?" has asked Natalie.

"Looks like twenty-five minutes ago."

Yeah, that's about when Sally returned from shopping. She must have let herself be seen. That's what he got for using someone who felt it more important to strut her stuff than be discreet. The cow.

Chapter Thirty-Six

He'd survived this far by trusting his instincts. Scenarios flickered through his mind, edges and angles.

Searching through the desk drawer, Alejandro pulled out what he needed, stuffing items in his pockets. Extending his hand to Natalie, he offered, "Coming?"

She didn't hesitate.

Opening the door quietly, Alejandro peeked out. The hallway was empty. He led his daughter down the hall to the stairwell. Again, cautiously checking, he went down a flight of stairs, then into the hallway. He walked to the first door and opened it with a key card. "I always book two rooms."

"Plan and calculate. I get it."

He liked this girl.

Natalie looked around. They were in a loft-like sleeping/lounge room. To the left were wooden stairs that led to an open area, kitchen, and living room.

Alejandro led her down that way. "This is a two-story suite. We'll go out this way." After again checking that the new hallway was empty, he led them out the exit into the parkade.

A late model, metallic blue Ford Mustang sat in the first parking slot. Alexander pressed a key fob and its doors unlocked.

Natalie's eyes flashed with excitement, and then a question. "Yours? Blend in much?"

"I call this hiding in plain sight. People pay more attention to the car than its occupants." He threw her the keys. "Get in."

"Me? I don't have a license."

"Are you going to tell?"

"Not me."

"On second thought, let me back out, then you can take over."

Getting back in, Natalie tried to be cool, but it was hard to keep the grin off her face.

"Ever driven before?"

"A few times. Dad, I mean Howard, took me to a parking lot in the evening and let me drive around a bit. But they wouldn't let me drive on the road without a license."

"Okay, here's the deal." From the glove compartment, he pulled out two identical baseball caps. "Put this on and pull it low on your forehead. Tuck your hair up under the cap." He placed one on his own head, tugging the brim low. "And wear these sunglasses. Now, just follow the painted lines on the floor. We'll go down the levels of the parkade. At street level, there may be a barricade." He pulled down Natalie's sun visor. "You may need to put this ticket into a machine or give it to the attendant."

Natalie put the lever into park and slowly stepped on the gas. It took a few lurches before she got the pressure just right.

Once he was confident that she could handle this, Alejandro gave her the rest of the instructions. "There may be cops. If so, say you're my daughter. I'm sleeping it off and you're driving us home. Keep your face in shadow. And smile at them. You can pull this off. You have to."

Buckling Liam into his car seat, Howard and Barbara drove to the police station. They'd heard nothing. Not one word on the whereabouts of their daughter, or about what exactly the police were doing to get her back.

Her looming birthday was at the forefront of their minds. Their internet research on missing kids told them that sixteen marked an invisible cut-off. Sixteen-year-olds were deemed able to make their own decisions.

As if, thought Barbara.

After age sixteen, runaways received far less attention. A week from today, at one-thirty p.m. to be exact, Natalie would turn sixteen.

Barbara undid Liam's carrier from the back seat of the car and passed it to Howard. Together, they entered the steps of the police station.

The desk sergeant paged Officer Hernandez.

Liam fussed, and Barbara took him out of his car seat.

Hernandez shook hands with Howard and Barbara, his face as grim as theirs. "Come on back. There's a room here where we can talk."

Howard followed his wife, tucking the carrier under his arm. From over Barbara's shoulder, Liam gave Howard a toothless grin. Howard tried to return it, but knew he failed.

"Yes," said Hernandez. "We have some news." He looked from one to the other. "Natalie has been spotted."

"Oh, thank god!" Barbara sank back against her chair.

Hernandez didn't change expression. "She's with a woman who is a known associate of Alejandro. They were both implicated in child abductions a year ago, if not more."

"Oh, no! How is Natalie?"

"There is no indication that she's been harmed. Nor is there any sign that she'd being held against her will."

This made no sense.

"We're still seeking the minor child, Amy."

Minor child. Did they know Natalie was almost sixteen?

Twisting the knife, Hernandez added, "The last time anyone saw Amy, was being led away by your daughter, Natalie."

"Where were they seen? Who saw them? Can we go get her?"

"The police are on their way."

Cynthia waited in trepidation. She was helpless to defend Amy while trussed up like this. Sally was an unknown quantity. Sort of. She'd conspired with Alejandro, and she'd been willing to sell her own children. Yeah, a lot of help she'd be.

Were Alejandro and Natalie coming back, or was she on her own with Amy against Sally?

The bedroom door opened. Amy's little face peeked out. "Momma! What are you doing like that?" Her little fingers fumbled at the ties binding her mom to the armed desk chair.

Cynthia mumbled at her through the washcloth.

Understanding, Amy pulled on the edges of the cloth, gently, so as not to hurt her mom. She used the white terrycloth to wipe up the drool that came out of Cynthia's mouth with the cloth.

Hoarsely, she whispered. "Do those bedroom doors lock?"

Amy nodded. "Like our bathroom door at home."

"Is there a phone in there?"

Amy left her to go check. "Yep. There's two. They have a phone beside the toilet!"

"What's Sally doing?"

"She's sleeping."

"Okay. Here's what I need you to do." Would their rescue depend on the actions of an seven-year-old? "Go into the other bedroom and lock the door."

"Without you? I want you to come with me, mommy. I haven't seen you in a long, long time."

"I know honey. It's been since yesterday and I've missed you, too. But I need your help now. This is important. Go in the bedroom and lock the door. Pick up the phone and dial 0. When the person answers, tell them we're in room 873. Say that back to me."

"We're in room 873."

"Good. Then tell them to send the police."

Amy's eyes get wide. "The police?"

"Yes, we need their help."

"Why?"

Why had to be the most common word out of Amy's mouth. Cynthia fought to hold on to her patience. "Amy, just do as I say. Repeat back to me what you are to do."

She did. The child's memory was not faulty. Cynthia had an uncharitable thought; she was glad she was not in stuck in this position with either Bonnie, Timothy, or Daniel, none of whom was comfortable speaking. But one thing Amy had going for her was her gift of gab.

"I'm thirsty."

Cynthia looked around. "Open the mini fridge and see what's there."

Amy got on her knees and peered inside. "It looks like grown-up drinks here. Can I have some of them?"

"No!" Craning her neck, Cynthia spotted a glass water bottle filled with reddish liquid. "What's that red stuff? Maybe it's raspberry juice. Try that."

"No," said Amy. "Every time I drink that, I go to sleep. I'm not tired now. And I have a job to do for you."

Oh, good lord. What was in that bottle? What had they done to her child?

They heard sounds from where Sally slept.

"Hurry, Amy," whispered Natalie. "Go lock yourself into that bedroom and dial 0. Remember, room 873 and tell them we need police help."

"Yes, mommy."

The other bedroom door opened, and a loud yawn preceded Sally's presence. She fluffed her hair with her hands. Blinking, she took in the fact that there was just Amy and Cynthia in the room.

"Amy, go!"

While Sally's sleep-and-wine-addled brain still tried to take in what was happening, the other bedroom door slammed shut and the lock clicked.

"What's she doing?"

"I asked her to take a rest."

They could hear a little girl's voice in a one-sided conversation.

"Who's she talking to? Are Alejandro and Natalie in there?"

Thinking quickly, Cynthia lied. She hoped Amy couldn't

hear her. "Sometimes Amy talks to herself. She's an only child, you know."

Sally seemed more perturbed by Amy's monologue than seeing Cynthia bound to a chair. And well, she should be worried about what Amy said, thought Cynthia. How long would it take before the cops arrived?

"Where's Alejandro?"

"He left."

"I'd better pack. He'll want me to be ready to go."

Chapter Thirty-Seven

Brendan was almost at the hotel. In the car behind him were Boyd and Hernandez. They'd tracked Cynthia's GPS to the hotel, the same hotel Alejandro had used before.

"Hey! It's moving." Hernandez's tablet's tracking homed in on Cynthia's cell phone. While it had been stationary for about the last half hour, it was now moving. It was still within the property but moving, and at a clip much too fast for walking.

What was she doing?

Bingo! Jake smiled for the first time in almost twenty-four hours. Got him.

Finally, finally, the computers came through and began spitting out data on Eduardo Arturo. A credit card under that name was used to book a suite at the hotel - suite 873. And someone had used the credit card at two of the hotel's shops.

Pulling one of the officers from the exit to the parkade to talk to the shop owners only took a few minutes. Yesterday's receipts were still in the register, and the officer learned that they had purchased several clothing items in four separate transactions yesterday. Two from the lingerie store contained items for a size ten woman. One sales slip showed clothing from their young adult line, in size six. The other store disclosed sales for size six and small.

Then, this morning, there had been more purchases charged to this credit card from outside the hotel. Toys and children's wear.

If they needed toys and clothes for her, that must mean that Amy was alive and with them.

"Detective Brendan James should be there any minute," Jake told him. "Just wait in the lobby for him. He'll tell you what he wants you to do then."

By the time she'd gone down two more floors, Natalie had the knack of this driving thing. She didn't know why people made such a big deal of it. Or maybe it was the car. Such a cool car inspired confidence.

"Okay, we're almost at ground level." Alejandro raised himself slightly from his slouched position. "I can see that the barricade is down, and someone in uniform is standing there. That means you'll need to give him that ticket. There should be no fee, but if there is, use this credit card to tap the machine." He set it on the console between them. He was trusting a lot to this girl. She was untried. But he had few options. If worse came to worst, he could shove her out of the car and drive off. This car had power, and if he took them by surprise, he'd be long gone before anyone thought to give chase. He'd hate to leave his daughter, but if he had to…

"Detective James?" An officer in uniform stopped him as Brendan strode through the revolving door of the hotel's main entrance.

"Yes?" He regretted his gruff tone. Patience, Brendan reminded himself. The guy was probably just doing his job.

"Detective Dean said to give you these." He held out the copies of the sales receipts charged to Eduardo Arturo's credit card.

"Yes, yes. Come with me."

Deflated that his significant finds warranted so little attention, the officer trailed behind Brendan, Boyd, and Hernandez.

Hernandez hit the button for the elevator. Boyd stopped at the front desk, announcing their presence. He requested that all exits from the hotel be locked. No one was to get in or out until the police gave the okay. The day manager was to watch until their elevator opened on the eighth floor, then lock all elevators, including the freight ones. While the manager was reluctant to take such drastic actions, inconveniencing who knew how many hotel guests, he'd already received orders from his boss to cooperate fully with anything the police asked for. He already had a key card made up for them that would grant them access to suite 873.

In the elevator on the ride up, a calm came over Brendan as it always did, just before the possibility of action. The only one showing his nervousness was the young uniformed officer.

The elevator dinged, signaling their arrival on the eighth floor.

Natalie tucked the visor of her cap even lower as she slowed and approached the barricade. She seated the sunglasses a bit higher on her nose. These were her only outward signs of nervousness.

She powered down her window part way. "Hey," she said to the officer in uniform standing beside the barricade. She gave him her most brilliant smile, the one she thought made her look older.

"Hey," he replied, his gaze torn between her and the car. "Nice wheels."

"Yeah, I know. Not mine, though." She pointed her thumb at the slumped form beside her, head wedged between the seat back and side window, ball cap blocking the sun from his face. "It's my dad's car."

The cop lowered himself to look through Natalie's side window.

Alejandro emitted a faint snore and shifted his body into a more comfortable position. The hat slipped even lower over his face.

"Geez, that's embarrassing," said Natalie. "Snoring in broad daylight."

The cop still studied the slumbering form, his gaze swept the interior of the car.

"He really tied one on last night and it was all I could do to get him to the car this morning. He's sleeping it off. Mom's going to kill him." She gave him her conspiratorial grin. "But at least I get to drive his car."

The young cop returned her smile and slapped his left

hand on the car's roof. "Well, drive safely then. Have a good day." He raised the barricade to let them through.

They were off.

About half a mile up ahead was a mall. "Pull in there," Alejandro instructed. While Natalie had done great so far, he wasn't sure her driving would avoid scrutiny on busier streets.

Pulling Cynthia's cell phone from his pocket, he removed the battery. Opening the passenger door, Alejandro got out. Dropping both to the asphalt, he brought his heel down hard on the pieces of plastic and metal. Bending down, he picked them up. He hated litter, had hated seeing the debris strewn around the town where he grew up. It wasn't right.

"Trade places with me."

Natalie hated to admit that even though driving the car was cool, she had been just a tad nervous once out on the street.

Alejandro drove over to the dumpster along the mall's west side and heaved the pieces of mangled mobile phone into it. He pulled another cell phone from the glove compartment, along with its car charger. Plugging it in, he waited for it to power up and show bars. He pressed some numbers. "Meet us at the jet in thirty minutes." He listened. "No, don't file a flight plan."

Chapter Thirty-Eight

When the scanner clicked open as it read the key card, then the door to suite 873 opened, Sally expected Alejandro. Instead, three men in suits and one in uniform surrounded her, all with weapons drawn. She obeyed their order to get down on the floor.

Ignoring the opulence of the room, Boyd and Hernandez cleared the living area, the bedroom whose door was open, and the en suite bathroom. They stood in front of the locked bedroom door.

The uniform, on the detective's instructions, finished untying the knots holding Cynthia to the chair. She'd managed to loosen them enough that she could move both legs but was still working on the bindings on her arms. The left one would have been free soon.

"What's in there?" Brendan asked, indicating the closed door.

"Amy. I told her to go in that bedroom, lock the door and not come out until I told her to."

"Can you get her to unlock it for me?"

Cynthia raised her voice. "Amy, honey, Brendan's here. Will you unlock the door for him? He wants to see you."

"Sure," a little voice said, followed by the click of the lock.

Holding his weapon behind his back, Brendan slowly opened the door.

Amy snatched the knob out of his grasp, reaching for his hand. "Come. Come with me." She pulled him toward the ensuite's bathroom. "You've gotta see this. They have a phone on the wall beside the toilet. Have you *ever*?"

Sally's luck with men was lousy. They left her. They were not to be depended on.

This time, she thought she'd found a better specimen in Alejandro. At least he was richer.

But he'd done the same as other men in her life. When she needed them, they let her down.

She spilled.

The detectives had no trouble convincing her to talk. Once she realized the possible charges she faced with abduction and child trafficking, she had nothing to lose. She was not, repeat *not* going down for Alejandro's schemes. After all, she'd just gone along with him, trying to make a better life for herself.

And for her children, she reminded herself. Yes, best put that spin on it.

Sadly, Sally didn't know as much as she thought she did. Alejandro had only allowed her tiny glimpses of his business

undertakings. Other than the one credit card in her posses-
sion, she had no access to his funds, nor did she know where
he stored them.

She could give them the approximate location of his
estate near Ensenada, the one closed down after the raid
when Anna and Bonnie had escaped.

She did not know the location of the airstrips Alejandro
used, nor where he kept his plane. She'd simply been along
for the rides.

What she knew was that the jet was white on the outside
and a delicate blue on the inside, with comfortable furnish-
ings. The helicopter he sometimes used in his business was
dark green or brown; she wasn't sure which.

Despite Sally's belief in the value of her information, and
how little she actually offered, they now had a respectable
case against Alejandro Ramon, Eduardo Arturo, or whatever he called himself these days. The Mexican officials shut
down Uniendo Familias. They now had the records of the
families awaiting adoptive children.

The records of children who had already been adopted
were not stored there, either in physical or electronic form.
Bonnie still mourned the loss of her youngest brother,
Benjie. They had no clue where he was.

A For Sale sign hung from pickets pounded into the lawn of
the house two doors down from Cynthia's home. The
McDaws were moving again. Cynthia almost felt sorry for
them.

No, she felt for Barbara. This had to be tough on her

and on Howard. But Cynthia could not shake her resentment at the havoc their daughter had wreaked. How could they not have known that they were harboring a monster?

That was harsh, she chided herself. Still…

Her doorbell rang. The first of her guests arrived.

Amy bounded down the stairs, racing to the front door.

"Amy, remember…"

Amy slowed, hands on the deadbolt, and placed her eyeball as close as she could to the peephole that was at just her height. "It's Timothy," she yelled, opening the door.

Timothy barreled in, followed by Elizabeth and Brendan, both with their hands full of wrapped dishes.

Pulling up in front of the house was Anna's van. Murph held the door for Anna, then slid open the back one for Bonnie and Jordy. Bonnie gave Cynthia a shy smile and a hug. She nudged Jordy to do the same. The two raced off to find Amy and Timothy in the backyard.

They'd just started arranging the food when the bell rang to announce Keira, Daniel, and Jake.

But they weren't alone. Officer Gordon Boyd accompanied them. He looked slightly uncomfortable, as he did each time he'd dropped by in the last month. His shy smile widened as his gaze met Cynthia's. Blitz danced around his feet with happy yips, claiming his share of the man's attention.

Through Barbara's open kitchen window came the sounds of children's giggles, the deeper voices of men sharing stories and laughs. And there was the conversation of women, the women she had so recently thought of as her friends, but no longer.

Yes, she'd run into Cynthia or Elizabeth a few times on the street, and there had been one awkward time when Cynthia knocked on her door. In her arms she had a cardboard box containing Natalie's school work. Cynthia had kept careful records of all the assignments Nat completed, the curricular outcomes she'd met, and written a progress note for the next teacher, should Natalie return to school. Their conversation lasted less than two minutes.

Barbara could understand Cynthia's feelings, really, she could. They said that Natalie had helped abduct Amy. From what they now knew about Alejandro's business dealings, nothing good would have been in store for poor Amy.

But what about Natalie? She was just a child herself. She would not have known what was going on, what was in the drink she gave Amy, what was about to happen. She was just doing what she was told, under the spell of a man.

A man they had let into their home. A man *Howard* had brought into their lives. Howard, who recently moved into a bachelor suite on the other side of town.

Barbara now missed not only her daughter, but her husband. This was temporary, though, a blip. Soon all four of them would be back together, she was sure.

She continued to pack their glassware, emptying the kitchen cupboards one by one.

Keira was the first to notice. "Elizabeth! What is that sparkly thing on your ring finger?"

Self-conscious, Elizabeth hid the hand behind her back. Brendan was having none of that. Clasping her hand in his, he held it over their heads, turning it so all could see. He'd shout it to the world.

While everyone clapped and cheered, Boyd made his way to Cynthia's side.

Epilogue

Dear Barbara & Howard,

Thank you. I think you loved me as best you could and that you tried hard.
It wasn't working, though, was it?
I need to be with someone who gets it, who understands me.
My father, my biological father.

I'm okay. Good, even. This is the life I was supposed to have.
By the time you receive this letter, I'll be sixteen. I get to choose.

Have a nice day,

Natalie

P.S. Enclosed are the results of the DNA tests Alejandro and I did.

vinci-books.com/REASONS

A mother's love knows no bounds, but when desperation calls, she must decide between her children and her future.

Sally, a desperate mother, makes an unthinkable choice that will forever haunt her. Driven by the hope of escaping poverty, she sells her own children, setting off a chain of events that will test the very fabric of her being.

Turn the page for a free preview…

REASONS WHY: Chapter One

PART I

It hadn't been bad while the sun was up, but now that darkness filled the car, it was damp and chilly. All three girls huddled in the back seat, using each other's bodies for warmth. Twelve-year-old Sally was in the middle, an arm around each of her sisters.

The streetlight across the road shone a beam into the dusty car's interior. Sally saw that Bethany's eyes were closed, her head slumped onto her chest. That kid could sleep anywhere. But she couldn't be comfortable like that. Gently, Sally eased the five-year-old down into a prone position, her head on Sally's thighs, her legs stretched across Laura's.

They waited. And waited some more.

"Geez, how long is Mom going to be?"

It had been several hours already. Mom said she was stopping in for a quick drink and a bite to eat with her friends.

"I'm thirsty." Laura was only voicing what played on Sally's mind, too.

Sally was thankful that they had no drinks in the car. If they'd guzzled pop or water, especially Bethany, who knew how many times she'd have needed to pee? As far as Sally could see, there was no store around where they could ask to use a washroom.

Although her eyes remained closed, Bethany stirred restlessly in her sleep. She brought her knees to her chest, inadvertently kicking Laura in the stomach.

"Get her off me! She kicked me! Little twerp. Thinks she can pretend to be asleep and get away with kneeing me."

"She *is* asleep. She didn't mean it." Sally looked at her little sister's soft face. Instead of her usual placid sleeping expression, there was a slight frown. Her hands were under her armpits, a move Sally had taught her to warm herself up. There was a slight vibration. There it was again, more regular now. The child was shivering. Quickly, trying not to wake the child, Sally stripped off her own coat and draped it over the sleeping little girl. Soon, the shivering stopped, and Bethany's face took on the relaxed repose only small children achieve.

Laura shuffled closer, her arm and side plastered to Sally's. She tucked her hands alongside Bethany's legs, underneath Sally's jacket. Although only ten, Laura's instincts for self-preservation were well honed.

Getting chillier by the second, Sally's hands joined her sisters' under the jacket, tucking them into the space where Bethany's upper arms met her shoulders. That warmed her hands a bit, but did little for the rest of her.

"Sally, you have to do something. We can't stay here all night."

True. This had happened to them before, but when the temperatures were warmer. Now it had to be in the low 50s

- not bad when you're walking around and dressed for it, but definitely uncomfortable for three girls huddled in the back seat of an old car.

Periodically the door of the bar opened, letting out a rectangle of light, raucous laughter and the stench of stale, spilled beer. As the door let out another burst of forced hilarity, the girls instinctively ducked. This was not their first rodeo. Mom gave strict orders to stay out of sight and silent so no one would know they were there. They'd had experiences before of strange men trying to get into the car with them. Even though she had checked, rechecked and checked yet again, Sally glanced at the door locks to make sure they were fastened. Sally appreciated that their mother had taken care to park the car away from any direct pool of light that illuminated the contents of the car.

The shaking started again, this time not from the smallest sister, but from Sally.

"Keep still," Laura complained. "You are so annoying."

"I'm shivering. I can't help it."

"Well, you're the dummy who took off her coat."

Sally glanced at the features of her sister that were visible in the murky light. How could Laura be so self-centered? Sally was positive that at ten, she'd had more consideration for others than Laura showed.

"I gotta pee." This from Laura, again.

"You'll have to hold it. I don't see any place around here with a washroom."

"If I pee my pants, you'll be sorry."

True, thought Sally. All of us will be sorry and the car would stink for weeks. It had happened before.

"When did Mom say she was coming back?"

"She didn't, just that she wouldn't be long."

"But this is long, isn't it?"

To Sally, it sure seemed it. Neither of them had a watch, but it had been dark for almost two hours now. It felt like at least nine o'clock, but who knew.

"I'm hungry." Laura, Miss Obvious.

"Who isn't?"

"I bet he isn't." Laura pointed to the older man leaving the bar on wobbly legs. He rested one hand along the brick exterior of the building to get his balance, before shaking his head and making a serpentine line for the car two spaces ahead of them. After a lengthy period of fumbling, he managed to get the car door open and pour himself behind the driver's seat. He sat there with his head back for a while, the door still ajar.

"What's he doing?" Laura asked.

"I dunno. Resting, maybe?"

"He just came from the bar. Mom says the place relaxes her. How can he need to rest if he's just been in a relaxing place?"

Sally had no answer.

Bethany made little noises with her mouth as she exhaled in her sleep. Sally wasn't positive, because the windows were down, but she thought the man made *big* noises from his mouth as he caught some zzz's behind the wheel of his car. With a snort and a gasp audible two cars away, the man came to. Seconds later, there was the sound of his engine starting. Then his car swung away from the curb, veered to the far side of the street, then righted itself into the correct lane, and was gone.

At least that broke their boredom for a few minutes, but now that that distraction was gone, Sally's brain reminded her once again of the distress her body was in. Her shivering was non-stop now, and intensifying. If she couldn't get it under control, she'd wake Bethany. A rudely woken

Bethany was a cranky Bethany; no one wanted that, especially when they were confined to the interior of an old car.

Sally needed to do something. Trying to do a brain meld with their mom was not working, at least not so far, and she'd really tried.

The orders were to not leave the car. But what if the three of them turned into icicles before their mom returned? What if she forgot about them? What if she went home with someone else? She didn't always come home from the bar, especially after meeting some friends she wanted to get closer to.

As gently as she could, Sally eased her legs out from under Bethany's head and shoulders. She made herself as skinny as she could in the small space between the little girl's dark curls and the door. "Here, you move over and let her use your legs for a pillow," she told Laura.

About to refuse out of sheer habit, Laura realized that it might be a warmer position. She wormed her way under Bethany's body without disturbing the child's slumber. She, too, did not want to wake up Bethany. "What are you going to do?"

"I'm going to see if I can find Mom."

"About time." Laura leaned her head back against the stained seat and closed her eyes.

———

The door was heavy and required wrapping both of her hands around the vertical bar and heaving. Maybe it would have been easier on another day, but Sally's hands were partially numb from the cold and she hadn't eaten since breakfast.

Once inside, Sally froze to the spot. Then, she moved

into the shadows at the side to scout the place. There were lights, but not nearly enough to see clearly. There was noise, all kinds of noise, especially that funny kind of barking laugh people gave when they'd been drinking. Or, at least her mom did and the gentlemen friends she brought home.

Although some establishments employed a ban on smoking indoors, this one obviously didn't. Or, if it did, no one heeded the rules. The wafting layers of smoke made it hard to make out individual patrons seated around the tables.

It would help if Sally knew the friends her mom was with, but Mom's friends changed rapidly, depending on her mood, she said. So, Sally had no idea who her mom was relaxing with.

Relaxing? This was not Sally's idea of relaxing. Relaxing was that odd moment when she could sneak off the library alone, when she could browse the stacks, working her way through the Dewey Decimal system, filling her mind with whatever facts she wanted to study at the time. Relaxing was those rare moments when she and Mom would sit out on the back stoop, just the two of them and talk, really talk. Or, Mom would talk and Sally would listen; it was a way to get to know the different sides to the woman who had given her life.

But this place? The wavering lights filtering through the smoke. The incessant noise of laughing, boasting, and people talking over one another, vying for attention. The clink of the billiard balls in the corner. The ball game on the big screen TV in the corner by the bar. The country music blasting in the other corner. Relaxing? Her thumb rubbed against the side of her index finger, over and over and over again.

There were so many angles to this room, so many

people who didn't stay still. Realizing she'd never find her mother from this vantage point, Sally moved farther into the room, each footstep sticking slightly to the floor. It was like that time Laura spilled strawberry jam on the floor, but only wiped up the most obvious part of the red goo, thinking herself hard done by to have had to do that much. For days their socks would stick to the floor before Sally washed away all traces of the accident. Perhaps she could get a job here washing the floor. She'd need a mask, though, or some kind of breathing filter to hide the stench of old beer.

What did people here have against lights? Sally had priced them in the store - 100-watt bulbs costs the same amount as 40-watt ones. So, why not shine a little light in this place?

There! It didn't peal out often at home, but when her mom laughed, no one could help but join in. Freezing to the spot, Sally moved only her head, focusing her hearing on that particular sound. There! Her mom's laugh, followed by a bunch of deeper, louder guffaws.

"Hey! You don't look twenty-one."

A man set down the glass he was filling and came from behind the bar, wiping his hands on the stained white apron stretched over his girth. His pace quickened as he got closer to Sally, hands on hips, looming over her. Sally had seen friendlier visages from Laura when she was told she couldn't have something she wanted.

Taking a step backwards, Sally's foot slid in a puddle. Her efforts to balance herself splashed the liquid onto the hem of her jeans.

"Well, little girl? What are you doing in here? Trying to get me shut down?" He pointed to the door with the blinking, red and white exit sign over it. "Out! Git out of here, now!"

"Please sir, I'm trying to find my mom. I just need to speak to her, then I'll go. Promise."

Izzy's laugh rang out again, flying overtop the cacophony of sounds reverberating through this room. Before the man could grab her arm and throw her out, Sally ducked and pivoted, homing in on the sound.

There. At that crowded table. No wonder she hadn't seen Mom when she came in. Izzy was surrounded by people. Of course. Both men and women pointed their faces in Izzy's direction, hanging onto her words. Oh, this was mom at her best, eyes flashing, visage animated, in control and relishing the spotlight.

Sally stood at the edge of the group, peeking between heads. Even though the men were sitting, some of them still towered over Sally. Behind her, she heard the heavy stomp of the barkeeper coming up behind her. She didn't have much time. "Mom!" She tried for both volume and authority in her voice at the same time. "Mom!"

The gentleman in the chair closest to Sally turned his head. "Whoa, a kid. What's a kid doing in here?" He moved his chair back half a foot, as if she had cooties and he didn't want to catch them.

His chair banged that of the man next to him. That, and his words snagged the attention of his nearest neighbors. In a matter of seconds, all conversation around the crowded table stopped and all eyes turned to Sally.

Izzy's exuberant face turned Sally's way. Like a deflating balloon, all the animation drained away. She said not a word.

"Mom?"

The barkeeper was behind Sally now. His beefy hand

came down hard on her shoulder. "Does someone belong to this kid?"

No one spoke.

His grip tightened.

Izzy's eyes remained on the table where she swirled a sweaty bottle of beer and set it in its damp ring on the table.

More quieter now, "Mom?"

In the rest of the room, speech and laughter and braggart stories gradually died down as if some unspoken message had spread that there was drama about. All eyes turned Sally's way, that is, all eyes, but for Izzy's.

"Mom, we need to go. Bethany's been asleep for hours. We're cold. And Laura has to pee."

That brought a roar of laughter from the crowd. Finally, Izzy's gaze met that of her daughter's.

Oh, no. Sally knew that unfocused look, as if her mom was not quite in control of her vision. The rest of her body wouldn't be much more coordinated, either. Sally squared her shoulders. It was okay. They'd dealt with this before. She gave a brief thought for how they were going to get their mother up the three flights of stairs to their apartment, while carrying a sleeping Bethany. But, she'd worry about that later. For now, she had to get her mom out to the car.

"Lady," the voice boomed from above Sally's head. "We don't allow no kids in this place. She doesn't even *look* twenty-one. You're gonna get me shut down. Take your kid and get out of here." When Sally didn't move, he released his hand from its grip on Sally's shoulder and took a step towards Izzy. There was a shuffling of chairs as both men and women tried to make way in the crowded space.

Sally smelled his body odor as he brushed by her. "Mom, come on." Izzy didn't move. What would this guy do to her if she didn't? His face was not friendly. Nor did he have what Sally called a leer, but mom called it bedroom eyes. Instead, his look was plain nasty. Living where they did, Sally had learned to avoid those types.

"Mom." Sally tried to use the tone she employed when trying to make Laura do something she didn't want to do. "We have to go *now*! The kids can't wait any longer."

"Wait." The hand on her shoulder spun Sally around. "Do you mean to tell me that you kids have been waiting in the car whole time your mom's been in here?"

Sally didn't mean to tell him anything. She just wanted to get her mom and leave. But his eyes left her no choice. They clearly stated that she was not moving an inch until she answered his question. So, she nodded.

The man narrowed his eyes at her, but his grip on her shoulder loosened. Instead, he turned that ugly look onto Izzy.

Uh oh. Now Sally'd be in for it if she got her mom into trouble. "Please, mister. It's all right, but we need to go now."

He gave a quick glance at Sally, then returned his glare to Izzy's wobbling head. "Are you trying to ruin my business? You can get me shut down for having an underage kid in here." His chin pointed at Sally. "Second, the cops don't look well on me having patrons who dump their kids in the car outside while they get sloshed in here."

"I'm not sloshed," insisted Izzy. But there was an extra "SH" at the beginning of the word. She heard it herself, and tried to correct it. "Shoshed. No, shloshed." She tried again. "I'm not drunk." There. She nodded, pleased with herself for getting it right.

The barkeeper approached Izzy's chair. Men quickly shoved their chairs out of the way, giving the looming giant easier access to Izzy. Not one of them attempted to interfere with the beefy hand that wrapped around Izzy's upper arm. Giving a tug, he joisted Izzy out of her seat.

In her semi-boneless state, she came up easily, listing to the side, and would have face-planted, if not for his hold on her arm. "Get your hands off me!"

Almost in unison, came "Get your hands off my mother!"

Izzy's and Sally's eyes met. A slow smile spread across Izzy's face.

Half a second later, it was rewarded with Sally's smile. They may have their difficulties, but they were a team.

As Izzy braced herself on the table, Sally squeezed past the bartender and put her arm around her mom's waist. Supporting most of the woman's weight, she began the slow process of leading her mother toward the exit sign.

Sally's feet wouldn't work right, and kept sliding in front of one another, slowing their progress and making it harder for Sally to keep both of them upright. But, the door loomed closer.

In the bar, all was silent as the patrons watched their stumbling path, as they wove their way through the occupied tables. About ten feet from the exit, Sally gave a yelp and jumped to the side. In her efforts to keep her mom in an approximate vertical position, she'd forgotten to watch out for the men watching their spectacle. One reached out and pinched her bottom, giving it a squeeze and a nasty twist. Only able to turn her head long enough to give the guy a glare, she kept on.

REASONS WHY: Chapter Two

Holding her mom up while using both hands to open the exterior door would not work. Sally propped Izzy against the wall and tried to hold her in place with her hip as she yanked at the door. Izzy began a slow descent to the floor. She likely wouldn't hurt herself at the rate she was falling, but it would be a struggle to get her back on her feet. Sally let go of the door handle and caught her mother under the armpits

As she righted the woman to a mostly upright position again, a hairy arm stretched over their heads. The stench of stale cigarettes overwhelmed Sally's senses, but she'd suffer through that to get out of there. The bartender's hand grasped the door handle and pulled, letting in the darkness and the sort of fresh air. "Good luck, kid," he said. "You're gonna need it."

Sally nodded at him once, then dragged her mother across the sidewalk to where Laura's face was plastered to the back seat window.

Sally hammered on the window to get Laura to unlock

the door for them. Laura gave her a two-handed shrug. What? Didn't the useless kid even know how to unlock the doors? Didn't matter. They needed the car keys anyway; they weren't going anywhere without them.

Izzy never took her purse with her to the bar. She'd left it behind far too many times, losing all her IDs plus any cash or credit cards she had on her. These days, she was smart, she said. She chose pants not so tight that the pocket couldn't hold her car keys. In her other hip pocket, she'd slip her credit card, although she rarely had to pay for her own drinks.

Now, to figure out which pocket held the keys. Shoving her mom against the car and trying to hold her there with her body hindered Sally's skill at patting her mom down.

Again, that stale smell came closer. "I'll hold her up, kid, while you look for the keys."

Sally didn't want this man touching her mother. Thinking quickly, she couldn't see any alternative, short of laying her mom flat on the crumbling sidewalk. "Thanks."

She found the keys right away, in her mom's front, right pocket. Their shape was unmistakable; the trick was trying to ease them out of their hiding place.

Realizing her problem, the guy hoisted her mom by the rib cage, holding her straight up and down. There. Now that Izzy wasn't hunched over, Sally could slide the tips of two fingers into that pocket and start to wiggle out the keys.

"You're not going to let her drive."

Sally didn't know if the man asked her a question or made a statement. Either way, he had a good point. If Izzy couldn't walk, couldn't hold her head up, how could she drive?

"Let's put her in the back seat here. Maybe if she sleeps it off for a bit, then she can drive." The man's suggestion might have been helpful, if Sally hadn't known how her mom passed out for hours when she was like this.

Nodding, Sally used the key fob to click the locks open, then held the back door open so the barkeeper could lower Izzy to the seat.

"Whoa!" He stopped. "Where am I supposed to put her?"

"Laura, go out the other side and get in the front seat. Prop Bethany into the corner to make room for Mom." For once, Laura did as asked without arguing.

After allowing Izzy to flop onto the back seat, the man straightened. "Better put a seat belt on her and on the little one." He stood back and watched as Sally did as he suggested. All the while, he regarded Sally. "How old are you?"

"Old enough."

"Do you know how to drive?"

"Of course," Sally lied.

"Yeah, right." He turned his back. "I don't want to know about this. Gotta go see how much these stinking customers robbed me of while my I was outside fiddling around with your mess."

Easing herself behind the steering wheel, Sally looked at the familiar interior. Except, it didn't look quite so familiar from this side of the front seat. She'd watched her mother do this thousands of times. How hard could it be?

"You're not going to drive this thing, are you?" Usually annoying, this time Laura had a legitimate question.

"Maybe."

"Wake up mom and she'll drive."

Sally looked at her younger sister. "Right. You go wake her and get her up here." Surprisingly, Laura obeyed. Or, tried to. While she rested her head on the steering wheel, Sally could hear Laura's voice in the back, imploring Izzy to wake up and take them home.

After a fairly persistent time for Laura, Sally heard the back door close, and the front passenger door opened and shut. Laura stared straight ahead. "She won't wake up." She turned to her older sister. "What do we do now?"

Good question. Glancing over her shoulder, she saw that Bethany was sound asleep, wrapped snuggly in her own coat, plus Sally's. That reminded Sally. In the struggle to get their mom out of the bar and into the car, Sally had forgotten how cold she was. Now that she wasn't exerting herself so much, the shivering began again. How long did it take for someone to freeze to death? Could she stay like this all night, until their mom woke up in the morning and took them home?

"I gotta pee."

Right. That had been the complaint that drove Sally into the bar in the first place.

"You'll have to hold it while I figure something out."

"I can't!"

A car stinking with pee from a five-year-old was bad enough. How much worse would it be if ten-year-old Laura wet herself on the car seat - the seat where Sally always sat?

"Let me think." It only took two tries for Sally to insert the key into the ignition. She'd watched mom do this thousands of times. Maybe millions. How hard could it be? She turned the key to the right and held it there. There was the sound of the car starting up, then a grinding noise. The latter startled Sally enough that she pulled her hand back to her chest. The grinding stopped. Well, so far, so good.

She put her hands on the steering wheel, near the top. It was a stretch, but her hands latched firmly onto the wheel. Now what?

Straining, she peered over the dashboard. She had a good view of the night sky and the streetlights up ahead, but not the road in front of her.

"I think you have to adjust the seat." At least it was a helpful comment from Laura.

"How?"

Laura shrugged.

Sally jiggled on the seat and bounced a bit. Yeah, maybe if she sort of stood, she could see out the front windshield.

"I think I remember mom fiddling with something under her seat. Remember when she dated that guy, Bennie, and he'd use her car? She hated when he left it so she couldn't reach the pedals." Uncharacteristically, Laura was on a helpful roll. Maybe she really was desperate to pee.

With her left hand, Sally felt under the seat. Her hand brushed stale popcorn kernels, some gravel, candy bar wrappers and something sticky she didn't want to think about. The back of her index finger brushed against a bar that seemed to run the width of the seat. Sally pulled up on it, and her seat shot backwards, eliciting a moan from their sleeping mother. Well, that moved the seat for sure, but the wrong way.

She tried again, raising the bar as high as it would go, then trying to squirm her seat into a better position. Nothing. Maybe if she held onto the steering wheel and pulled. She tried, but with one hand on the bar and one on the wheel, she wasn't strong enough to move herself. "Laura, you'll have to help. Get down here and pull up on this bar."

"Do I have to? I need to pee?"

"If you want to find a bathroom, we have to move this car and I can't do that if I can't see."

Grumbling, Laura positioned herself on the floor of the car, draped over the console, and grasped the bar with both hands.

Sally pulled and the seat came forward.

"Ow! You're squishing me!" Laura let go of the bar and edged herself out from beneath the steering wheel.

"Sorry." This new position helped a bit, but she was still too short to see over the dashboard without straining her head. Making herself as small as possible, Sally pressed into the back of the seat and pulled her left leg up under her. There. If she sat on her leg, she gained another few inches. Not ideal, but it would do.

Where was her brain. Here she was freezing, and she'd not even thought to turn on the heat. She knew how to work it as Mom often got her to do it, especially if she was busy putting on her lipstick.

Soon air blew out of the vents, then warm air.

Mom hated what she called parallel parking and refused to do it. She always looked for spots where she could drive in and out without any of that 'stupid back and forth stuff'. Today Izzy had parked with an alley entrance in front of her. There were no cars parked on the other side of the entrance either, so no tricky maneuverings should be needed to drive off.

Sally grasped the level sticking out of the console and tried to pull it back. Nothing. It was stuck beside the letter P. What did Mom do to get this thing moving?

Yeah, she did something with her feet. Sally knew that the pedal on the left was the brake; everyone knew that. Peeking under the dash, she located it, along with the longer, narrow pedal that must be the gas.

Hanging on to the steering wheel to pull herself as close as possible, and rising up slightly on her bent leg, Sally pressed the gas pedal. The engine revved. She tore her foot away. Then she gently pressed the brake pedal. No sound, nothing at all. Okay, she needed to get used to how these felt. She put weight on the gas pedal again, gently this time. The engine's sound changed but it didn't roar. She tried the brake again, pressing and releasing it several times. Now, what was it Mom did to get this thing moving?

Sally thought she recalled seeing Mom's leg move as her hand moved the lever on the console. But which pedal did she press?

"Come on, let's go!" Laura jiggled in her seat.

Deep breath in. Okay. It would probably be better to try the brake pedal first. What if she used the gas and the car shot forward before she knew how to control it? Clasping the steering wheel tightly in her left fist, Sally pulled herself as far forward as she could. She pressed the brake pedal and kept her foot there. With her right hand, she tried moving the lever again. This time it moved. It slid to the R position. R. Did that mean reverse, a fancy way of saying go back-wards? No, they didn't want to go backwards because there was a pickup truck there. It probably belonged to some drunk, bad-assed dude in the bar who'd rip her head off if she banged into his truck.

Keeping her foot on the brake, Sally eased the lever back more. Now it rested beside the letter N. N. What would that be for? No go? She skipped it and aimed for the D. That had to mean drive. Hopefully.

The lever settled itself into the D's slot, like it was meant to be there. Sally relaxed her hands. Oops. That meant that her foot no longer pressed so hard on the brake and the car slowly inched forward.

Sally grimaced. Yeah, she meant to do that, she told herself.

Turning the wheel slightly to the left, Sally slowly, ever so slowly steered the vehicle into the street. Funny. When she saw this car beside others, it seemed small, but from behind the wheel, it seemed like she was driving a tank far too big to fit on this city street.

With the brake off, the car crept along. Bethany as a toddler, could have crawled faster.

"Let's go! I need a bathroom like now!"

Okay, keep calm, Sally told herself. Use your brain. In Health class in school, they said to take a deep breath, then several more when you got anxious or scared and didn't know what to do. You need to engage your brain, and to do that you have to breath.

Sally pushed her shoulders back. Nope, that wouldn't do because she needed to hunch forward to grab the steering wheel. But she could breathe.

Stretching her right foot as far as it would go, she pressed down on the gas pedal. The car shot forward. Both Laura and Sally screamed. The jolt loosened Sally's foot, and without the pressure on the GAS pedal, the car returned to its former sedate pace.

Sally tried resting her right heel on the floor and pressing down with her toes. This meant that she took most of her weight on the hands wrapped around the steering wheel. Okay, she told herself. This was doable.

"Red light, red light!" Laura yelled, holding up her hands as it to stop the car's forward motion.

Sheesh! There was so much to pay attention to at once. She was trying to get the hang of how to drive this stupid car and forgot about anything outside of the vehicle. "Thanks," she said to Laura.

Laura muttered under her breath, but Sally didn't have the time nor the brain power to worry about what she said, with all her effort going into jamming that brake pedal as hard as she could.

From behind came the short blast of a car horn. Had they been caught? Was someone going to arrest her for driving underage? The horn came again, longer this time.

"I think they're trying to tell you to go. The light's green now."

Just as Sally eased her foot off the brake and planted her heel on the floor to push on the gas pedal, there was the sound of squealing tires. The car behind them pulled out into the opposite lane and whooshed by them. Good, thought Sally. She had enough to concentrate on without having to worry about someone behind them.

As the car went by, it flashed its lights over and over. On, then off, then on, and off.

"I think they're trying to tell you something," said Laura.

Couldn't she just come out with it? Sally didn't have time to play guessing games.

"Lights. I think you're supposed to have lights on when you drive at night."

"How do you make the lights come on?"

"Why ask me? I'm just a kid."

Sally shot her sister a look.

Up ahead was another intersection and a yellow light. Sally slowly eased her foot off the gas, the car creeping to the corner. "Quick, look. How do we turn on the lights?" Jerking her head around, Sally saw that there was no one behind her. No traffic at all in sight. She could take a few minutes to figure this out.

Laura sat on one leg, rocking back and forth. "I really

need to pee." But she at least looked at the driver's area. After only a few seconds, she pointed. "There. Is that supposed to be a picture of a light bulb?"

Finding the area Laura meant, Sally turned the knob one way, then the other. The lights on the dashboard lit up and beams of light pointed out in front of the car. Thank goodness.

Sally had concentrated so hard on keeping the car in the right lane, that she hadn't paid much attention to where they were. Up ahead she saw the yellow arches, indicating a McDonalds. Now she knew where they were. Next to McDonald's was a Walmart. Walmart had bathrooms.

The entrance into the Walmart parking lot was on the right. Good. She would not have to cross the road to get there. Carefully, and ever so slowly, Sally guided the vehicle in between two sets of white lines. Well, maybe she straddled one of them, but it was near the edge of the parking lot, with no other cars around. She slumped over the steering wheel, relaxing her arms for the first time in ten minutes.

Beside her, Laura jigged up and down.

"Well, go. We're here. Go use the washroom in Walmart."

"Will you come with me?"

Sally threw her head back against the seat. Now she knew why her mother sometimes muttered, "Lord, give me strength." "Can't you just go by yourself."

"I'm scared and it's dark."

"You want me to leave Bethany and Mom here alone in the dark?"

"Lock the door and they'll be fine. Please?"

Sally sighed and tried pulling the key from the ignition. It wouldn't budge. In her efforts to tug on it, her foot dislodged from the brake, and the car edged forward. Quickly, Sally slammed on the brake, throwing both herself and Laura toward the dashboard.

"I think you're supposed to put the car in park when we stop."

Oh, yeah. That made sense. Laura was on a helpful streak. Keeping one foot firmly on the brake, Sally shoved the lever up to the P position. Tentatively, she eased her foot from the brake. Nothing. The car didn't move. This driving stuff was nerve-wracking.

Laura's jiggling sped up.

Glancing at their slumbering mother and little sister, both snoring quietly, Sally agreed that it might be safe enough to leave them locked inside the car. Both seemed out for the night and it was warm enough in there now that the heat had been blasting at them. Besides, she could use the excuse to stretch her legs; her muscles were cramping from their awkward positions, trying to reach the pedals while hoisting herself high enough to see to drive.

Exiting the car, Sally used the fob to lock the doors, checking again that Bethany and Mom were asleep. "Let's make this fast."

She didn't need to warn Laura. Laura led the way, speed-walking toward the entrance doors. Once inside, she stopped dead, partially dazed by the lights, unsure where to go.

"This way," said Sally, pointing to the sign to the left that indicated the public washrooms.

The lavatory was far from pristine with soap smeared on the counter and faucets, paper towels littering the floor. Laura didn't seem to care. She didn't even take time to lock the stall door before finally letting herself go. She peed on and on and on.

"Hurry up. We'd better get back to Mom and Bethany." There was a rustling of clothes, then the toilet flushed and a much relieved Laura headed for the washroom's exit. "Aren't you going to wash your hands?" Sheesh. At ten, she shouldn't need reminding, should she?

As they walked back to the car, Sally ran over in her mind all the steps she needed to take to get the car moving again. Her right thumb attempted to soothe itself by rubbing up and down the side of her index finger. It was exhausting working out all that had to be done. She was tempted to settle in for the night, all four of them sleeping in the car.

But, what if someone saw them. Was it even legal? Would Mom get in trouble? Would Sally get arrested for being the person behind the wheel? No, maybe they should get home.

REASONS WHY: Chapter Three

It wasn't quite as hard this time. Sally got the car in motion, and in the right direction. She knew the way home from here since Mom often shopped at Walmart. At least, she thought she knew the way. Things looked different from the driver's seat. And in the dark.

Sally squinted. She'd been telling Mom that something was wrong with her eyes. Not that she *wanted* glasses or anything gross like that, but lately she could not read the board at school. Now, when she needed lots of warning to be able to plan her moves, she couldn't quite see where they were until they were almost right at the street corner. This was exhausting. How come teenagers were always eager to start driving?

The leg she sat on was going to sleep, doing that pins and needles thing. Well, it would just have to bear up. She used her hands on the steering wheel to hoist herself up just a bit higher. There. Now her neck was not kinked at such an awkward position, trying to peer over the dash.

Ah, Value Village up ahead. Now Sally definitely knew

where she was. In two blocks was the police station. Dare she drive by it? Her shoulders slumped under the weight of the decisions. Did they never stop?

Would cops be outside their station? Would they notice someone really short driving by? Maybe they had secret cameras. Nah, probably not. Or, would they? Would they take a picture of her and keep it until she was sixteen and tried to get a driver's license? Spring it on her, like they'd had her under surveillance all along, waiting until she was old enough to be arrested for impersonating a driver.

Maybe they'd feel sorry her, think that she was just a kid and it wasn't her fault that she had to drive her family home.

She unclenched her back teeth as she eased up to the next stop light. This time she braked without throwing Laura into the dashboard. Served her right for not putting on her seat belt when Sally reminded her. As the light turned to red, she let her bottom rest on her leg, relaxing the tension on her arms from gripping the steering wheel with all her might. They had a long ways to get before reaching their apartment building. Then what? It was all she could do to keep this machine in the correct lane. There was absolutely no way she'd be able to back it into their parking spot in the tiny, tight parking lot. Would this night never end?

Ahead, light pooled from the front of the cop shop. Then another thought struck. What if? No, she couldn't do it. But what if she just drove right up to their front door. She could lay on the horn, and surely someone would come out to see what the ruckus was about. Then an adult could take over, someone else make the decisions, someone else keep them safe.

But what had mom always said? If the law or the

government got involved, it would split them up. They'd never see one another again. The three kids could taken into the foster care system and mom, well, mom might get in big trouble for not looking after her kids. Could she be thrown in jail?

But at least in foster care, they'd always have something to eat, wouldn't they? There would always be a safe place to pee. There would be no nasty old man hand on her body. Maybe life would be easier for all of them. At least it would be easier for Sally, not having to be the responsible one.

She glanced over her shoulder at her slumbering little sister. Bethany was angelic in the halo created by the streetlight. From her driver's seat, Sally could not see her mother, but she could hear her snores. Mom always snored when she'd had too much to drink. Sometimes she farted, too.

The light turned green. Sally took in a deep breath and squared her shoulders. Hands planted firmly at ten and two o'clock on the wheel, she pulled herself up, balancing on her folded left leg, pressed her right heel into the floor and pushed with the ball of her foot. The car shot forward through the intersection, startling Sally so that her foot jerked from the floor and the car slowed. Okay, she told herself. You can do this. She tried again, but too lightly this time. The car barely budged and the car behind them honked.

Laura made a tsk sound with her tongue and rolled her eyes. "This is *so* embarrassing. Can't you even drive right?"

The police station rolled on by. With a car trailing right behind her, Sally couldn't think of a way to turn in there, even if she wanted to. Oh, some part of her really did want to, but she couldn't do that to their mother. Mom trusted her, needed her to help look after the kids. And her.

Mom would be worth little tomorrow morning and

Sally would have a monumental task trying to get her out of bed and off to work. She hoped they had plenty of aspirin left from the last time this had happened. Mom could not miss work or she'd be docked a day's pay. She'd already missed far too many days. She might even get fired if she didn't show up. Sally's grass-cutting job was definitely not enough to support them.

Funny, but Sally had never noticed how very far away their apartment was. The drive seemed to go quickly when someone else was behind the wheel. But finally, finally, it was in sight.

"Hey, you went right past the entrance." Laura, queen of the obvious, informed Sally.

"Yeah, I know. I don't think I can park this thing in our spot. It involves backing up and maneuvering the way Mom does."

"How lame." Laura sighed and stared out the side window.

But her sister had a point. Now what?

Sally swung the wheel to the right at the corner. Too much to the right and the right front tire hit the curb, then propelled them off, back into the center of the road. Good thing no cars were coming. There was still room to make the turn. Or so she thought.

Yep, there was. Now she'd driven past the parking lot entrance, past the apartment building and onto the side street. Vehicles were parked all along the road on the side of their building. Easing her way along, Sally spied a long open space near the next group of buildings.

Carefully, ever so carefully, Sally steered the boat of a car toward those spots. Surely she could make it. She didn't want to hit the curb going in, because that would mean she'd either have to back out and try again or leave the ass end of the car hanging out in the street. Neither option sounded doable.

Boosting herself up as high as she could, her sweaty fingers clutched the steering wheel. She knew now why these wheels had bumps on them, to prevent your fingers from slipping around and losing their grasp.

Pulling the wheel so that they were now parallel to the sagging fence that ran by the sidewalk, Sally removed her foot from the gas pedal and trod on the brake.

This time Laura's seatbelt kept her in place but didn't stop her from complaining.

Sally rested her head on her hands and let her body sag. Home. They'd made it. And, without any of them getting arrested.

Laura opened her door and stepped out. "Are we supposed to be this far from the curb?"

Sally tilted her head in her sister's direction. Through the open passenger door, Sally could see several feet of the paved road, and the entire sidewalk. "It's fine." She knew it wasn't, but there was nothing she could do about it. The ordeal was over and she was done in.

She shut off the car.

Wiggling, she used her hand to help drag her unresponsive left leg out from under her. Ignoring the pins and needles shooting down her appendage, she used her hand to rub away some of the numbness.

When she thought that her leg would support her weight, she opened her door and touched that foot to the ground. It buckled. Swinging her right leg out of the car, she used that as her pivot point while she worked the life back into her left leg.

Then she noticed her sister. Laura was about fifty feet down the sidewalk. "Hey, where are you going?"

Laura turned around, but kept walking, backwards. "Home. I'm tired."

Sally hunched into the car and plucked the keys from the ignition. Holding them up, she dangled them in the air. "How do you think you're going to get in without these?" The streetlight reflected off the shiny metal.

Reluctance in every step, Laura returned. "Give me those." She tried to snatch them from Sally's hand, but Sally was taller and in no mood to be messed with. "You have to help me get them upstairs." Then it struck Sally. How were they going to do this? They lived on the third floor of a walk-up building. Maybe, just maybe, they could carry Bethany all the way, but Mom? No way.

When she was first learning how to cook and clean, she read a book. It talked about life skills being like how to eat an elephant - one bite at a time. They'd take this step-by-step, too. But she was *not* relinquishing the keys to Laura.

Opening the back passenger side door, She unbuckled their smallest sister and shook Bethany. Nothing. That kid would not be roused once she fell asleep. Sally hoisted Bethany into her arms. Five-year-olds might not be huge, but this one was like a leaden sack. The child's head rolled. Sally bounced her and rearranged her hold until Bethany's head rested on her oldest sister's shoulder.

Turning, she looked at their mother, slumped in the other corner of the back seat. "Wake her up, will you?"

Laura put her head into the car and yelled, "Mom!"

Izzy snorted, shifted her head, then resumed her snoring.

"Shake her to get her up," Sally instructed.

"Why does it have to be me? You know she'll hate

whoever wakes her." Both girls knew this from past experience.

"Would you rather carry Bethany?"

Laura scooted over the seat, grabbed her mom's arm and shook it. "Come on, Mom. Get up." No response. "Mom!"

On the sidewalk, Sally juggled Bethany's weight again. She didn't know how long she could keep holding her. "Leave Mom for now. We'll come back for her."

"Gladly."

Sally staggered as her foot left the sidewalk and met the uneven, patchy grass. She'd have to be careful where she put her feet. Bethany could get hurt if they fell.

They almost made it to the back door of the building. There were seven steps to mount before they reached the door. Sally turned and planted her butt on the second step from the bottom. She was done in. How could she get the child up the next five steps?

Then a scary thought occurred. These seven steps were nothing. They had three whole flights of stairs to navigate before getting to their apartment door.

The chill of the night air and the dampness of the concrete under her started to seep in and Sally shivered. She should have taken her coat back from Bethany. On the other hand, she was exercising hard, and so would keep warm. Wrapping her arms around her burden, she pushed up with her feet. Scraping the front of the flaking concrete step with her back, her butt came to rest on the third step.

This would work. She repeated the process until she reached the stoop with a sigh.

"Give me the keys," demanded Laura.

No way, Sally thought. She didn't trust her sister to take off with them, go to bed, and not come back to help.

Bracing her little sister against her chest, Sally balanced, bringing her legs under her and straightening. She groaned.

"Do you know how unladylike that sounds?" Laura's disgusted comment.

Thanks, Laura, thought Sally. "Here, take her." She tried to pass Bethany's weight to Laura.

"Why do I have to hold her? She weighs a ton. I'm only ten."

True. "Just while I get the door open." This lock was always finicky. She got it open. Leaning her back against the opened door, she reached her arms for Bethany.

Laura didn't complain about passing over the child.

They made their way down the stained, linoleum floor, from experience stepping around the spots most likely to have attracted urine, or worse. Reaching the middle of the hallway, Laura held open the door to the stairwell without having to be asked.

Looking up, Sally counted the steps. Eight stair treads, then a landing. Turn, and another eight steps. That would take them to the second floor. Do the whole thing again, and they'd reach their floor. Whatever possessed Mom to pick an apartment on the top floor?

At least there were handrails. Shifting Bethany so that her right arm bore most of the weight, Sally grasped the railing with her left hand and hoisted herself up a step. Yeah, this would work.

She was sweating by the time she reached the first landing. She shifted Bethany so that the child's legs wound around Sally's waist and Sally's arms cradled the little girl's upper thighs. As long as she leaned slightly backwards, Bethany's head remained on Sally's shoulder. Sally backed up against the wall, letting that wall bear some of both of their weights.

"Come on, let's go," urged Laura. She was already one landing up.

This time Sally used her left hand to support Bethany and pulled them up with her right. Now she knew why Physical Education teachers tried to make them do deep knee bends in gym class. Maybe she should have paid attention to that whole physical fitness thing.

There. They were halfway up. Just one more flight of stairs. Well, two sets of stairs actually, with a nice landing in between.

She lay Bethany on the floor, the child laying bonelessly. Nobody slept the way Bethany did. Except maybe for Mom when she'd been drinking.

"I'm not sure I can do this." Sally hated admitting it, but she really wasn't sure she had the strength to make it up the remaining sixteen steps.

"Are you going to just leave her there?"

Geez. What was Laura thinking? "No. Look, you grab her feet and I'll take her arms. We should be able hoist her up between us."

With a glare, Laura complied. Sally was careful of Bethany's head. On the first step the child's bottom smacked the tread and she made a sound. "Lift her higher."

"I can't."

"Bring her back down to the landing." She thought about it. "You lift her under her knees and I'll grab her armpits."

There. That worked better. They wouldn't injure the little girl, but progress was slow. Gently, they set the sleeping girl onto the next landing, panting.

"It was better when just you carried her," Laura said.

Sadly, that was true. "Okay. I need to catch my breath for a minute."

"We need to hurry up. It's late and I'm tired."

Sally eyed her sister. She didn't have the energy for a retort. Besides, she still needed Laura's cooperation.

Bethany on her back was a different problem. While it was one thing to pick her up from a sitting position, this was much harder. Sally raised the child's shoulders. "Here. You get behind her and prop her up so that I can lift her."

Reluctantly, Laura scooted behind Bethany and held her upper body erect. Then, without being asked, she draped the child's arms over Sally's shoulders.

Wrapping her arms around Bethany's waist, Sally tried to stand. Their combined weights were too much for her legs. Another reminder to practice those deep knee bends. "You're going to have to help. I can't lift her on my own."

The more tired Laura got, the less energy she had to argue. Maybe they should keep her tired more often, thought Sally. Together, they got Bethany into the initial position and Sally ordered her screaming calf muscles to push them higher, one step at a time.

She didn't even realize they'd made it to the top, until Laura opened the creaking door. Sally would know that sound anywhere.

It wasn't far from the stairwell to their door. Bracing Bethany's body against the wall, Sally twisted the key in the lock. With little effort, it opened. Just a few more steps, Sally told herself.

Soon the front of her knees hit the twin bed that Bethany shared with Laura. "Pull down the covers," she instructed Laura. Laura did as asked, then toed off her own shoes.

Her arms shaking from the strain, Sally tried to gently lower the dead-to-the-world five-year-old onto her pillow. Really, she should undress the child and put her into pajamas but removing Bethany's shoes plus her own coat as well as Sally's were as far as Sally's energy reserves went. Before she could pull the covers up over their little sister, Laura was in bed, a nightdress over her head and her arm cuddling the pillow.

"What about mom?" Sally asked.

"What about her?" Laura mumbled.

"How are we going to get her up here?"

One of Laura's eyes opened. "We're not."

She was right.

Sally needed to make an attempt, though.

Ignoring her fatigue and wobbling legs, Sally locked the children in the apartment and made her way down, down, down to where she had left the car.

"Mom! Mom!" Sally yelled and tried shaking their mother. Nothing, not a movement, other than her head lolling with the vigorousness of Sally's shakes. Izzy was passed out. They'd seen this before. There would be no waking the woman, at least not for a goodly number of hours.

Sally shivered. She still had not put on her coat. Well, she'd be inside soon.

She felt her mom's hand. Although she had her coat on and Sally had buttoned it up, her exposed skin was a bit chilly. It wasn't yet midnight and the night would grow colder. Since it had taken all Sally had to get Bethany upstairs, she knew that there was no way they could get Izzy up there, even with Laura's help.

Facing the apartment building, Sally made a decision. Boy, it felt like that's all she'd done tonight.

Turning, she went back to the building, let herself in

and trudged up all three flights of stairs. It was easier without her little sister's weight, but her legs still protested.

Once in their suite, she stripped the bedspread and comforter from her mom's bed. Folding them into a loose roll, she locked the apartment door behind her and made her way back down the stairs, to the car.

Throwing the blankets onto the front seat, Sally reached for the large bedspread. Shaking it into the night air, she folded it in half, then tucked it around her mom, covering the woman from her neck down. Next, she took the comforter, wrapping it around Izzy, raising first one shoulder, then the other, tucking the warm duvet under the her body, hoping that the weight would keep the covers in place.

Drats. She'd forgotten a pillow. For a moment, just a moment, Sally debated going back for one. But, eyeing the angle her mother's head was at, she told herself it wasn't needed. Mom would be fine without it.

While she might have forgotten a pillow, she hadn't forgotten a note. She worried that mom might wake up in the night and not know where she was. Sally taped the note to the back of the driver's headrest. Then she locked the car door. Without looking back, she headed to her own bed.

Grab your copy…
vinci-books.com/REASONS